DIG DEEP FOR MURDER

A SMILEY AND McBLYTHE MYSTERY

Dig Deep For Murder
Text copyright © 2024 Bruce Hammack
All rights reserved.

Published by Jubilee Publishing, LLC
Paperback ISBN 9781958252185

Cover design: Streetlight Graphics
Editor: Teresa Lynn, Tranquility Press

DIG DEEP
FOR
MURDER

A Smiley and McBlythe Mystery

BRUCE
HAMMACK

1

Heather rubbed her temples as she turned to Steve and lamented, "Work on the project is on hold until the police tape comes down."

The former Houston homicide detective gave his head a single nod. "That should come as no surprise, and you're exaggerating. They won't shut down the entire project, only the street where they found the woman's body."

Steve pulled the wooden lever on the side of his recliner and lowered his feet. He rose and moved toward the kitchen.

"Where are you going?" asked Heather.

"Didn't you hear the flap on the cat door? Max finally woke up and he'll raise the roof if I don't feed him. He's getting more and more demanding the older he gets." He paused. "Now that I think about it, I am, too."

"I know what you mean," said Heather. "I'm a decade and a half behind you and caught myself snapping at the new attorney I hired."

"Did she deserve it?"

"I thought so. She asked for half a day off because she and her boyfriend have tickets to a concert in Houston. She said I might as well let her off because she'll likely be too tired and hung over the next morning."

Steve's chuckle bounced off the hard surfaces of the kitchen. He spoke loud enough for his voice to travel into the living room of his two-bedroom condo. "Give her the time off. A truthful attorney is hard to find these days." He chuckled again. "Present company excluded."

She rose and followed his path into the kitchen. "That was the most backhanded compliment I've received in quite a while."

Steve opened the door to a small pantry. His voice echoed as he asked, "Can you help me? I don't feel any cans of cat food."

Heather moved to look. "That's because you put them on the floor."

Steve spoke under his breath. "That's just great. I'm not only blind, but my memory is fading."

She knew that wasn't the case. Steve's mind was sharp as a surgeon's scalpel. He could remember the most minute details unless something important distracted him. The challenge was getting him to talk about it before he was ready.

Heather waited for his normal change of subject after a self-deprecating statement.

Right on cue, he said, "Tell me about the body they found. The report on the six o'clock news was vague."

Heather arranged her thoughts as Steve moved out of her way and she unloaded a case of cat food tins onto the proper shelf. "I met Jack for lunch and was halfway through my salad when Lee Cockrell called me. You remember my general contractor, don't you? He asked us to help him find out what happened to his dog and cat at Christmas."

"Ah, yes. It started as a simple case of discerning whether one of the guests could have stolen his retriever and his wife's cat. It morphed into a murder investigation when one of the guests turned up dead. I believe you're now reaping the reward of ten percent off his contractor's fee for finding his animals."

Defensiveness tinged her words. "That should have been a

simple night of getting to know the other guests to see if one of them was an animal-napper. How was I to know someone in that group had murder on their mind?"

Steve spoke with emphasis. "We're back to our agreement of no animal cases and I'm adding no Christmas parties for me."

"Anyway, back to what happened today. By the time I arrived, deputies and state police had the street leading into the subdivision blocked off. I talked my way into the area, but not onto the street where they found the body."

"Not surprising," said Steve.

"Lee met me and said detectives had already questioned him. It seems Lee's son, Clay, was running an excavator when he uncovered the body."

"Did they take Clay in for questioning?"

"They'd hauled him away by the time I got there."

"Did you tell Lee to get his son an attorney?"

"I told him to call Jack."

"Why was Clay digging there?"

"Concrete drainage lines. They didn't bury a short section deep enough. As construction mistakes go, it wasn't a big deal, and it wasn't Clay's fault. His father told him where to dig the trench and how deep, so that's what he did."

"When did he put in the line?"

"Almost two months ago."

"That would make it the end of January." He added, "It may take a while to establish the victim's identity if they didn't wrap the body in a tarp or something similar."

An insistent meow came from the giant ball of black fur at their feet. Max, Heather's chubby Maine Coon cat, looked up with eyes that telegraphed impatience.

Heather moved to the cabinet and took down a clean bowl for his food. "I'm sorry, Max. Steve fell down on his job tonight. Don't worry, your momma will feed you."

Steve said something unintelligible under his breath. He followed it with, "Don't blame me if he missed lunch. He's been next door in your condo all afternoon and evening. All he had to do was come through the pet door and ask."

"It's good that he didn't. You wouldn't have found his food."

Steve mumbled again, which was out of character and confirmed that something else was on his mind.

Before she could explore what was bothering him, he asked, "Have you talked to Jack since lunch?"

Heather opened the tin of cat food and scooped it into a bowl. She spoke as Max rubbed his face against her leg. "I called him this afternoon. He's been interviewing candidates to replace his mother. It's going to take a full-time receptionist and a paralegal to fill her shoes. Another attorney would also be a good idea, but I haven't mentioned that yet."

"I thought he had a receptionist."

Heather placed the bowl on the floor and gave Max a stroke down his arched back. "She didn't work out. It seems she had designs on Jack, not the job."

"Ah. Not good." Steve quickly changed the subject. "How's Briann adjusting to her new life?"

"Not great. I can't imagine how tough it's been for her to lose her mother and having to move in with a father she didn't know existed. If it weren't for Cora taking her grandmother role seriously, I'm not sure what Briann would do."

"Add to that the rejection she must feel because none of her relatives in Louisiana would take her in."

Heather lamented, "I was so careful to never date a man who'd been married or had a child. That hasn't worked out so well, has it?"

Steve ran a hand down his face. "We make our plans, then life comes along and changes them."

Heather considered the man in front of her who spoke from experience. His career as a homicide detective and going home to his wife every night ended in a Houston parking lot when drug-addled thieves jumped them. The attack ended Maggie's life, and left Steve for dead. He survived but lost his sight and so much more.

Compared to what Steve had lost, a delay in her relationship with Jack seemed trivial. She shook off the introspection.

Steve's next question helped her to refocus. "How is Briann adjusting to her new school?"

"That's one of those good news, bad news stories. Her mom was a talented attorney and Briann's role model. She's coping with her mother's death through perfectionism. Not only does she make top grades, she does so to the exclusion of everything else. Absolutely no social life."

"Give her time," said Steve. "She's only twelve." He lifted his chin. "Are you sure she wants to become a lawyer like her mother?"

"According to Jack, it's an obsession."

Heather knew it wasn't an idle question. He'd been thinking about Briann and Jack's situation. Even though he didn't have children of his own, Steve had a knack for helping families find win-win solutions.

His next question verified her suspicions. "What's your plan?"

She tilted her head. "I don't have one, but you obviously do. What is it?"

"Right now, you're a role model for Briann, but you're dating her father. That means she admires you and resents you at the same time. Give her another role model."

Heather let out a huff. "Sometimes you're so obtuse I can't follow."

Steve lifted his chin. "What does Jack need most in his practice, a paralegal or another attorney?"

"Both. He's the best defense attorney in the county and turns away a ton of potential clients."

Steve rubbed his hands together like a mad scientist. "Here's a plan you can take to him. Any or all of those you mentioned would free him to spend time with his daughter, plus increase profits. If Briann wants to hang out in a law office, let her. She can start as a helper to the secretary and paralegal. If she's as smart as you say, she'll soon be an asset to Jack's practice."

Heather looked for holes in Steve's plan as he kept talking.

"If you help him hire those three, you can choose women who'll be good role models for Briann. You're used to hiring and firing people. Jack isn't."

"That's true. He's always been a one-man shop, except for his mother."

Steve spoke with confidence. "Everything changed when he found out he had a child. He might as well go all the way and expand his practice. It's the only way he'll have time to be a dad."

Heather whispered, "Consequences."

"What?"

She raised her voice. "Consequences of our actions bring about changes."

He nodded in agreement.

Heather ran the plan through her mind, looking for flaws. There were several, but the benefits outweighed the potential deficits. "I'll take your plan under advisement and sleep on it tonight."

"Smart move," said Steve. "I hate to admit it, but my plans for other people's lives don't always work out. That also applies to some of my own plans."

This was the opening Heather had waited for. "Does that include whatever has you distracted tonight?"

He lowered his voice. "Was it that obvious?"

Heather didn't want to sound too condescending. "The misplaced cat food gave you away." She added, "Do you want to talk about it?"

"Might as well." His pause told her he was collecting his thoughts. "I received a phone call from Kate today."

Heather's mind shifted to Miami, Florida, which was the home of Steve's former writing coach and editor, Kate Bridges.

She was also the closest thing to a romantic interest Steve had had since his wife died.

Steve continued, "Kate called to congratulate me on publishing my short stories under a pen name."

The information stung Heather like a wasp. "Why didn't you tell me you were publishing your stories? You and your secrets will be the death of me."

Steve held up his hands for her to stop. "I didn't tell you because I never considered using a pen name."

Heather was glad he couldn't see her lower jaw drop. "Are you telling me someone stole your work?"

"It appears so."

"Don't say another word," said Heather. "I'm making us each a mug of tea and we're going into the living room, where you'll give me the details."

2

Heather filled two mugs with water and placed them in the microwave. She then retrieved two tea bags from the cabinet. Her goal was to take some time doing a mundane task in order to bring her anger under control. She failed. The more she thought about someone pirating Steve's stories of his days as a homicide detective, the more her blood boiled.

While she stewed, Steve went into the living room. She called out, "I'm going next door for a legal pad."

Steve didn't reply, which meant he was arranging his thoughts to give her his version of the events leading up to the theft. She looked down at Max, whose wide head was still in his bowl. "Stay here, Max. I'll be right back."

A phone call from Jack showed on her phone as she opened the door to her condo. "Can I call you back?" she said before he could utter a word.

"What's wrong?"

"I'll tell you when I know more."

"It sounds like we both have problems."

She promised to call him back. With the door thrown open, she made quick steps to the kitchen bar and retrieved a legal pad from her valise.

In mere seconds, she returned and lowered herself onto Steve's couch with pen and paper in hand. Steve sat in his recliner with feet flat on the floor.

"I'm ready. How did this happen?" said Heather.

"After Kate and I realized we needed to take a break from our friendship, as well as our author/editor relationship, I found a guy who was publishing books for other people to be my coach."

"I remember you telling me about him. Isn't his name Buck?"

"Bucky. Bucky Franklin. I chose him because he's nearby, knows Houston, and is a former cop."

Heather looked over at Max as he entered the room, settled onto the carpet, and began the post-supper ritual of licking his paws and washing his face.

"Bath time?" asked Steve.

Steve's hearing was a constant amazement to her. He always seemed to know what was going on around him. "Don't worry about Max. Tell me about Bucky."

"When I hired him, he asked me to email all my stories to him. He wanted to study my level of competency as a writer."

"When was this?"

"I'll need to check the exact date, but it's on my computer."

"Do you have a contract with him?"

"No."

Heather allowed a huff of exasperation to escape, but didn't chide him. She'd save that for a time when she wasn't so angry.

"Tell me about your phone call with Kate."

Steve pulled the lever on the side of his chair and his feet rose. "She called this afternoon about two. Someone told her about a new book of short stories from a Houston cop. The person who contacted Kate knew about me and told her to check it out. She did and immediately recognized the stories. After all, she taught me how to write them."

Heather jotted down notes and practiced breathing techniques to release stress.

Steve folded his hands in his lap. "That's the short version. What can I do about it?"

She tapped her Mont Blanc pen on the legal pad. "My initial thought is to find a hit man and put Bucky in the Houston ship channel wearing concrete boots."

Steve's belly jiggled. "That might be a little extreme."

"How about I make him regret the day he was born?"

"I can live with that."

"Let's call Kate," said Heather.

Steve held up a hand. "Do that without me. I didn't know she had such an extensive vocabulary until I told her Bucky published my work without my permission." He heaved a sigh. "She blamed herself for not helping me publish them and started crying. If you would, tell her I don't blame her. This is my fault for not insisting on a contract."

Heather had heard enough. "Listen to me, Detective Smiley. The only one to blame is Mr. Bucky Franklin. He's a thief who broke all kinds of copyright and possibly criminal laws."

Heather reviewed her notes as Steve took another drink of tea. He asked, "Do you have a plan?"

"Not yet, but that's something you don't need to worry about. The wheels of justice are going to grind Bucky into a fine powder."

"More consequences?" asked Steve.

"That seems to be the theme for the day. Someone will have to pay for committing a murder, Jack is paying for fathering a child, and Bucky will have to pay for being a thief." Heather rose. "Where's your computer?"

"In my bedroom."

"I'll bring it back to you in the morning."

"Leave it on your dining room table and I'll get it. Max and I don't get up as early as you."

Heather thought about Steve and Kate's relationship as she shut the door to her condo. She had been so happy to see a friendship develop between them as they worked on Steve's stories. After the encounter with Kate's abusive ex-husband and her subsequent arrest for his murder, their relationship wasn't the same. Even though the real killer was found, Steve and Kate decided to go their separate ways. Apparently, neither one of them were ready to commit to someone new.

Heather sighed and placed a call to Kate. The distraught author began the conversation by saying, "I was hoping you'd call. I'm alternating between explosions of anger and self-loathing."

"No need for the second. The first is optional if it makes you feel better. I called to let you know Steve told me about Bucky Franklin. He said he only had a verbal agreement with Bucky to coach him and edit his works."

Kate spoke in quick sentences. "I did some snooping on my own. Bucky is a small, independent publisher. Steve's stories are only available in eBook format and print on demand. That could change if it proves to be a money maker."

Heather added to her notes, then asked, "What else could it become?"

"Large print, hardcover, and audio book are next. After that, you're looking at television or movie rights. The odds of that are more than a million to one, but it could happen."

Heather scribbled more notes and said, "Tomorrow morning I'll find the best intellectual property attorney in the state and get the ball rolling on teaching Bucky not to steal another author's work."

"I'm so glad to hear it. Please tell Steve his former coach and editor wants him back."

Heather wondered if there was a double meaning to her words. She put that thought on hold. "Thanks for the information. I miss seeing you."

"You, too." Kate paused. "I'm serious about helping Steve with his writing again."

"I'll tell him he has a friend, and he'd be a fool not to accept your offer."

The call ended on a positive note. Heather put the legal pad aside after making notes of action steps she'd take.

Then she stepped into her bathroom and turned on the bathtub faucets. She needed to unwind before she talked with anyone else.

Twenty-five minutes later, she donned loose-flowing pajamas and dialed Jack's number. He answered with his usual greeting of, "Hello, beautiful."

She responded with, "Hello, handsome."

The terms of endearment were their way of telling each other it was safe to have a private conversation. If either of them used any other words to open a conversation, they'd know someone else could hear.

Jack followed the salutation with, "You go first."

Heather sat cross-legged on her bed with two pillows supporting her back and Max beside her. "Sorry I took so long to get back to you. I had to take a hot bath and light three candles to get the mad off of me."

"Three candles? This is serious."

Heather launched into what sounded like an opening statement by a prosecuting attorney. "The accused man is Bucky Franklin, and the victim is Steve Smiley."

Jack remained silent until she finished pouring out the story then asked, "Does this Bucky character have a death wish? Is he aware that you and Steve are business partners?"

"Steve has a habit of compartmentalizing his life. I pressed him about how much Bucky knows about him. You know Steve. Unless he's known someone for a long time and trusts them, you'll get a lot of questions but few answers. Twenty years as a cop taught him to extract information from others and keep his mouth shut concerning his personal life."

Heather then threw out two names of attorneys she knew who specialized in copyright litigation. "Do you have a recommendation?"

Jack didn't hesitate. "Constance Banks. Her office is in Houston. She looks like a harmless grandmother, but she's a cross between a barracuda and a piranha. Politicians ask her advice when drafting new intellectual property laws."

"I'll call her first thing in the morning."

She added the name to her legal pad and moved on. "Your turn. Were you able to get to Clay Cockrell before the detectives grilled him?"

"Afraid not. The good news is, they didn't read his rights to him until they got him into an interview room. The bad news is, they had him for two hours before I got there and put an end to their questions."

"Why so long?"

"I told you at lunch about the job interviews I had scheduled. What a waste of time."

"Two hours being grilled by the cops," mumbled Heather. "That's a long time. Did they use the standard tactics to trap him with his own words?"

"Of course. Not enough to arrest him yet, but plenty if they can make a connection between Clay and the victim."

Heather thought about how the police could legally use deception and intimidation to twist a suspect's words to fit a narrative of their own making. The courts may assume a person is innocent until proven guilty, but that isn't the case with the police.

She then asked, "What evidence do they have?"

"He dug the original trench with an excavator, put in the concrete drainage pipes, and covered it up. Today, he discovered the body when he had to correct the mistake."

"Who did he call first?"

"9-1-1. The sheriff's department responded immediately. After he made the initial call, he called his dad."

Heather shook her head. "That's one suspect for the police to start with. I wonder how many more there will be?"

"None, if the police have their way."

The sound of a girl's voice came through the phone's speaker, but not loud enough for Heather to make out the words. She assumed it was Briann.

Jack ended the conversation with, "Got to go. I promised Briann that I'd look over her algebra homework before she moved on to Latin. She's on her own with that one."

"Lunch tomorrow?" asked Heather.

"Sounds good. See you at the same place, same time."

The call clicked off. It had been almost four months since Jack learned he had a daughter and his life turned upside down. After that, the engagement ring he'd given her took up residence in her jewelry box. They'd agreed to put a permanent relationship on hold for the foreseeable future. The new arrangement suited Heather fine, and Jack seemed satisfied—sort of.

Heather's thoughts turned back to the murder and how it might affect the biggest housing development project she'd ever undertaken. Having the son of her general contractor on the verge of being arrested for murder didn't bode well. If the police weren't interested in looking for other possible suspects, perhaps she and Steve could lend a helping hand.

3

I t was one of those nights that Steve hated. The Earl Gray tea that Heather fixed tasted so good he had a second cup. Whether it was the double dose of caffeine, hearing of a murder, or the unauthorized publication of his stories, it didn't matter. Sleep eluded him. He awoke in the recliner with a stiff neck and needing a shower.

Hot water pounded on his head. It felt good but ushered in thoughts of the woman's body found by Clay Cockrell. In an imagined scene, he saw the nineteen-year-old operating an excavator as the bucket pierced the ground. Metal clanked and bumped as the claw extended. It continued downward, taking out full scoops of rich soil and casting them aside. Next, a helper affixed a chain on the concrete pipe with a loop of chain hooked over the excavator's bucket. The bucket lifted the pipe and the helper guided it to a resting place beside the trench.

The young man was looking into the trench as the claws of the bucket sank deeper into the sandy soil. As the bucket full of dirt rose from the trench, he saw more than dirt.

Steve dismissed the scene from his thoughts and felt in the shower caddy until his hand found the bottle of shampoo. He lathered up his hair and moved on to a fresh scene of the sheriff's deputies' arrival and calling for backup. It was natural for suspicion to fall on Clay. He remembered many homicides he'd worked where the person reporting the crime turned out to be the killer. The adage that a guilty dog barks first came to his mind.

Those cases, however, were the exception. He'd arrested many more suspects who'd killed in fits of passion. Mind-numbing alcohol or drugs were common to those crimes.

He then thought of the unusual cases, the ones involving premeditation and planning. Some schemes were elaborate and pointed to multiple suspects. Others involved deception, lies, false alibis, and planted evidence. Memories of old cases swam laps in his mind as the water beat against the suds on his head. He wondered which category this case would fall into.

As quickly as he asked himself the question, his mind shifted to his purloined stories. A smile crossed his face as he took a fluffy towel and dried. Heather would handle it and show no mercy. He'd offer to pay the attorney fees, but she'd scoff at him. Having a multi-millionaire next-door neighbor and business partner came in handy.

Thoughts of breakfast rose to the forefront after shaving and selecting clothes for the day. He knew they would match if he selected the first pair of pants on the left side of his closet and the first shirt on the right. Heather had made sure the woman she hired to clean and wash clothes for them knew the system. Before Heather came along, he had no system other than feel and smell. She'd accused him of dressing like a gypsy.

On his way to the kitchen, his phone rang. He had to retrace his steps to the bedroom and retrieve it. It was announcing, "Call from Bella." He told it to answer.

"How's married life?" he asked instead of issuing a standard greeting.

"Totally awesome. Adam and I found the cutest house to rent in Puerto Rico. Mom and Dad are still in St. Croix. After they close on the sale of their resort this week, they'll pack and join us."

Bella was the closest thing to a daughter Steve was likely to have. It was always good to hear from her, but he had a feeling this wasn't strictly a social call. He waited for her to tell him what else was on her mind. It didn't take long.

"I was wondering if you know what Heather's schedule is next week. I'd like to come and spend a few nights."

"I'm sure it wouldn't matter what her schedule is. She'd never turn you down."

"If she's busy or traveling, I can get a hotel. Do you know if she has any business trips planned?"

"She's focused on a huge project at Lake Conroe. I thought she told you about it."

"I think she did, but what was going on at my parents' resort had me distracted."

Steve couldn't help but respond in a tongue-in-cheek way. "I don't know why. All you had to think about were your wedding, a murder, and people trying to cheat your parents out of their life's work."

"Yeah, I don't know why I can't remember what Heather's schedule is eight months later," she teased.

He took a breath and continued, "If I remember right, you and Adam have a plan of living half the year in Puerto Rico and half the year in Texas. Is that why you want a place to stay for a few days?"

Bella's laugh sounded like liquid joy. "You're still way too good at reading my mind. The only thing that's changed is, Mom and Dad think it's such a good idea they're considering the same plan. They want us to scout out some possibilities in Texas."

Steve wondered why Bella didn't call Heather. There was one way to find out. "There's a reason you didn't call Heather. What is it?"

Bella hesitated before her answer stuttered out. "I... uh... I wasn't sure how she's doing emotionally. You know, since she and

Jack called off their engagement. I'm so happy I could bust, but I wanted to talk to you and see if it's too soon for her to be around a newlywed."

"You don't need to worry about Heather's mental state. In fact, both she and Jack seem relieved. He has his hands full caring for Briann. As usual, Heather's consumed with projects. The latest is an enormous investment on her part."

"It makes me feel better to know they're adjusting. Tell me about the new project."

"You'll need to see it to believe it. I'll tell Heather to expect you. If she can't put you up, plan on staying with me."

"Are you sure? I don't want to intrude."

"There you go again, making foolish statements. There will always be a place for you and Adam. Of course, I'll need to get a larger place if you and Adam have children."

"Don't rush us on that, but we agree on having two, a boy and a girl."

The thought of Bella as a young mother pushing a stroller made him smile. He shifted his thoughts back to the conversation. He had a feeling there was more. "There's something you're not telling me about this spur-of-the-moment trip to come see us." He took a stab. "Do you know yet where you'd like to put down the Texas half of your roots?"

Bella let out a coy giggle. "We have the first part of the plan in place—living part-time in Puerto Rico to take advantage of the lower taxes. That may change when a baby comes along. My parents can't wait to be Gramps and Mimi."

"You didn't exactly answer my question. What about the second part of the plan, living in Texas? It's a big state. Have you narrowed down the location?"

"Well." Bella started slowly, "We'd both like to be near you and Heather. If that's all right with you?"

He had to clear his throat before he said, "I'd like that."

"Oh, good. It would be so awesome to be near the two of you. If we can get Mom and Dad close by, we'll be all set."

"Do you want to rent or buy?"

"We'd like to have something similar to what you and Heather have, but bigger. Something we can grow into, with Mom and Dad next door."

Steve could see a scene of the future in his imagination. "I assume you want a room each for the two children you're planning, a guest room, a home office, and a double garage. I'm sure your folks could get by with one less bedroom."

She giggled. "Yeah, that's pretty much what we were thinking. It would be so nice to have them close and to have built-in babysitters."

"You could design and build something custom if you can't find what you want." He paused. "Heather's new development might be a good option."

Excitement filled her voice. "Okay. Now you have to tell me about it. How did she start a local project? Most of the ones I know about have been outside of the Houston area."

Steve took a breath. "A long time ago, when Heather was a child, her father bought an old trailer park on Lake Conroe. It was an entire subdivision designed for single-wide mobile homes. The original owner had no idea the land would appreciate like it has, or I'm sure he would have done something a little classier. It's some of the most sought-after property in the state. To make a long story short, the county condemned the last trailer last year. After Heather had it hauled away, she approached the county to rezone the property for single-family residences with a few condos. She's putting in paved and curbed streets, underground utilities, and all the amenities that go with a high-end housing development."

"That sounds wonderful. My mind is racing."

"I'm sure Heather will be glad to show you around when you come."

"It could be perfect," said Bella.

"Perhaps not as perfect as you might think."

"Why not?"

"A worker discovered a woman's body buried under a drainage line yesterday."

After a long pause, Bella asked, "Are you and Heather solving another murder?"

"Not yet." His voice carried a hint of hesitation.

"You will," said Bella with absolute confidence.

Steve laughed. "What makes you so sure?"

"It's what you do."

"I could say the same about the police."

"They're all right for the simple cases. You and Heather get the tough ones. Do you have any details yet?"

"Only that the son of Heather's general contractor found the body when he was digging with an excavator. Also, the police are looking at him as their chief suspect, and Jack's representing the young man."

Even more excitement filled Bella's words. "Keep me posted. If you need a helping hand with the case, I'm in. It's only a matter of time before Jack tells you and Heather he's in need of top private investigators."

Steve didn't argue. The same thought had crossed his mind. He tried to change the subject. "When do you think you might arrive?"

"I was thinking in two weeks, but we may have to move that up."

"Oh? Are you in the middle of a project yourself?"

"Not yet, but I may have good news soon."

Steve couldn't help but tease her. "It must be top secret or you'd be gushing to tell me about it."

"Adam made me promise not to jinx it by blabbing about it."

"Fair enough," said Steve. "Come whenever you can. If Heather's swamped, I'll be your tour guide. Just don't ask me to be your driver."

"I'll rent something at the airport," said Bella. "By the time I arrive, you'll be working on the case."

"I hope that's all I have to work on." Steve hadn't intended to burden Bella with his other problem, but the words seemed to slip out before he could stop them.

"What's going on that you don't sound excited about working a murder?"

He imagined her taking all the slack out of her posture. There was no use trying to avoid telling her. "It's a minor problem that Heather's handling for me."

"Tell me," her tone mixed concern with insistence.

"It seems my new writing coach published a book containing my short stories under his name."

Her response was immediate. "He stole your stories?"

"It appears so."

"That dirt-bag."

"Heather's taking care of it."

"She may need help. I'm calling her as soon as I hang up. How did you find out?"

"Kate called me."

"I'll call her first."

4

The next day, Heather breezed into *RUBIO'S BISTRO* and found Jack waiting for her in a booth. After the standard greetings, she slid into the booth opposite him. He always appeared handsome to her, but the scowl wasn't his best look.

She spoke the first thing that came to mind. "The creases on your forehead tell me you didn't have a good morning."

He slid a finger down his glass, chasing a drop of water that had condensed on the side. "Are there any decent secretaries left in the world? This morning I interviewed two airheads. The first was an unemployed used car salesman searching for anything he could find." He paused. "Did you notice the gender pronoun I used?"

"I noticed. Did he have nice legs?"

Jack played along. "The bib overalls blocked my view."

They traded grins. Hers lasted longer than his.

"The second was a single woman with three children. She was at least seven months pregnant and didn't know how to turn on a computer."

"Other than that?" asked Heather.

"Briann wants to work in the office after school and on Saturdays. I'm tempted to let her."

Heather acknowledged the server and ordered a bottle of mineral water. With that chore taken care of, she turned back to Jack. "I can help with the secretary/receptionist position, and Steve has an idea that you might find interesting."

Jack tilted his head. "I'm open to anything that will get my practice running again. Start with how you can replace Mom."

"No one person can replace Cora Blackstock, but I have a file of applicants that my personal assistant can send your way. I tasked her with keeping updated files on people seeking employment for various jobs."

"Does that include secretaries and receptionists?"

Heather nodded. "All positions, including attorneys. I talked to Steve last night about your practice. He suggested you hire a good secretary/receptionist, a paralegal, and another attorney. He's right. You need all three."

"But I'm a small shop. I like it that way."

Heather reached across the table and covered his hand with hers. "It's a new season of life for you. Changes need to take place. Do what's necessary to free up time to be with Briann *and* keep the money flowing."

He grumbled under his breath but kept his gaze fixed on her. "I'm still listening. How do you and Steve recommend I rearrange my practice?"

"I just told you."

"That's too many employees."

"Not if you do it right."

He cut a sideways glance at her. "What's that supposed to mean?"

Heather gripped his hand. "Please don't get defensive. I'm trying to help you."

Jack closed his eyes for several seconds before opening them again. "Sorry. Give me details."

"Like I said, my PA has already interviewed applicants. I can have her call the best ones and see if they're interested in interviewing for the open positions in your office."

"When did I agree to multiple positions?"

"It's necessary if you want your practice to survive, thrive, and give you time to spend with Briann. Your mother was really filling three positions: secretary, receptionist, and paralegal."

"Are you sure I need another attorney?"

The server interrupted with order pad in hand. Heather made a quick decision. Lunch would be comprised of a strawberry-pecan salad and a dinner roll. Jack followed her lead but added grilled salmon.

"Back to your question," said Heather. "You need another attorney to bring in the extra income to fund the clerical and paralegal help we're going to hire."

"We?"

Instead of responding to his comment, she teased him about something else. "What does Briann want most?"

He didn't need to think about the answer. "To become an attorney like her mother."

Heather gave her head a firm nod. "You and I both want her to succeed, but how can we do that?"

Jack leaned forward with elbows on the table. "You seem to know the answer. Enlighten me."

"Steve gave me the idea. You need role models. Briann's too young to do the work of a paralegal, but she could watch and learn the duties of a receptionist and a secretary. She can type, can't she?"

"Of course. She's a wizard on the computer."

"All it takes is the right person teaching her and she'll look forward to coming to your office every day after school. She can start with receptionist duties, then move into the more technical secretarial duties. The older she gets, the more responsibility you can give her."

She could tell Jack was warming up to the idea, but his next words showed she hadn't sold him on the entire package. "I'm on board to let her shadow the secretary and gradually take on other tasks. Another attorney in the office is something that makes sense, too. I've known for years I needed someone to cover for me. Scheduling time off and appearances in court has been difficult. Now it's next to impossible."

"With the right women, Briann will have two exemplary role models."

Jack cast his gaze to a passing woman and brought it back just as quickly. "Why does it have to be a woman?"

"It doesn't, but either way, the person will need to be exceptional."

Heather sensed Jack had reached his limit of change. His next words proved her right.

He pursed his lips in a way that made her believe he was looking for reasons to object. "I'm on board with hiring another attorney, but I doubt you'll have any applicants on file that fit my needs. As for a paralegal, I don't see it happening soon."

Heather shrugged. "Then pass on hiring a paralegal for now. You and the new attorney can do your own work as long as you get someone as good as your mother to run the clerical side of things."

Jack let out a low moan. "Let's discuss adding another attorney a little more. Are you sure you can screen qualified applicants?"

"Attorneys apply for employment with McBlythe Enterprises all the time. All shapes, sizes, and backgrounds. I know for a fact that we have applications from several who are working in various district attorney's offices."

"Yeah, but—"

She didn't allow him to finish. "I'll tell my PA to get you the lists of secretarial applicants. We'll concentrate on the office help first. I suggest both of us interview the top three applicants."

Jack sat back in the booth and spoke as if offended. "Don't you think I can hire a secretary?"

She chuckled. "You're a brilliant defense attorney, but you

need help in replacing your mother. Let's look for someone who isn't trying to take you to the altar."

Jack dipped his head and brought it back level. "You make a good point, counselor. When can we start the interviews?"

"How does three days from now sound?"

"Like two days too many."

Their salads arrived, which put a temporary end to the first thing on Heather's agenda. As Jack was chewing his first bite, she said, "I heard from Bella. She's coming to visit."

"Bella and Adam? When?"

"Next week, and only Bella. She talked to Steve and believes we're on the verge of having a murder to solve."

"Why isn't Adam coming with her?"

"He's booked. Some sort of conference for professional stock traders."

Jack put his fork down and leaned toward her. "Bella might be right about the murder investigation. I met again with Clay and his father this morning. Clay revealed more than I thought to the detectives yesterday."

Heather's head shot up. "What did he say?"

"Enough to incriminate himself. He denied recognizing the victim, which may come back to bite him. What he did recognize was the high school letter jacket the girl was wearing. It was his. Unless some other girl was wearing it, the victim is April Brewer, his former girlfriend."

A tingle went down Heather's spine. "You said, 'former girlfriend.' That tells me they broke up. Didn't she give the jacket back to him?"

He shook his head. "Clay graduated last year. It's not cool to wear high school letter jackets after you graduate, so he didn't make a big deal of trying to get it back. Now he's wishing he had."

"And he didn't tell the detectives he recognized his own jacket?"

Jack stabbed another bite and shook his head as he chewed.

"He said it was muddy and water-damaged. I'm expecting them to arrest him in the next few days. He discovered the body and wasn't forthcoming with vital evidence. He'll be their primary suspect."

"Do you think he did it?"

"He says he didn't."

"Do you believe him?"

"He's convincing in person, but it's a strong circumstantial case. Clay didn't do himself any favors by saying he didn't recognize the jacket. It has his name embroidered on it. I can make a case that mud obscured it, but that's a long way down the road. A lot of things can happen between now and a trial." Jack put his fork down. "If the police settle on Clay as the killer, I'll need the services of a top-notch team of private investigators."

Heather shook her head. "Bella told me she had a premonition that we were on the verge of another case. She's coming to look for property and to help with the case if we need her."

"That's amazing," said Jack. "Clay's still walking around free and Bella's making plans to help."

"She's an amazing young woman in so many ways."

Jack didn't argue.

Heather thought back to how they became acquainted with then-seventeen-year-old Bella, who had the looks of a Nordic goddess. A man kidnapped her from her parents' resort in St. Croix when she was a toddler, then assumed the role of her father. All through her life, she was raised to be an outdoor hunting television personality. Steve and Heather were heading into a mall when a shot rang out, killing the man Bella thought to be her father. This led to a murder investigation and a request from Bella to find her birth parents.

Jack was stabbing another bite of salad when Heather came back to the present. Her thoughts went to Steve. He needed to hear about the new information she'd received from Jack. "Pardon me, but I need to call Steve."

A wave of his hand kept Jack from having to respond with his mouth full of strawberries, lettuce, feta cheese, and pecans.

Steve answered on the fifth ring. "Talk fast. I'm meeting with LeAnn."

"LeAnn Cockrell?"

"Uh-huh. We're discussing Clay and his relationship with April Brewer."

"Did LeAnn call you?"

"I called her."

As usual, Steve was a step ahead of her. "Are you gathering background information?"

"Guilty. I'm sure you're doing the same with Jack. We'll compare notes tonight."

The phone call cut off, leaving Heather to pull the device away from her ear and stare at it.

Jack swallowed and asked, "Did Steve sniff out another murder to investigate?"

"He's already working on Clay's case and is talking with LeAnn Cockrell."

"Good. It would help if you two could come up with someone else who could have murdered April. Preferably the person who did kill her. For now, I'll take anyone with motive, means, and opportunity to get the spotlight off my client."

Heather put down her fork. "Steve continues to amaze me. I thought he'd be so involved in his own problems that he wouldn't get us involved in a murder investigation."

Jack tilted his head. "What problems?"

Heather told him again about Bucky Franklin taking Steve's stories and publishing them under his name.

Jack's fork dangled in the air throughout Heather's recounting of the details, including her phone call with Kate. His expression soured the longer she spoke.

"I wasn't paying much attention to the story last night. That guy is toast. What have you done about it?"

"I hired Constance Banks. She said she'd call Steve and get his side of the story before she takes any action."

"What's your opinion of Ms. Banks?"

"The jury's still out. She sounds like a grandmother who bakes fantastic cookies but has the reputation of being ruthless and relentless when it comes to protecting copyrights."

"Did you make it clear you wanted this Bucky character to suffer?"

"Oh, yeah. She got the message loud and clear."

"How did she react?"

"She let out the cutest giggle and told me she'd get extra creative."

5

Steve called LeAnn to make sure she was already at the restaurant and could meet him when his Uber dropped him off. She met him at the curb and guided him inside. It was a mid-priced establishment with good chicken-fried steaks, the kind of restaurant Steve felt the most at home in. His white cane made a sweep in front of him, helping to ensure he didn't come into contact with protruding chair legs.

It wasn't a surprise that LeAnn jabbered nervously as they walked. He expected either excessive talk or complete silence. Both were signs of worry.

He hoped to score a booth, but the server told him there were none available. To gain a small measure of privacy, he spoke to LeAnn. "Sit next to me and not across the table. This place sounds crowded, but there's always someone who wants to listen to others' conversations. I have exceptional hearing, so you can keep your voice low."

"I'll try," said LeAnn. "Clay finding April's body has me in knots."

Steve interrupted. "They've identified the victim?"

"Yes. It's April Brewer, a girl who went to school with Clay. She's been missing for several weeks."

"I think I remember hearing about it on the news."

"You were the first person I thought of when Lee told me we should prepare for a rough ride with the police. What did he mean by that?"

A waft of perfume swept Steve's way, telling him LeAnn had moved closer. "Jack Blackstock is representing Clay. He's a wise defense attorney. It may not be fair, but the first person or persons the police rule out as suspects are the ones who reported the crime or found the body. It's standard procedure."

"Standard procedure? If they'd just look at him, they'd know Clay's not like other young men his age. He's never had a parking ticket, let alone been involved in a murder."

The server arrived and took drink orders, giving him a few seconds to gather his thoughts.

LeAnn picked up where they'd left off as soon as the server left. "It may be standard procedure to you, the police, and Mr. Blackstock, but it certainly isn't to me. I've not been the same since Christmas Eve when you solved the murder on our property. Now this! There may not be enough hair dye in the state to cover all the gray this is causing me."

He knew he needed to take control of the conversation or LeAnn would rattle on like a metronome stuck on a fast setting. He raised his voice and put some starch in it. "I did research on your son this morning. Why isn't he in college?"

The pause told Steve the question put LeAnn on her back foot. Her words leaked out at a reduced rate. "Clay's birthday is on August thirty-first. If he'd been born one day later, he'd have been in the next year's graduating class. He gravitated to the students in the class behind his. His best friends are more his age, but they don't graduate until this year."

Her words picked up speed. "Besides, he's a deep thinker... perhaps too deep. He questioned the benefit of going to college and is taking a gap year after graduating last May."

"How were his grades?"

"Top ten percent of his class, so that's not an issue. Like his father, he loves the outdoors. Any sort of job that would lock him in a building would drive him nuts. He loves heavy machinery. Lee had him running a backhoe as soon as he could reach all the pedals and levers."

"Was he popular in school?"

LeAnn let out a sigh. "He's a bit of a loner, but not overly so." She paused a few ticks of the clock. "Clay is the type of young man who attracts girls without trying. It's his crooked smile and sleepy cobalt-blue eyes. He also comes across as uninterested in relationships, which seems to drive young ladies batty. The more he acts like he doesn't want a relationship, the more the girls chase him. As for work ethic, you'd be hard pressed to find a more diligent worker, which means he has money to spend on whatever he wants."

Steve summarized. "He sounds like an independent thinker."

"An independent, deep thinker," said LeAnn, with a mixture of pride and frustration in her voice. "He can be very stubborn once he sets his mind to something. He's also incredibly loyal."

"With boys or girls?"

"Both. His first childhood friend moved when Clay was in the sixth grade. Jeremy and his family relocated to Spain. I think Clay made some sort of promise to himself that he wouldn't lose track of him, and he's kept that promise. Since then, his two best male friends are Luke Paulson and LaShawn Moody. My husband calls them the three amigos."

Steve committed the names to memory and moved on. "Tell me about his girlfriends."

LeAnn released a sarcastic laugh. "Clay's path through life is littered with the broken hearts of girls who thought they could keep him interested in them."

"Do any stand out?"

"Unfortunately, yes. The most recent one was April Brewer."

Steve wanted to moan. He didn't want to distress LeAnn any more than she already was, so he maintained a flat, unemotional tone to his words. "What makes her stand out?"

He could tell the distraught mother had leaned closer to him when he caught a strong waft of her perfume. Her volume decreased. "She's the only girl that ever ended the relationship with him. He was always the dumper, not the one getting dumped. Like Luke and LaShawn, she was in the class behind his. They started going to dances together before he graduated, then she broke it off in the summer."

"Do you know why she ended the relationship?"

"Clay never talked about it."

The longer LeAnn spoke, the worse things looked for Clay. The police would dig until they found out about April ending the relationship, and motive would stare them in the face. Clay certainly had the means and skill to put her deep in the ground. The only thing that might save him from arrest was an airtight alibi. That presented problems of its own. The body was in the ground for months, and establishing the time or even date of the murder would be broad. Unless Clay was out of town on an extended vacation, the proverbial noose was tightening.

The server arrived, which gave Steve a few seconds to come up with a plan to keep Clay out of jail. The best way was to find an additional suspect or two to give the police someone else to look at.

After ordering the restaurant's signature chicken-fried steak, Steve turned his attention back to LeAnn. "Who were Clay's other romantic interests besides April?"

"There've been so many, but one that stands out is Janie Polk. She's a gorgeous young lady and, like April, a senior this year."

"What can you tell me about her other than she's good looking?"

"Not good looking," said LeAnn. "I'm talking about magazine-cover beautiful. She has long, raven-black hair with azure eyes and a flawless complexion. She's on the track team as a distance runner. Whatever picture of perfection you can imagine of her long legs and slim figure, it falls short of how she looks."

"Why did Clay break off the relationship?"

"I'm not sure he did. Veronica Polk, Janie's mother, has quite the reputation as a helicopter mom. If half the stories other moms tell about Veronica are true, Janie's on a very short leash."

Steve tucked that answer in a mental notebook. If the police arrested Clay, and he and Heather were called upon to help Jack solve the case, they'd have questions for Janie Polk.

He found his glass of iced tea and took a drink before moving to the next question.

"Has Clay ever mentioned any of April's other boyfriends? Did she date anyone you know before or after Clay?"

"Clay isn't the most talkative child in the world."

"What teenagers are?" asked Steve.

"Exactly." She paused. "My source isn't Clay, but JoAnn Paulson."

"Peter Paulson's wife?"

"That's right. You met them at the ill-fated Christmas party. Clay's friend Luke is her son."

Steve dredged his memory. "If I remember right, Peter's a master plumber and works for Lee."

"You have an excellent memory, but Peter is an independent sub-contractor. It's a subtle difference from him working for Lee."

She got back on track. "Luke dated April before Clay did. The reason I know about that is JoAnn told me how upset she was with April's mom. She and her husband made April break up with Luke because he was the son of a plumber. They assumed Luke would follow in his father's footsteps and make a living with his hands. Apparently, they had bigger dreams for their daughter that included a college degree and a husband with at least two degrees."

Steve felt the need to lighten the conversation. "Master plumbers make more money these days than most people with college degrees."

"I know they do," said LeAnn with certainty. "I help keep our books. Dependable craftsmen with excellent skills are in high demand. Keeping projects on schedule is critical to general contractors. We have a reputation of paying top dollar and keeping the best subcontractors."

LeAnn's voice lowered again. Her words held a mother's concern. "Do you think it's only a matter of time before the police arrest Clay?"

It was a question that deserved an answer, but Steve hated to be the one to give it. He tried to think of a way of breaking it to LeAnn gently but came up short. It was best he told her the unvarnished truth, without overstating the situation.

"Based on what I've heard so far, I'd say Clay is the primary suspect. Unless the police discover additional evidence that rules out your son, they'll arrest him." He held up his hands. "However, I don't think it will happen right away."

"But it will happen?"

Steve shrugged. "Prepare for it, but that doesn't mean things are hopeless. Investigations have a way of turning up all kinds of unexpected information. Many times, it's information that can cause charges to be dropped."

"What should we prepare for?"

"Posting bond if he is arrested. Jack will fight hard for a moderate amount. The district attorney will want a higher number because of the seriousness of the crime and the fact that a young woman is the victim. The judge will probably find a middle ground because of your stability, standing in the community, and the fact that Clay has no criminal record."

A sniffle told him LeAnn's heart and emotions had cracked. He wondered if he'd been too direct and stolen her hope. He raised his voice and brightened his words. "You realize that I'm giving you a worst-case narrative. The police are, as we speak, chasing down leads and discovering fresh evidence. There's so much we don't know yet."

He felt LeAnn pat his hand. "Nice try, Steve. General

contractors are used to bad news and dealing with it. There are three rules to any construction project: It takes longer than you think it should, it costs more than projected, and there are always problems. With the Lord's help, we'll get through this."

Steve appreciated the statement of faith. It reminded him so much of his late wife's optimism.

LeAnn had another question. "If they arrest Clay, will you and Heather get involved in the investigation?"

Steve ran a hand over his chin. "We already are. All we need to do is formalize it."

"Do Lee and I need to sign a contract or something?"

"Not yet, and it may not be necessary. Heather's meeting with Jack today." He paused a moment. "Let me explain how these things normally work. You hire an attorney, who then hires private investigators and any other specialists needed. If Clay isn't arrested, we won't be needed." Steve rubbed his chin. "I hadn't realized it, but if we are needed, it will create quite the unique situation. Heather and I will work for Jack while you and Lee are working for Heather on her project, while Jack is working for you."

"This sounds like a game of financial ring-around-the-rosy." LeAnn tried to clear the lump from her throat. "Sometimes I think that's all we do... trade money with everyone else."

Their food arrived, giving Steve time to ponder the information he'd received. He had at least three leads to follow up on: Janie Polk, Luke Paulson, and LaShawn Moody. Also, he'd need to speak with Heather and make sure they were in agreement regarding the investigation. He wondered if she was ready to commit to it or wanted to wait until Clay's arrest. His money was on Heather wanting to start now. Things weren't looking good for the young man.

Instead of going home and calling from his condo, Steve told the Uber driver to drop him at Heather's office. It was really *their* office because he had a desk, chair, and telephone there, but his spot remained unused unless they were working a case. It had been a while since his shadow darkened the door of the McBlythe Building in The Woodlands. It was time to check in with Heather and decide if they would take the case or not.

6

Heather looked up from the blueprints she'd spread across the conference table in their office. Steve walked in with his cane leading the way. "Hello, stranger."

Steve acknowledged her greeting with a left-handed salute.

Heather kept goading him. "It's been months since you've been here. Do you remember where your desk is?"

It was a tongue-in-cheek question that didn't deserve an answer, but she got one anyway. "No thanks, I came to take a nap while you work. How do I get to the bedroom you added? The chicken-fried steak I had for lunch with LeAnn has my eyelids drooping."

Heather considered his words. Even without an official contract, he'd taken significant steps to begin the investigation. "Did you learn anything interesting?"

"Some, and none of it is good for Clay. I figured since you and Jack were starting without me, I'd need to earn my keep."

"Your desk or mine?"

"Mine... if I can remember where it is." He then walked in a straight line across the room, circled the desk, and sat in his leather chair. She followed him to the lone chair that sat in front of his modest workspace.

"Let me go first," she said. "I'll not take long."

He folded his collapsible cane and placed it on his desk. "Go ahead."

"Jack's convinced Clay's arrest will come sooner than later. Clay wasn't exactly truthful when he told the police he didn't know the victim."

Steve nodded. "LeAnn's expecting it. She also told me April was wearing his letter jacket. Is that the same story you heard?"

"You already know it is. It was Lee, LeAnn, and Clay in Jack's office yesterday afternoon when Clay gave the details."

Steve drummed his fingers on top of his desk. "Any other revelations?"

"Jack gave Clay and his parents a homework assignment of a daily accounting of Clay's location and actions for each day in January and February."

Steve leaned back in his chair. "It would help if we could prove Clay was somewhere far away. A long cruise would be a great alibi."

"No such luck," said Heather. "Clay loves to work, especially running heavy equipment. He was working steadily on my project from mid-January until yesterday, running either an excavator, a backhoe, or a bulldozer."

Steve expressed his feelings by letting out something between a moan and a huff. He followed this with, "Nothing else?"

"Not that you haven't already heard."

Heather crossed her left leg over the right. "In other news, I called Kate. She feels horrible about your stories being stolen."

Steve responded with a grunt that could mean something or nothing. It was one of his few infuriating habits. He used the tactic when he had to acknowledge something but didn't want to divulge anything.

Heather broke the silence when it became apparent that he'd said all he was going to. "Kate said she wants to be your coach and editor again."

Another grunt.

"Her exact words were, 'Tell Steve I want him back.'"

Steve came out of his shell. "Tell Constance Banks to call Kate. I don't want my mind cluttered with details about what you're going to do with Bucky. Call Leo, too."

Heather's mind raced to keep up with Steve's words. Leo, his former partner in Houston homicide, would move heaven and earth to help Steve. He could also be a great help to Constance. Nothing like having a homicide detective's assistance.

Steve asked, "Did you hear me?"

"Sorry. I drifted away for a few seconds. I was having pleasant thoughts about what Leo might do to Bucky. It wasn't pretty, but I certainly enjoyed it. By the way, is there anything special you want me to say?"

"It occurred to me that it might help if the attorney you hired has a good connection in the police department. Leo can get the official and unofficial scoop on Bucky. I'm wondering why he's an ex-cop. Ask Leo to find out what he can."

Heather tilted her head. "I'm surprised you don't already know Bucky's background. Didn't you do any research on him?"

"I was writing my stories, not his. Looking back, he avoided my questions about his work history. He got around it by telling me I had too much to learn about writing to be wasting our time talking about him."

Heather made a mental note to make two phone calls, one to Kate and the second to Leo. She added an email to her to-do list. It would inform Constance Banks of the two sources of information she could use to build her case against Bucky—Leo and Kate.

"What else?" asked Heather.

"I didn't hear you writing notes. You'd better grab a pad and pen."

She scurried to her desk, retrieved a legal pad, and returned to her chair. "Got it. What's the plan?"

Steve folded his hands on top of his desk. "I need to tell you about my talk with LeAnn Cockrell." As usual, he recounted their meeting in detail, taking extra care to focus on April Brewer and Janie Polk, Clay's former girlfriends. He also mentioned Luke Paulson and his mother.

Heather had questions. "Let me make sure I have this straight. Luke Paulson is a senior in high school who dated the victim, April Brewer, before Clay did."

"Correct."

"And April ended the relationship with both boys?"

"Right. First Luke and then Clay." Steve paused. "According to LeAnn, April's parents didn't think Luke had the right pedigree because he's the son of a plumber."

Steve took a breath. "Another of Clay's former romantic interests was Janie Polk."

Heather wrote the information. "Let's wait a minute before we move on to another girlfriend. Did Luke hold a grudge against Clay when he started dating April?"

Steve shifted in his chair. "That's something we need to find out. If so, we may have a suspect. High school romances can run white-hot."

Heather looked down at her notes. "Next we have Janie Polk. She had the hots for Clay?"

"She and Clay dated before her mother flew in on her broom and put an end to the relationship. We need to find out if Janie blamed April for the breakup, even though LeAnn told me Clay never was serious about April."

Heather looked again at her notes. "We need to find better suspects. The chances of Luke or Janie killing April are next to zero."

Steve shrugged. "We have to start with what we have and work out from there. Let's begin with Janie. She may be the hardest to get information from."

"What makes you say that?"

"Her mom has the reputation of being overprotective. We

need to find a way for one of us to talk to her without mom listening to every word."

"What do you suggest?"

Steve issued an impish grin. "A smart woman like you should be able to come up with something."

Heather sensed a set-up wrapped in the gushy compliment. She threw one back at Steve. "Houston's former top homicide detective must have a few tricks up his sleeve."

His head wagged side to side. "I'll take Luke. That leaves you with Janie and her mother, Veronica. It will give you an opportunity to get creative. Find out what interests Janie."

Heather loved a challenge, but she was too many years away from being a teen. A thought bubbled to the surface. It took shape and morphed into a plan. She cast her gaze to Steve. "This may not be as difficult as I think."

She scribbled another note on her pad, which read, *Call Jack. Enlist Briann to search social media.*

Looking up from her notes, she said. "We still don't have a client. Jack and the Cockrells are talking to us, but no one has pulled the trigger to officially hire us."

Steve waved away the statement. "Neither one has waved us off, either. At this point, I think they're all assuming we're in."

Heather didn't like what she had to say next but steeled herself and let it ease out. "I may have to renegotiate my contract with you."

"Oh?" said Steve. "What did you have in mind?"

"I can't drop everything this time and work only on the murder case. This project I'm working on is too big. I can give you half time, but not full time."

Steve rubbed his chin. "That's no problem. I'll call Bella and ask her to come as soon as she can."

"That occurred to me, too. I'll draw up a contract with Jack and see if he's ready to pull the trigger on hiring us."

Steve nodded. "Keep our standard agreement of no charge with Jack, and I'm sure he won't charge Lee for our services.

Since Lee's giving you a ten percent discount on construction because we solved the murder in December, we'll all just pass our money in a circle. Nobody will get rich off this deal."

"Misunderstandings over money can ruin relationships faster than anything I know," said Heather. She smirked, even though he couldn't see her. "I know a guy who wrote a bunch of stories but didn't have a contract to protect him. He regretted it."

"That was a low blow, even if it's true."

"Sorry. Couldn't help myself."

Steve stood. "Just for that, I'm going to take a nap. Show me to the apartment you had built. I was up most of the night thinking and I don't want to take another ride in an Uber today. The last one smelled of vomit."

Heather settled Steve in the tiny apartment that had reduced the size of her office, but not by much. He took off his shoes and lay on the Murphy bed. She turned on a white noise machine to block out the street sounds with a recording of waves coming to shore. She closed the door, went to her desk, and told her phone to call Jack.

He answered with, "Blackstock Law Office."

"You need a receptionist."

"Tell me about it. Please say you have applicants ready to interview tomorrow morning."

"Three, starting at nine o'clock. All qualified, and two are excited about the prospect of working in a small office."

"You're a lifesaver. Is that why you called?"

"It isn't the only reason. Steve dredged up a couple of potential suspects. They're not likely to have killed April, but interviewing them should give us good background information."

"Better than nothing."

"There's more. I want to hire Briann to do some research for me."

"I don't know..."

Hesitation seasoned Jack's voice, so she moved on quickly. "The two suspects are seniors in high school. I'd like Briann to search social media and give me a report on their interests, hobbies, and what's important to them."

"Social media only?" asked Jack.

"Or anything else she can find on the Internet. I'll need to talk to Janie Polk without her mom. It's our understanding she's a little overbearing." She launched into the tale of Steve interviewing LeAnn Cockrell and the information he gleaned about Janie Polk and Luke Paulson.

When she finished, Jack said, "Did you and Steve agree to start a formal investigation?"

"If you're ready, we're ready."

"I like it."

"Good. I'll bring a contract with me tomorrow morning. We'll be working *pro bono*. Lee's giving me such a deal on the project, it's like he's prepaid for our services. That includes any subcontractors Steve and I might hire."

"Like Briann?"

"Her and Bella. It's likely she'll help us, too. I have a feeling Steve has something in mind for her."

She heard Jack's chair creak. That meant he'd leaned back and most likely had his boots on his desk. He wouldn't have done that if he hadn't felt some of his burdens lift.

"I'll let Briann know to expect a call from you. It will thrill Mom to hear we'll interview her potential replacement tomorrow. She trusts you a lot more than me to make a good choice."

"Is it all right with you if we wait until next week to interview attorneys?"

"I'm in no rush for that."

"You'll need time to train your new secretary."

"That's Mom's job. She'll train Briann with light receptionist duties at the same time."

Heather closed the conversation. "I'll keep you posted on anything else we turn up in our investigation."

"Thanks. I'll send you a text if I hear anything."

The call ended and Heather went back to the table covered

with blueprints, a scale model of the project, and a folder titled *Strategy for Sales and Marketing*. She was on the third page of the marketing plan when she received a text from Steve.

Who will benefit from Clay Cockrell being in jail?

The question stopped Heather in her tracks. All thoughts of her project took flight. Leave it to Steve to come up with such a question. Perhaps April's murder had nothing to do with teenage romances or bruised egos.

She quickly sent her own text.

You're supposed to be sleeping. Figure it out yourself.

Steve replied with an emoji of a smiling face wearing sunglasses.

7

Heather arrived at Jack's office, a renovated home on a major street leading to downtown Conroe. The size, location, and lack of mortgage suited Jack. He'd owned it free and clear for years, and it was big enough to hold additional staff. Two more attorneys, a paralegal, a secretary, and a receptionist would pose no need for expansion or renovation. Only one of those positions was on today's schedule.

Heather pulled into the space beside Cora's car. She smiled as she thought of the warm-hearted woman who had received her into their family. Cora had gotten used to the idea of Heather being her daughter-in-law and wasn't giving up hope. The surprise arrival of Jack's daughter was an unexpected delay in what the older woman thought to be an inevitable marriage.

On the bright side, Briann's arrival had eliminated Cora's hunger to have a grandchild to dote on, which had the unexpected benefit of reducing the pressure on Heather and Jack to marry.

As she put the car in park, Heather took a moment to examine her relationship with Jack. Her feelings for him hadn't changed, but Briann's arrival in Jack's home had certainly changed the dynamics of her relationship with him. She was no longer the center of Jack's attention. Heather was focused on business while switching back into the role of steady girlfriend. All three were finding their footing after experiencing emotional earthquakes.

Cora and Briann had hit it off from the start. This relieved a ton of pressure from Heather to play a role in the girl's life she wasn't sure she was ready to handle. For now, Heather was content to have a wonderful, very part-time companion in Jack and a challenging career... probably for a long time to come.

Heather closed the front door and Cora met her with a warm hug. Removing her jacket, she asked the silver-haired woman, "Did you get Briann off to school with no trouble?"

"She grumbled a little, but I think it's only because her classes aren't challenging enough. Jack and I are pushing the school to get her into more advanced classes, but it's like pushing mud uphill. I'm exploring other options, but it's quite a learning curve for me."

Heather gave a nod of commiseration. She wanted to help but wasn't sure about the new boundaries in her relationship with Jack. It seemed best to tread lightly with Briann and allow time to heal the sting of grief caused by the loss of her mother to cancer.

Instead of getting into a circular discussion about educational alternatives, Heather focused on hiring a secretary. "Did you look over the job applications?"

"I arrived early and studied them. On paper, they look excellent."

"You know the job better than anyone and what Jack needs. I hope he asked you to be a part of the interviews and selection."

She chuckled. "It must have slipped his mind."

Heather shook her head. "Isn't that just like him? Sometimes he can't see what's right in front of him." She issued a sly grin. "I have a plan."

The sound of Jack's boots clomping down the hall reached the co-conspirators. "Are you two talking about me?"

Heather looked into brown eyes. "You have a choice today. Option one is all three of us will conduct the interviews. We each get a vote on selecting the best candidate. Majority wins. Option two is your mother and I will do it without you."

"That's not what I had in mind."

"It's good business practices," said Cora. "The pressure is off you from making another poor decision."

"Thanks for the vote of confidence, Mom."

"Don't mention it."

"I won't, and I'll take option one. That will at least give me the illusion that I have some say-so in the running of my practice."

Heather kissed the left side of Jack's face as his mother kissed the other at the same time.

Cora backed away to arm's length. "See there, son. You're already making better decisions."

Jack led Heather to the conference room while his mother stayed in what had been a formal living room when the home was built. It now served as the secretary's office and seating area for clients. On the way down the hall, Jack asked, "Did you bring the contract regarding you and Steve working for me?"

Heather reached into her valise and withdrew papers. "All ready to sign."

Jack took them but made no move to read the pages. "Any progress on the case?"

"Bella's flying in tomorrow. Steve believes she can help, but he hasn't shared his plan with me yet. The next step may depend on what Briann uncovers in her social media search on Janie Polk, Luke Paulson, and LaShawn Moody."

Smile lines radiated from Jack's eyes. "Briann may put on a good show to pretend she doesn't like you, but you pushed the right buttons by asking her to help with a murder investigation. Last night, I had to tell her to turn off her computer at eleven thirty."

"Did she find anything juicy?"

"She told me she was working for you, and you were working for me. It would be your responsibility to tell me after she submitted her report to you."

"Wow. Her mother trained her well in chain-of-command procedures."

A hint of regret seasoned Jack's next words. "It sure wasn't me."

Heather ignored the inflection of his voice. "That's because you're a one-man show. Get used to the idea of change and a more formal structure."

"You keep saying that. I hope you're not trying to mold me into a corporate bureaucrat."

"I'd be wasting my time. Besides, I like the slower pace when I come here. Sometimes I wish I wasn't so driven, but I get bored easily." She looked away. "I guess it's true that opposites attract."

Jack took two steps toward her. "Apparently so."

Heather held out her hands to stop him from drawing closer. "I heard the front door. It wouldn't do to have the first applicant catch the prospective boss in a clench with a hired hand."

Jack grumbled but retreated. Seconds later, his mother arrived with the first applicant.

By ten thirty, the trio had interviewed, discussed, and selected a new receptionist. Jack's first choice was a woman with thirty years of experience in a large California law firm. What gave Heather pause was the woman's reaction to Jack's adequate time off policy. During the interview, Heather traded travel stories with her. It became apparent the woman was more interested in time off than working. She revealed her husband had already retired and he wanted to see the world.

The second applicant exaggerated her skills. When pressed, the truth came out. She could whip up a mean cup of espresso latte but didn't know the difference between litigation and libation. Six years ago, she'd grown tired of working for a law firm after three weeks and gone to work in a coffee shop. It was a brief interview.

The person selected for the position was a minister's wife with kind eyes, a pleasant voice, and ten years of transferable experience. Her name was Francesca Calderon, and she was bilingual. Jack was concerned that she had three children. Heather knew that with one in college and the other two in high school the woman's job of child rearing was almost done. She was confident Francesca could handle the duties of secretary and receptionist with no trouble. Heather hoped she would also be a good role model and mentor for Briann.

Fran, as she preferred to be called, would start the following morning. In addition, she lived nearby and had dependable transportation.

Phase one of Heather's project to re-imagine and re-engineer Jack's law practice was a success. It was time for her to take care of her own business. She declined an invitation to go to lunch and moved on to the next item on her to-do list. Making sure the installation of modern infrastructure at the Lake Conroe development was back on track required a trip to the job site.

Her Mercedes SUV pulled to a stop in front of the construction trailer at the turnoff into the sub-division. Lee Cockrell's truck was there along with several other vehicles, all pickups.

Heather entered the single-wide trailer and faced a desk that Lee sat behind. He hadn't shaved and possibly hadn't bathed. A white hard hat sat on the desk, giving her a clue as to the reason for his disheveled look.

Instead of greeting her, he held his cell phone mashed against his ear. His voice had the tone of a bear rudely awakened in mid-hibernation.

"Let me get this straight. You're telling me you can't deliver the first load of road base for three more weeks? Did I hear you right?"

It must have been a one or two-word reply because Lee quickly lowered his voice and spoke as though it hurt to talk.

"Listen good. I don't know who told you to call me, but it wasn't the company president. I spoke with him the day before yesterday. He gave me his word that trucks would roll on time. Did you speak with Andy before you called me?"

Another short answer.

"I didn't think so. I have a contract with your company to have that base here in ten days. I have Andy's word that he'll make it happen. If you need to talk to the woman funding this project, I'm looking at Heather McBlythe. Do you know that name?"

An even shorter response.

"Would you like to explain to her why you're going to cost her thousands of dollars because you took it upon yourself to reschedule?"

Lee looked up and smiled. His gravelly voice ground away at the caller. "That's what I thought. Tell whoever told you to pull this on me that I'm not new to this game. I don't appreciate having to play it."

The conversation ended. Heather asked, "Trying to bump a customer to make another sale?"

Lee nodded. "Everybody's building and trying to maximize profits. Supplies and subcontractors are in such demand they pull out all the stops trying to get bonuses. Integrity is often the first casualty in the construction business."

Heather pointed to the door. "Care to take a drive with me?"

He reached behind himself to grab a hard hat off a peg and handed it to her. He took his in hand as he rounded the desk. "I need a break. I've been trying to check on the crime scene all morning. One thing after another kept me chained to the desk."

Heather and Lee thought enough alike that he must have known she'd want to visit the trench where Clay found April Brewer's body. She also wanted to know the status of tearing up the streets. Lee's worry lines told her his thoughts were elsewhere.

"How's Clay coping?" she asked as she buckled the seatbelt in Lee's truck.

"Scared, silent, and sullen. Do you want more?"

"No. I get the picture and I'd act the same."

Lee glanced her way. "Sorry. I didn't mean to snap. I never thought I'd be waiting for a phone call telling me my son's been arrested for murder."

Heather wanted to console the distraught father, but refrained. She'd learned a long time ago that platitudes had the sound of counterfeit coins—hollow and worthless. Instead, she focused on a question Lee could answer. "Is Clay working today?"

"He's on a dozer ripping up streets. At one time, asphalt covered them. They're more like rutted trails now due to years of neglect."

"He's not running the excavator?"

"It was his idea to trade with another man. He's sure a jail cell is in his immediate future and wanted to make sure the other guy was comfortable with the new machine I leased."

"That's a responsible thing to do, even though it might not be necessary."

"Like I said, Clay's convinced it's only a matter of time."

Lee slowed to a stop on a rutted road. She stated the obvious. "The tape is still up."

A huff of air came from Lee. "Working at the sheriff's department must not be that different from a construction job. Things take longer to get done than they should. I was told the tape was coming down early this morning." He paused. "At least that's what the detective said."

A pickup that looked like it would fall apart if someone washed it came to a stop behind them. Lee glanced in his truck's side mirror and provided a couple of details. "It's Rusty Brigs. He's the excavator operator taking over for Clay. He's rough around the edges but a skilled dirt mover."

Lee lowered his window as the man came even with the

driver's door. "I heard the road was supposed to open. Were the cops telling lies again?"

The words brought Heather on point. She inspected what she could see of the man and judged his age at thirty-three, give or take a few years. She estimated his height at about five seven. A dirt-and-oil-stained baseball cap shaded his narrow face and shifty eyes. His black hair was pulled into a pony tail. She wouldn't be surprised if the local police had him on their radar.

Lee responded to Rusty's question. "I heard the same thing. Stay here and wait for them. We're days behind on getting the drainage line reburied. If you don't know how important it is to stay on schedule, I'll give you a refresher. Get caught up and you get a bonus. If you don't, look for another job." He looked in his mirror. "Where's the rest of the crew?"

"Finishing lunch. They should be here any minute."

Heather spoke for the first time since Rusty approached Lee's truck. "I'll call and see what the delay is with the sheriff's department."

Heather knew the ranking officers and the detectives at the sheriff's department. She scrolled through her phone until she found the lead detective on April's murder investigation. It rang twice before a woman said, "Detective Blake."

"Loretta, this is Heather McBlythe. I'm at the crime scene trying to get some work done. Does the forensics crew need more time?"

"Didn't someone take the tape down?"

"I'm looking at a blocked road and an excavator that isn't running."

"Sorry. Take the tape down and throw it away."

"Thanks. Good luck with the investigation."

"Based on a rumor going around, I should say the same thing to you. Don't forget to let me know if you and Steve discover anything interesting."

Heather slipped her phone back into the pocket of her jacket. She cast her gaze past Lee to look at Rusty Brigs. He'd positioned himself to stare at her, listening to every word of her conversation. He dug into the pocket of his jacket, retrieved a toothpick, and slipped it into the corner of his mouth.

Lee started his truck and looked at Rusty. "Call the others in your crew and tell them I said lunch is over. Take the yellow tape down and bury it deep. It's not a souvenir."

"You got it, boss. Anything else?" The toothpick rose and fell with every flick of his tongue.

"You have until the end of the day tomorrow to get caught up on this street."

"Then you'll put me back on my old job?"

"Don't push me, Rusty. You'll work wherever I need you."

Lee pushed the button on the door handle and his window rose. Heather asked, "Ex-con?"

"Yeah."

"Is he more trouble than he's worth?"

"Not yet, but men like him don't last long."

8

Heather watched Rusty Brigs walked back to his truck. His gait was that of a man who looked for angles to play, a little bit shifty with a tablespoon of cocky. Heather ran her tongue across teeth that felt like they could use a good brushing. She turned to Lee. "Steve and I are gathering information on suspects. One of Jack's strategies is to give the police other people to consider. Correct me if I'm wrong, but Rusty's not one of Clay's fans."

"The cab on the excavator is air conditioned in summer and heated in winter. Most all the other pieces of equipment I own or lease are open to the elements. Rusty believes he should work in comfort and doesn't like it that the boss's son received preferential treatment. Clay is every bit as good an operator as Rusty, and I trust him a heck of a lot more. Rusty's the one Clay traded machines with."

"I'll add him to the list of suspects and do a thorough background check on him."

The last Heather saw of Rusty was when she and Lee pulled away. The former convict was taking down the police tape. She said, "What do you bet he takes that tape home with him?"

"Wouldn't surprise me a bit. Things go missing wherever he works. If he weren't such a good heavy equipment operator, I'd have fired him a long time ago."

Heather realized Briann would need to search social media for one more person. Rusty was the type of man who couldn't stay out of trouble for long. He might not be the killer, but he was bad news waiting to happen.

Lee drove street by street and gave her updates. He stopped on a side street and pointed, "That's Clay on the dozer."

Heather lowered her window and watched as a bulldozer lowered metal claws into a road of weeds, dirt, and asphalt. The machine tore into the road as the metal tracks clanked and rattled.

She turned to Lee. "Can you think of any other workers who might have something to gain from Clay going to jail?"

"I've thought about that long and hard. I can't think of anyone but Rusty."

"What about former classmates? Did Clay ever get in a fight with someone from high school, or since he graduated?"

Lee dragged his hand over his stubbled chin. "He and LaShawn Moody used to be close friends, but that cooled when Clay was a junior in high school."

"Do you know why?"

He shook his head. "If I heard, it went in one ear and out the other. LeAnn probably knows what it was about. Call her."

Heather made a mental note to dig deep into LaShawn Moody's background. It occurred to her she'd have to find someone to infiltrate the world of high school seniors and recent graduates. What wasn't clear was how she'd do that.

The morning had gone better than expected. The project was getting back on track, and she'd added more names as possible suspects. Bella would arrive tomorrow morning and be available to help Steve. In addition, Jack had added a secretary to his payroll. She hoped the rest of the day would be equally productive.

Her stomach clenched. Was it hunger pangs telling her to keep her blood sugar up, or something else? The image of Rusty Brigs flashed in her mind.

STEVE SLEPT LATE, WHICH WASN'T UNUSUAL. SINCE HE LIVED IN a dark world, keeping on a regular schedule was often overlooked. The banging on his front door jolted him from his recliner as he sipped the day's first cup of coffee.

He lowered his feet and padded to the front door, still wearing pajamas, a robe, and house shoes. He hollered, "Who is it?"

"Delivery," came the reply.

"I didn't order anything."

"It's flowers from someone named Kate."

He unlocked the door and stood back. "Come in."

The door opened, letting in cold air and an even colder voice.

"You're slipping, Smiley. A washed-up, blind cop like you should be more careful."

The voice was familiar, but the tone wasn't. Steve kicked his mind into gear. His hand went into the pocket of his robe and felt his phone. He immediately withdrew his hand and put both where the uninvited visitor could see them.

"Hello, Bucky. I smell flowers. Did you bribe the delivery person or pretend you were me?"

The question didn't receive an answer, so Steve kept talking. "I hope you didn't have to wait long at the door."

"Not long." His voice held a malevolent tone. "Aren't you going to offer a cup of coffee to your writing coach?"

"I'm fresh out of arsenic to put in it."

"You're making jokes now. You won't be when I'm through with you."

"In that case, I'll get that cup for you. Have you ever tasted Honduran coffee?"

"Can't say that I have."

"Go into the living room and have a seat on the couch. I want you to be comfortable while you threaten me."

The lack of noise from footfalls told him Bucky hadn't moved.

As he turned to go into the kitchen, Steve withdrew his phone, keeping it out of Bucky's line of sight. He whispered into the microphone a single word. "Record." He hoped the noise from the television would be enough to cover the command as he slipped the phone back into his robe pocket.

Steve kept talking in a calm voice. "That was a slick move to get inside."

"Child's play for an old cop like me."

"How do you take your coffee?"

"I'll take mine poured over your head. You made a huge mistake when you sued me. This isn't the first time someone's tried to cross me. I only had to break a finger or two and they came around to my way of thinking."

"Perhaps you're right. I'm a reasonable guy. We might work out something we can both live with."

"You're in no position to negotiate. I've already shown you how vulnerable you are."

Steve poured Bucky a mug of coffee and placed it on the bar overlooking the kitchen. "Be careful, it's hot."

"That's what I was hoping for."

Steve heard Bucky move behind him. The coffee pot rattled. Hot liquid slapped Steve on top of his head and stung as it trickled over his ears and face.

He gritted his teeth and choked down the desire to scream. As coffee dripped from his chin, his arm was jerked behind his back. Bucky had him by the wrist and pushed upward until Steve thought his shoulder would come out of its socket.

A cruel voice whispered in his ear. "The last writer that crossed me can't type anymore."

"I don't type," said Steve through his pain.

"I know. You're a special case. Think what life would be like if you couldn't talk. I'm used to making up all kinds of ways to hurt people in my stories. Believe me, I can get very creative."

"Tell me what you want," said Steve.

"That's better. Drop the lawsuit, and you'll never hear from me again."

"I'll do it."

His hand came down a couple of inches, then immediately went back up. Pain shot through his shoulder again.

"Don't think about crossing me again. It will be your word against mine and I was never here. I have two cops that will swear I was with them."

He heard Bucky chuckle. "By the way, Smiley. You need to find another writing coach. Your stories don't have enough grit in them to make me want to publish any more of them."

Steve responded with silence as his arm dropped to his side. The front door opened and slammed shut. He told his phone to stop recording. With his uninjured hand, he picked up the cup of coffee he poured for Bucky and brought it to his lips. "Good thing the coffee pot turned off twenty-five minutes ago. If he'd tasted it, he might have hurt me."

A dishtowel dried his hair and some of the mess in his kitchen. He'd do a better job of cleaning after a shower and putting his coffee-stained clothes in the washer.

One thing being blind had taught him was patience. He rejected the knee-jerk reaction to call the police. Revenge would require a plan. While cool water pounded his head in the shower, he also dismissed the thought of calling Heather. She'd be too angry if he told her about the assault. The temptation to feed Bucky to the fish in small bites might be too tempting to her.

One thing was clear: Bucky had to be stopped. Steve smiled. "He isn't the only person who can be creative."

As cold water took away any residual stinging from his face,

Steve weighed his options on what to do. Bella would arrive tomorrow morning. Could he use her to set a trap for Bucky? What about Leo, his former partner? Yeah. That was a better idea.

Heather called while he was running a mop over the kitchen floor and relayed the news about additional potential suspects. She wouldn't be home until late and asked him to come to the office for an after-hours meeting with Jack. She promised to have coffee waiting for him.

"If you don't mind, I've had my fill of coffee today. Iced tea sounds much better. I'll be there in about an hour and start doing background on the potential suspects you discovered."

"I was hoping you'd say that. My day is getting out of control. For everything I finish, two more crises take their place. The only thing I'll have time to do on the investigation is to ask LeAnn Cockrell why Clay and a young man named LaShawn Moody are no longer friends."

"I'll call for a ride and be there in about an hour. Max is full of cat food and sleeping."

"Anything else going on?"

"Some coffee spilled in the kitchen and I'm mopping the floor. I'm also doing a load of laundry."

Heather's last words had a wistful tone of sarcasm to them. "Oh, to be retired and carefree. It must be nice." A sigh came through the phone. "No time to talk. See you later."

Steve's mind had already moved on to his next call. He kept his phone in hand and told it to call his former partner, Leo. He answered on the fourth ring.

"Are you busy?"

"Why do you bother asking?" said Leo. "There's no shortage of people killing each other in Houston."

"I'm calling to make sure you're not currently working a homicide. If Heather finds out what happened to me today, she'll come unglued and you'll for sure have one tomorrow."

"I'm listening."

Steve told Leo the story of his visit from Bucky. His reaction was what Steve expected. There was one major difference between working with Leo and working with Heather. Leo was more likely to follow Steve's instructions on what to do with Bucky.

9

Steve rose early enough to give him plenty of time to dress, eat breakfast, and be ready for Bella's arrival. His phone call to Leo the previous day had gone well, but took longer than expected. First, he had to peel Leo off the ceiling.

After Leo finally stopped cussing in Spanish long enough to listen, they made a plan to approach the assault as they would any other investigation of a serious crime. They'd gather facts and find out what there was to know about Bucky. That would give them time to put raw emotions aside.

After taking care of Leo, his mind shifted to Constance Banks. He sent her the audio recording of the assault, but didn't want her to do anything yet. He wanted Bucky to think he'd won. The delay would give him and Leo time to put a better plan in place that would teach the bully a lesson he'd never forget.

Constance suggested they drop the lawsuit until Steve and Leo could find additional victims, especially the one Bucky said could no longer type. A flurry of civil lawsuits and criminal complaints from multiple people would harm Bucky more than Steve's alone.

Bella called at ten thirty. "I'm on the ground and scored a brand-new SUV. My bags are in the back."

"Perfect. Be careful. There's no shortage of wild drivers."

"You sound like Dad and Adam."

"That's because you're precious cargo."

A horn sounded, and Bella let out a squeal. "You weren't kidding about insane drivers. Is there an epidemic of mental illness?" The excited tone of her words faded. "I'll see you in a few minutes."

"Call me when you get here and I'll unlock the door."

He knew Bella would think the instruction odd, but after yesterday's fun and games with Bucky, he wasn't taking any chances. Leo had made him promise to be extra vigilant. He'd even extracted a commitment to install additional audio and video cameras in his and Heather's condos. Technicians were installing tiny cameras when Bella arrived.

Bella gave him a two-armed hug and a kiss on the cheek, then asked, "What's with the extra security?"

"Nothing for you to worry about."

The dismissive response didn't cut it with Bella. "You already had a decent security system. Why the upgrade?"

Steve put his hand behind his back and crossed his fingers. "Leo thinks Heather and I are making too many enemies by being private detectives. Also, there have been a couple of break-ins in this complex."

It wasn't a total lie, but he hoped she wouldn't press him for details.

"That doesn't sound good."

"It's not. Crime is spreading out from Houston. Of course, there's crime everywhere. You pay your money and take your chances."

Steve didn't want to get stuck in a conversation about property crimes. "How's Adam?"

"Wonderful," she said with genuine joy in her voice. "He's super excited about Heather's new project. Do you think we could go there today?"

"Nothing's stopping you and me from taking a nice, long

drive. I don't know if Heather can break loose, but we can check. Do you want to put your bags in her condo before we go to her office?"

"They're in the back of the rental, out of the way. I'm ready to see her and to hear all about the investigation."

Steve slipped on a light jacket as best he could with his sore arm and grabbed his cane.

Small talk about the sale of Bella's parents' resort in St. Croix and the move to Puerto Rico filled the rental on the way to The Woodlands. This suited Steve and he sensed Bella had bigger news to tell, which she'd prefer to tell later when Heather could hear, too.

They rode the elevator to the fourth floor of the McBlythe Building, Heather's corporate headquarters. Her father's McBlythe Building in Boston was older and larger, but Heather hadn't outgrown this one yet.

Steve knew it would be a noisy reunion between Bella and Heather. They didn't disappoint as both squealed with delight, hugged, and talked over each other.

They soon gravitated to the scale model of the project, with Heather giving a street-by-street tour. Steve had heard the plans so many times that he could almost name all the streets. He went to his desk, put on headphones, turned on his laptop, and told it to check emails.

HEATHER STOOD BESIDE BELLA WITH A POINTER IN HER HAND. "This is the community center with exercise rooms, spa, and juice bar. There will be two pools, indoor and outdoor, as well as a splash pad for the little ones. Over here will be a retail center with a bank, shops, and a convenience store. There's also a second community center for social gatherings and conference rooms."

"Are those tennis courts?"

"Tennis and pickleball courts. I'm also putting in an eighteen-hole putting course for the golfers."

"With real grass?" asked Bella.

Heather answered with a smile. "It's Jack's contribution to the project. He insisted on real grass. Did you see the walking trails?"

Bella's blue eyes opened wide with delight. Heather took a moment to inspect her. She'd braided her white-blonde hair into a rope that hung down her back to her trim waist. If possible, marriage had brought about an even warmer glow to her face. She'd effortlessly morphed from a breathtaking teen into a woman. Tall and willowy, she moved with the grace and flow of a ballerina.

Bella's voice tinkled with excitement. "There are lake-front lots? Are they reserved for the mansions?"

"More like mini-mansions," said Heather with a wink of her eye. She used the pointer to draw attention to a peninsula. "I thought you and Adam might be interested in this lot. It's zoned for a duplex. One side could be a four bedroom and the other a three bedroom."

Bella's mouth hinged open. Heather continued, "It will be up to you and Adam to fill the bedrooms with children. Steve and I thought your parents might enjoy living next door to you."

Bella had to sit down. Her gaze didn't shift from the model on the table. Heather filled the void of silence. "Steve and I had such a good time selecting the lot and playing with ideas about what your future home might look like. Of course, the decision is yours. We certainly don't want you to feel we're planning your life for you."

Heather put a finger up to her lips to signal Bella not to speak. The dumbstruck newlywed rose to her feet as the pointer shifted to a second lot on the peninsula. It was like a game of charades when Heather used her finger to point to herself and then at Steve. She then handed Bella a drawing of another duplex.

Revelation hit Bella like a club as Heather's meaning became clear. Her family would live next door to Steve and Heather's condos.

Bella slumped into the chair again, tears of joy rolling silently down her face. Heather grabbed tissues and handed them to the beauty.

Steve still had his earphones on. Heather leaned into Bella and said, "Steve doesn't know it yet, but he's getting a new three-bedroom condo next door to mine. It'll be similar in design to what we currently have, but with an extra bedroom, a home office, and a large back porch overlooking the lake."

It took time and several hugs for Bella to compose herself. All the while, Heather pointed out more details of the meticulously planned community. She finally put the pointer down. "Do you want to take a ride and see it?"

Bella shouted out, "Heck, yeah!"

"You'll need to use your imagination. Road and infrastructure construction is in full swing."

"I need to see it to prove this isn't a dream."

"I'll get my purse. Tell Steve we're leaving."

He spoke as he took off the earphones. "It's about time. We also need to decide where we're eating lunch."

Bella took steps toward him and they met as he rounded his desk. "You still have the best hearing of anyone I've ever met. Latch onto my arm. We're going to check out my new home."

Steve extended his hand, and Bella placed it on her arm. "Will you tell us your big news on the way to the lake?"

Bella came to a quick stop. "How did you know I have big news?"

Steve chuckled. "I didn't know for sure until now. It must be good news."

"You tricked me again. One of these days, I'm going to learn."

"You sort of gave it away with all the small talk on the drive here. It sounded forced, so I figured you had something to tell us but wanted to wait."

Heather spoke up. "Never forget how sneaky he is. Just for that, I'm putting him in the back seat on our trip to the lake."

"To lunch first," said Steve. "If not, you'll hear me gripe all afternoon."

"I want Texas barbecue," said Bella.

"Me, too," said Steve. "There're three places between here and the lake."

Heather couldn't help but say, "Who needs a phone with a program that gives restaurant locations when we have Steve?"

Bella didn't wait until they arrived at the restaurant before she blurted out, "I'll need to go to Houston while I'm here. A major sportswear company hired me to be their spokesperson and model."

Heather was the first to respond. "That's wonderful. Have you signed a contract yet?"

"I brought it with me. Adam and my parents read it and said it looked good to them."

"Do you want me to look at it?"

"Do you mind?"

Steve chuckled from the back seat as Heather reached over to pat Bella's hand. "Of course, I don't mind. How much travel do they expect you to do?"

"Not more than once a month. Most of it will be studio work and a large social media presence. I'm also to recruit models of all ages. Mom and Dad will be my first two for the mature adult demographic."

"Is that how you say *old people?*" asked Steve.

Heather dipped her head as she glanced at Bella. "Ignore the guy in the back seat. Your parents will be perfect models for active wear."

Bella expounded on the line of clothing. It was a full line of apparel—everything from hiking boots to ski caps. They discussed fashion styles and trends as the miles clicked by.

It occurred to Heather that Steve hadn't joined in the conversation as she wheeled into a parking spot. Instead of making a move to get out of her SUV, Steve said. "There's an idea rolling around in my mind. I've been wondering how we can interview some of the high school students who might be suspects or have information about the victim."

"How old are they?" asked Bella.

"Three are eighteen. All are seniors in high school."

Heather asked, "What's your idea?"

"Let's talk about it over lunch. I think better when my stomach isn't growling."

10

The smell of smoke from barbecue pits hit Heather as soon as she opened the SUV's door. If it smelled good to her, she could only imagine how the aroma affected Steve. He answered her unasked question. "There has to be barbecue in heaven."

"Agreed," said Bella as she led Steve across the parking lot.

Steve didn't need any help in ordering once the woman behind the counter asked, "What will it be today?"

"A plate of moist brisket with potato salad, pinto beans, three slices of bread, pickles, and sauce on the side."

"Pickles, onions, and jalapeño slices are on the salad bar. Sauce and paper towels are on the tables. Spicy and regular."

"Yummy," said Bella. "Do you want the cook to cut your meat into bites?"

Steve shook his head. "I'll make half-sandwiches. You'll need to squirt the sauce on the bread for me. I made quite a mess the last time."

"Yes, you did," said Heather. "And it cost me a very nice blouse."

Bella took her turn and ordered a duplicate of Steve's.

Heather ordered lean brisket and a trip to the salad bar. It wasn't long before they dug into their feasts. Both women knew better than to interrupt Steve with questions until he was at least halfway through his meal.

At the three-quarter mark, Steve swallowed, took a drink of sweet iced tea, and wiped his mouth with a paper towel. "Here's what I'm thinking. Bella is looking for models of all ages. I know of at least three eighteen-year-olds that we need to interview. Why don't we use the office Heather uses for interviews and get LaShawn Moody, Janie Polk, and Luke Paulson in for a pretend screen test?"

Bella and Heather traded glances. Bella spoke first. "I need to start somewhere in finding teenage models."

Heather asked, "How are you planning on interviewing them?"

Steve answered. "You and Bella will need to do it. We'll coach her on what to ask beforehand."

Heather tilted her head. "I know she can do it, but what about the kids' parents?"

Steve waved a plastic fork over his plate. "At eighteen, they're all adults, but you make a good point. Their parents might want to accompany them. Why can't we put them in the adjoining office, listening and watching through the one-way glass? You do it all the time when your PA interviews job applicants."

Bella leaned forward. "What a cool idea. Should we get more kids to come in so it wouldn't look suspicious?"

Heather joined in. "Younger and older models both might be a good idea."

Steve asked, "Why don't we include Briann in the mix and let her in on the plan?"

Heather took in a deep breath.

"What's wrong with her being a part of it?" asked Bella.

"Yeah," said Steve. "You already have her doing social media reports."

Heather's response eased out like she was unsure of her words. "I'll need to clear it with Jack."

"Of course," said Bella. "This may sound mean, but it's hard to find girls her age that don't look like gangly horses. She's unique in a beautiful sort of way."

Steve added, "She's plenty smart and has great listening skills. I think she could bring the guards down on the older ones."

Heather held up her hands. "You two slow down. I need some time to think about all the things that could go wrong. After all, she's only twelve."

"Almost thirteen," said Steve.

Bella added, "I was shooting big game in front of a camera and doing commercials when I was twelve."

Heather didn't have a good argument to make, but the unease of including Briann remained. "I'll talk to Jack about it and get back to you. Otherwise, I think it could work. And it's pretend with her—you won't present her as a model, right?"

Bella shrugged. "I don't know. She might be really good."

Heather's eyebrows rose.

"Don't worry about it. She probably wouldn't want to do it anyway," said Bella.

Steve dug into his potato salad but didn't lift his fork. "You two have a photo shoot to arrange. I'll be responsible for training Bella in the finer points of gathering information related to a murder. The trick is for the models not to suspect anything."

Heather puffed out her cheeks. "I hope Briann can pull it off without spilling the beans."

"Speaking of spilling beans," said Bella. "Someone decorated Steve's shirt with bean juice." She dipped a paper towel in her glass of ice water. "I'll get it."

"Sorry," said Steve. "I don't have this problem when I have a big napkin. If I can tuck it under my chin, it's like a child's bib."

As Bella removed the stain with cold water, her gaze shifted to Steve's face. "Have you been out in the sun? Your face looks pink."

He cleared his throat. "It must be the lighting in here, or it's old age setting in."

Heather inspected him with more care. Bella was right. Steve's face looked sunburned or flushed. She didn't notice Bella's complexion looking any different. She thought it strange but didn't pursue it.

They finished their meals with Bella carrying the conversation. It was mainly excited chatter about her job and the desire to look at the lot that might become the site of her forever home.

It was a fairly quick trip to the lake from the restaurant. While Steve expressed his pleasure about the meal, Heather looked into the future and knew she'd one day make frequent stops on her way home from the office to get Steve brisket.

Instead of stopping at the construction trailer, Heather wound her way through the future neighborhoods. At one point, she stopped. "It's hard to imagine because of all the trees, but this area will be the community center. Did I tell you it will also include tennis and pickleball courts?"

"I can't wait to see the walking trails," said Bella.

"I insisted on them," said Heather. "It presented a bit of a challenge because we had to sacrifice the size of some lots, but I think it's worth it. We'll pave some of the shorter trails, but the longer ones will be trails through a wilderness."

"You thought of everything."

As they drove, Heather noticed that many streets bore the scars of heavy equipment. She continued in the general direction of the lake until they approached the peninsula of land that Heather believed would make Bella's heart skip a beat.

Instead of the pristine lots shown on the model, trees, and undergrowth covered the land. They watched an excavator take a swipe at the earth and dump the contents of land that would become part of Bella's driveway.

"Rats," said Heather. "I wanted you to see the land before they started burying drainage lines."

"Can we walk to the lake? The trees and brush are so thick I can't see the water."

"Sure." She parked where the street curved. "Do you want to come, Steve?"

"No, thanks. I'll get out and shake down lunch, but you two tromp through the sticker-bushes without me."

"What was I thinking?" said Heather. "I didn't dress for the occasion. Of all days to wear a skirt, heels, and jacket."

"Don't worry about it," said Bella. "Can you point out the property lines?"

"I can do better than that. I have a plat of the lots in the back."

Heather met Bella at the back of the vehicle. She took out a roll of papers and found the correct page. "You probably don't need this, but take it anyway." She then pointed to the excavator. "Where he's digging is very close to the property line that divides the two lots. Your lot has water on two sides. It goes to where the land curves back into the relatively straight shoreline."

Bella nodded. "I understand." Off she went, down the street, past the excavator, and onto the property. It was as if the woods swallowed her.

Time passed. Heather spent it responding to phone calls, texts, and emails.

Steve opened the passenger door, invading her makeshift office. "You need to check on Bella," he said.

She stopped typing into her phone and asked, "Why?"

"The excavator stopped running eight minutes ago."

Heather bolted from the car. Rusty Brigs wasn't a man to be trusted, especially with a woman as beautiful as Bella.

Heather ran down the road, cursing herself for not paying closer attention to the noise of the machine. After yelling for Bella, she rounded the excavator. Without hesitation, she thrashed her way into the thicket, giving no thought about her shoes or bare ankles.

By the time she heard Bella respond, sweat ran down her face and her ankles bore evidence the lot contained an undergrowth of thorns. Bella was weaving her way through the woods, with Rusty following behind at a slow lope.

"What's wrong?" asked Bella.

Heather stood up straight. Her ragged breathing came in and went out of her mouth. She tried to quell her emotions by saying, "Nothing's the matter. I lost track of time and allowed my imagination to run away with me."

Rusty ambled up with a toothpick waving up and down. "What's all the hollerin' about?"

Heather fixed her gaze on him and returned his question with one of her own. "Why aren't you digging the trench?"

He pointed. "I went as far as I could before the land dipped. If I'd kept going, Bella would have gone through a briar patch to get back to the road." He looked down at Heather's legs. "I see you found another patch."

"Don't worry about my legs, and her name is Mrs. Webber."

Rusty had the look of a confused dog but soon replaced it with a piercing stare. "Don't worry, *Miss* McBlythe, I'll get back to where I belong." He pointed. "There's a path you can use unless you enjoy walking through stickers." He chuckled as he brushed past her.

Heather waited until he was well ahead before she turned to Bella. "I'll explain in the car."

Bella took hold of her arm. "The lot is absolutely perfect." She paused. "At least it will be once it's cleared."

Heather wanted to say, *"Of both unpleasant plants and one human in particular."* Instead, she held her words inside.

Bella looked back toward the lake and then returned her gaze to the excavator. "If I had a dollar for every creep who came on to me, I wouldn't have to work as a model. It's nothing new, and he didn't touch me."

It should have been one of the most perfect moments in Bella's life. Instead, the foul odor of exhaust from the excavator's

Dig Deep For Murder

diesel engine wafted over them. The two women walked down
the path to the road side by side. Neither spoke.

Rusty waited until Heather and Bella were back on the road
before he slammed the bucket into the ground. The metal hand
pierced a fresh chunk of ground, curled, and withdrew a full
scoop of earth. Once the machine had its way with the ground, it
discarded the soil off to the side and went back for more.

Steve slipped into the back seat and remained silent until
Heather was two blocks away from the site of their future
homes. A single word came from behind her. "Trouble?"

The answer came to Heather in a flash. "Nothing that I can't
handle."

It must have been the tone of her voice that tipped Steve off.
Instead of focusing his attention on her, Steve asked, "Are you all
right, Bella?"

Bella met the question head-on. "I've had people staring at
me so long it doesn't hardly register. It's the things guys say that
bother me."

"Ah," said Steve.

Heather added, "I don't want him on my lot."

"Your lot?" asked Steve.

Heather rolled her eyes. The proverbial cat was out of the
bag. She stopped her car, put it in park, and shifted in her seat
until she could see him. "I should have said our lots. This was
supposed to be a surprise, but my big mouth gave it away. We're
moving, but not for a while."

"Who's we?"

"Me, you, and Max. I'm building each of us a condo on the
land we just left."

"On the lake?"

"Overlooking the lake, next door to Bella and Adam."

A wide smile parted Steve's lips. It didn't last long. "I'm with
you, Heather. When Rusty Brigs finishes putting in the drainage
pipes, he needs to move on."

"Let's stop by the construction office and talk to Lee."

Heather drove on but didn't make it to the office. Two law enforcement SUVs and an unmarked car sat on a side street. Lee's pickup slid to a stop ahead of them. She explained the scene for Steve's sake. "Detective Blake and two officers have Clay handcuffed. They're putting him in the back seat. I need to call Jack."

11

Warm, soapy water helped loosen the dried blood on Heather's legs. She grimaced but was thankful she'd included a shower in the tiny bathroom of her remodeled office. By adding a bathroom and a small closet, she could get a full makeover if circumstances warranted. They did on this occasion. It would be weeks before she could wear a skirt again.

Flesh-colored tiny bandages dotted her legs, but slacks covered them so no one would be the wiser. Her ill-advised sprint through the briars would remain the secret of a select few. With the damage repaired as much as possible, Heather exited the bedroom and stepped into her and Steve's office.

Bella looked on with an expression that mixed approval and surprise. "What a great idea to renovate your office. I love the outfit. Are you sure you don't want to model? I'll need women in their mid-thirties."

"No thanks. From what you've told me, the job requires travel. That's something I don't need more of."

Steve put an end to their discussion. "Jack called me when you were in the shower. Lee Cockrell called, too. They both wanted the same thing: other suspects."

Heather and Bella traded glances as Heather directed her

gaze back to Steve. "I need to find out when they'll set Clay's bond."

Steve sat behind his desk, running a finger around the rim of his coffee mug. "They must have received the results of the autopsy. I don't think Detective Blake and the DA would have asked for an arrest warrant if they didn't have positive ID and approximate date of death. That means they know Clay has no alibi."

Heather added, "It tells me the forensic report from the scene revealed little."

"I've been thinking about that," said Steve. "It occurred to me the trench is likely a secondary crime scene."

Bella joined the conversation. "Are you saying someone killed that girl somewhere else, took her to Heather's property, and buried her there?"

"It's a theory. If Heather's right about a lack of evidence at the crime scene, it fits nicely." He added, "I hope she's right."

"Why?"

Steve brought his hand away from his coffee mug. "If there's a primary crime scene other than the pipeline, that means the killer had to transport the body to the trench."

Heather added, "That's two more places for evidence: The place of the murder and whatever was used to transport the body. It doesn't take much, only a smidgen of someone else's DNA, and guilt can point to another person."

Steve issued a word of caution. "The hard part is finding out where to look for the primary crime scene and the transport vehicle. That's why we need to start interviews as soon as possible."

It was Heather's turn again. "We already have a list and a plan. There's Luke, Janie, and LaShawn. They're our first step to getting into April's world of high school and all the relationships there."

Bella snapped her fingers to signal she had an idea. "There's someone else I could interview."

"Who's that?" asked Heather.

"That creep running the excavator."

"No way. He's nothing but trouble."

Bella stood her ground. "Exactly. He looks like someone central casting would send to play the part of a bad boy. You know, the type your mother always warned you about."

"That's because he is," said Heather.

Bella kept talking. "I could call him and say I'm looking for male models. I need a man who doesn't look like a malnourished wimp—a guy with an independent, dangerous look about him. The interview would take place here with both of you next door."

Bella hadn't convinced her of the sagacity of the idea. Too many risks.

Steve joined in. "I hate the idea, and I like it. Heather's right about Rusty being dangerous, but we need someone to take the pressure off Clay. If we don't give the district attorney something to think about, he'll fight hard for a high bond or no bond."

Heather huffed and paced as Steve and Bella hammered out a plan. Like Jack in selecting a receptionist, she'd been outvoted. She threw up her hands. "I want to include two more people in the room watching."

"Only one," said Steve. "Detective Blake can be with us, but not Jack. He'll be busy taking care of Briann. We'll give both of them a copy of the recordings."

"He's not going to like being excluded," warned Heather. A worry-knot tied itself in Heather's emotions. "I hope we're not making a huge mistake."

Bella's ringing phone put a temporary pause to the meeting. She pulled it from the back pocket of her skinny jeans. "Adam! You'll never guess what's happening here. We're getting a new lake-front home with Mom and Dad living next door."

Heather noticed Bella didn't mention the murder case or that she'd be in training with Steve to extract information from a dangerous ex-con. It was a marital crime of omission.

For the hundredth time, Heather wondered if keeping a secret or two improved a marriage or harmed it. She might never know for sure, but her vote went to supporting the occasional secret. Perhaps that was the reason she felt a small sense of relief when her engagement ended.

Bella ended her conversation and joined them at the conference table. The three of them pushed papers aside and fine-tuned a plan. It contained all the potential suspects and included interviews for Bella to conduct. They decided the only task for Heather was to talk with Jack and ask if Briann wanted to be a combination model and spy.

Heather called in her personal assistant and told her to assist Bella and Steve in setting up the interview rooms. Bella would practice interviewing until Steve was sure she could handle Rusty. Steve suggested they call out for supper.

It was mid-afternoon when Heather called Jack. He answered with, "Hello, beautiful."

"Hi, handsome. Any word yet on Clay's bond hearing?"

"Not yet. Please tell me you have good news."

"We're working on it." Heather spent the next five minutes telling him the short version of their plan for Bella to conduct a series of job interviews. Three would be high school students who had a connection to April Brewer. "We added an employee of Lee Cockrell's by the name of Rusty Brigs to the mix. He has the skills to operate heavy machinery. He's also a two-time ex-con who comes across as a guy who'd kill. I've met him twice, and he gives me the willies."

Jack responded with a measure of doubt. "I'm not sure the judge will take your 'willies' into consideration at a bond hearing. What else do you have?"

Heather knew her reaction to Rusty didn't count for much, but it was true and felt good to say out loud. She continued with relevant facts. "Rusty was working at the construction site the month April died, the same as Clay. He can operate an excavator.

In fact, he took Clay's place and was digging trenches and burying drainage lines today."

"I want to watch Rusty's interview."

Heather gave her head a quick shake, even though Jack couldn't see her. "Sorry. Steve's orders. You'll get a copy of unedited videos."

"I'd rather be there listening." Jack shot out. When Heather didn't respond, he sighed and said, "I guess the recording will be good enough."

Heather sucked in a breath and continued, "There's something else we want you to consider. We'd like Briann to interview to be a model. Bella needs two boys and two girls her age to audition."

Jack remained quiet for several seconds before asking, "What aren't you telling me?"

"How did you know there was more?"

"That little catch in your voice gives you away."

"I'll work on that."

"What else?" asked Jack with more bite in his words.

"We want to include Briann in the investigation in a very limited way. She won't arouse suspicion if she asks questions of the older teens we're going to interview. Steve wants her to sort of nudge them with a question or two. He believes she'd be perfect because they won't suspect a twelve-year-old."

Jack's next words came out with a mirthless laugh. "You want to use my daughter as a spy?"

"I wouldn't put it that way."

"How would you put it?"

"We want to include her to prove you trust her with responsibility. It will help her gain maturity by helping you keep an innocent young man out of prison."

Jack erupted in laughter. "You sure know how to put lipstick on a pig."

When his chuckles subsided, he said, "Let me get this straight. All you're asking Briann to do is sit in a room with three twelfth-graders and other kids her age, ask a few leading questions, and listen?"

"She may not have to ask questions if they're talking among themselves. She'll be there to lend legitimacy to the interviews and spark conversation if it lags."

"It's a fake interview?"

"Not at all. Bella needs models. She thinks Briann will be perfect."

"I don't know about that, nor do I know if she wants to audition to be a model. Are you sure she'll want to?"

"It's your job to help her make the best decision."

"What do you think?"

When she didn't respond, he said, "Any other fine print?"

"That's all."

Jack hesitated before asking, "I insist Briann is only speaking with kids her age or younger, or the high schoolers. Absolutely no contact with Rusty Brigs and I want to hear everything that's said."

Steve gave his head a nod of approval. Heather had the phone far enough away from her ear that he could hear the conversation.

"Of course. All other parents will be in a separate room."

"I assume this will take place at your building. What day?"

"This coming Saturday. The staff will be gone and the kids won't be in school. Be here at nine, but we won't start interviews until ten. We want the potential models to have time to talk among themselves."

Heather could hear Jack tapping something on his desk calendar. "I'll talk to Briann as soon as she comes in from school. It will be her decision."

A breath of relief escaped Heather's lips as she hung up. Jack was on board and she had a feeling Briann would be intrigued enough to agree. She hoped something useful would come from the interviews but had her doubts. If nothing else, Bella might get some suitable models for her new job.

12

The next day Bella made a casting call, of sorts. It consisted of getting word to a local middle and high school that she was looking for candidates to model. As expected, there was a small avalanche of applications. Thankfully, Luke, LaShawn, and Janie had applied, which negated the need for a secondary plan to include the potential suspects. Bella's trained eye made short work of weeding out all but a few besides the three they needed to interview.

On the day of the shoot, Heather, Steve, and Bella tried, with little success, to dodge raindrops as Jack's F-150 pickup slid into a parking space at Heather's building. Bella used Heather's golf umbrella to cover her and Steve until they made it inside.

Heather held the door open for Briann, who took cover under a small umbrella while Jack scurried toward the covered entry wearing a rain jacket with a hood.

Once inside, Bella focused on Briann by enveloping her in a hug before backing off to arm's length. She patted the preteen's hair. "You look absolutely scrumptious. This will be so much fun."

Briann dipped her head. "I'm nervous."

"There's no need to be. All you have to do is ask a few questions and pay attention to what people say."

"It's not that. Anyone can ask questions and listen. It's the modeling." She pointed toward her hair. "Look at this frizzy mess. Of all days for it to rain."

Bella dismissed the comment with a wave of her hand. "I thought I was the ugliest girl on earth when I was your age. Nothing but skinny arms and legs and the figure of a fencepost. Now I look back on past episodes of the hunting shows I co-starred in and realize it was my smile that carried the day. You have an advantage because your hair has loads of body and volume. The dusting of freckles across the bridge of your nose only enhances your awesome smile."

"I can't stand my hair."

"You'll feel better when the makeup and hair artist gets through with you."

Briann's eyes widened. "A real makeup artist?"

"The real deal. She's coming from Houston with the crew. They're bringing clothes for all the models. A perk of this shoot is, you get to keep what you model."

"That's awesome!"

Heather cast her gaze to Jack, who gave her a wink of approval. It was his way of saying thank you. She winked and said, "There's a slight change of plans. You're to watch the interviews and photo shoots in the room with Steve, Detective Blake, and me."

"All of them?"

"Not this afternoon's with Rusty. Steve has something special in store for you with that one."

An armed man wearing the uniform of a security guard approached. Heather directed her attention to him. "Good morning, Charley. I'm expecting several visitors today for a photo shoot. Point them to the elevator and tell them to go to the fourth floor. Someone will direct them from there."

Right on cue, a van sloshed its way through the parking lot

and backed into a *No Parking* space in front of the main entrance. Heather turned to the guard. "They'll move after they unload the racks of clothes and other things we need today."

"I'll give them a hand."

"So will I," said Jack. "No one asked me to be a model."

Bella met his flippant challenge, "I didn't know you wanted to."

"Thanks, but I'd rather go swimming with hungry sharks."

"Is that the punchline of a lawyer joke?" asked Steve.

Heather responded, "When Steve and Jack start making jokes, it's my cue to leave. Who's with me?"

The elevator doors slid open and Heather's personal assistant welcomed them on the fourth floor. After confirming that all was in order with her various businesses, Heather and Briann went into Heather's office while Bella and Steve walked to the interview room.

Briann cast her gaze around the office. "This is the biggest office I've ever seen."

"You should have seen it before renovations. I made part of it into an efficiency apartment."

"Why would you need that?"

"I'm a compulsive worker and have business dealings all over the world. It's not unusual for me to stay here overnight. One day blends into the next at times."

"Mom said everyone needs a good night's sleep."

"Your mother was a wise woman."

Briann's gaze focused on Steve's modest desk. "What's with the second desk and chair?"

"It's Steve's. He comes here when we're working on a case."

"He's amazing."

"That he is," said Heather. "He keeps me grounded."

Briann tilted her head. "How does he do that?"

She smiled. "By finding homicides for us to solve."

"You're weird."

Heather issued a gentle correction. "I'm unique... just like you're unique. Jack tells me your mother was unique, too. Everyone is, once you get to know them."

Briann then asked, "Did you make a deal with Bella to ask me to be a model?"

Heather thought this question might come. It was Briann's way of looking for someone to share the hurt of life kicking her in the teeth. Why not transfer part of the blame to the woman who was dating her father? She hoped this would only be a skirmish and not a full battle.

"Does it matter if I arranged for you to be considered as a model?"

Briann rolled her eyes. "Mom taught me that when lawyers answer a question with another question, they're hiding something."

Heather knew there was only one way out of the trap Briann had set. Only the unvarnished truth would do.

"Like I said, your mother was a wise woman. To answer your question, I do have mixed motives. I like your dad very much and I want to keep dating him without too much drama from you. I thought including you as a model, as well as in the investigation, might earn me a few brownie points. With your looks, you could make a good model plus you're smart enough to get information out of high school students without them becoming suspicious. If you get them talking about April Brewer and the case, it could help your father, Steve, and me, plus an innocent young man you've never met."

Heather knew she'd blunted the first attack when Briann said, "I still don't think I'll make a good swimwear model."

"You may be right. There's no guarantee Bella will select you. That part is up to her. I have no influence."

"Do you hope she chooses me?"

It was another question designed to trap her, but Heather was having none of it. "I think it's a unique opportunity. That's all I have to say about it. If she offers you the chance, that will be between you and your dad."

This earned a smile from Briann. "Dad's right. You're very clever."

The door opened and a line of preteens walked in. Heather concluded that speaking with Briann was like playing chess. It was a good thing she enjoyed the game. She leaned into Briann and whispered, "Practice on these guys. See if you can get them to talk about themselves, but don't reveal anything about you."

Her personal assistant herded the two boys and a girl into Heather's office. The foursome received instructions to sit around a conference table and fill out forms Bella had brought. The questionnaire was light on demographic information and heavy on personal likes and dislikes, preferences in music and movies, social media presence, and why they want to be a sportswear model.

While the young models filled out questionnaires, their parents were in a separate office filling out different forms and reviewing a boilerplate contract.

Bella and Heather allowed the children plenty of time to finish their assignment. The two adults then left Briann alone to practice what Heather had challenged her to do.

After twenty minutes, Bella took the four potential models to separate offices, where they dressed in their first outfits. They alternated between photo shoots and changing into the next selection of sportswear.

Meanwhile, the parents watched the four youngsters strut and pose on a monitor.

Once finished, the excited families reunited. Smiles abounded as they were told they could keep the clothes worn in the photo shoot. Bella answered questions and led three of the four families to the elevator. Their day was done and Bella seemed pleased with the results.

When Briann expressed her sympathy for the young boy who had a pimple on his nose, Bella's comment seemed to surprise Briann. "His bone structure is what I was interested in. We can take out the zit by airbrushing the photos. If the complexion gets worse, I can use him as a model for pants, shorts, and shoes. They take a lot of shots from the neck down."

Briann looked up at the ceiling. "That's where my future as a model lies."

"Absolutely not," said Bella. "You're the best of the bunch, and I'm not saying that to make you feel good. I can't explain why, but the camera loves your face and hair."

Heather spoke up, "I told her she was unique."

"Uniquely beautiful," said Bella.

Steve then brought Briann back down to earth. "You did very well on the modeling part of your assignment. How did you do on gathering information?"

Briann squinted her eyes like she was consulting a mental checklist. "The brunette's name is Stacy. She hates her mother and fights with her constantly."

"Why?" asked Steve.

"Stacy dreams of someday being allowed to eat more than one Krispy Kreme donut a month. She's been modeling all her life and is sick of it. She wants to be a normal kid."

Briann went on before anyone could ask another question. "Randy was cool, except for that big honker of a zit on his nose. His mom has perfect skin, but his dad had a severe case of acne in high school. Randy thinks you'll cut him."

Briann took a quick breath. "Last, but certainly not least, is Bryce. He's an advanced placement kid who likes to work on calculus problems for fun."

Steve asked, "How would they describe you?"

Briann shrugged. "Probably as an airhead. I asked Bryce what calculus was just to see how he'd react. He laughed and explained how to find the volume of a cylinder."

Heather concluded Briann passed the test. She could extract information from her peers. It remained to be seen how she would do with high school students, but her money was on Briann.

13

Bella sequestered the next group of models in Heather's office until they'd all arrived with their parents. Briann was already in the office when the older models arrived.

All went well until Bella announced parents would need to go to a separate office to fill out forms and examine contracts. A woman's voice shot forth. "You told me I could watch Janie during the photo shoot. You lied."

Heather took over. "That wasn't a lie. The room you're going to has a big screen monitor. You and all the other parents will see and hear everything that takes place. We've already completed one shoot with the younger models. Everything went off without a hitch and all four children have a contract."

"I don't care what's happened to others. I want to be in the same room with Janie."

Bella spoke in a soft tone. "We're on a tight schedule, Mrs. Polk."

"It's Ms. Polk or Veronica."

"Of course, Ms. Polk. It's in Janie's best interest if you go with Ms. McBlythe to the observation room. She's an attorney and can explain things in the contract that you might not understand."

"Are you calling me stupid?"

Janie put a hand on her mother's clenched fist. "Mom, please? This is a wonderful opportunity. Think of the money. Please go with them and try not to worry. These are all my classmates. I see them every day at school."

Veronica Polk pointed at Briann. "You don't see her at school every day. She can't be more than ten or eleven years old."

Briann sidestepped the question and answered with confidence. "I was in the first group. I can't believe how much they're paying to take pictures of me wearing cool clothes. Did you know Janie will take all the outfits home with her today?"

"Of course, I know."

Heather ignored the comment and made introductions. "Briann, this is Luke, LaShawn, and Janie." Her gaze moved to the three teens. "We had to hold Briann over from the first shoot with the twelve-year-olds. Some of her blouses need a slight alteration."

"Yeah," said Briann. "They were expecting a girl with something up top, not one that looked like an ironing board."

A snicker came from both young men. Janie Polk didn't react. Even with the worry lines creasing her forehead, the young woman lived up to her billing of being exceptionally beautiful.

Heather redirected her gaze to the other students. "Bella is going to check on the set up for the photo shoot. It will take a while, so talk among yourselves. Since she's been through the process once, Briann can answer questions."

She turned her gaze to the parents and said, "Parents, if you will follow me, I will get you settled in the viewing room and answer any questions you may have about the contracts."

Janie gave her mother a big smile and motioned for her to join the others. Between Heather's command, Briann tempting Veronica with clothes and a lucrative job, and Janie's comforting words, the reluctant mother joined the other parents.

Heather huffed a sigh of relief. She'd known helicopter parents before, but Veronica Polk was in a league of her own.

After giving Briann what she hoped was sufficient time to loosen up the trio of prospective models, Heather returned to her office. "They're ready for you now. Please follow me." She led the teens and Briann past the room where Jack, Detective Loretta Blake and Steve would watch the shoots through one-way glass and listen to the audio that was piped into the sound-proof room.

Heather preceded the group into the room and handed each of the young adults a clipboard that held a questionnaire similar to what the younger models received. The form for the older teens had extra questions about future plans, accomplishments in high school, and a few more personal subjects.

Once left alone, the three older ones worked through the questions. Near the end of the assignment, Luke Paulson asked, "Why do they want to know who I dated?"

Heather was in the observation room in plenty of time to see both LaShawn and Janie shrug. Briann offered an explanation of sorts. "I wondered the same thing. It was easy for me, because I don't date yet."

La Shawn pointed to Janie. "She's had guys chasing her since the sixth grade."

"Shut up, LaShawn. You're still mad 'cause your plan for the prom didn't work. Clay was a wreck."

Luke spoke in a serious tone. "That plan crashed and burned." He shot a knowing glance at Janie. "Someone's mom forgot to take her happy pills and didn't let you go."

Janie dipped her head. "I cried until I ran out of tears."

Silence took over for long seconds that seemed to last minutes. "I'm not answering any question about my social life," said Luke.

LaShawn issued a toothy smile. "That's because you don't have one."

Briann jumped in. "If you don't fill it out completely you can't do the shoot and you won't get paid." She paused. "Just make something up if you don't want to tell the truth. They probably won't check."

Janie chimed in. "I'm not missing out on the money or the chance this might lead to."

Heather leaned into Jack. "She might be right. Janie's gorgeous. Bella hit the jackpot with her."

"Umm," said Jack as he stared. He then whispered, "Somewhere between beautiful and drop-dead gorgeous."

This earned him an elbow in the ribs.

Briann shot a glance at each of the high schoolers. "I heard a guy named Clay killed a girl. Is that the Clay you were talking about?"

"Yeah, that's him," said Luke. "And for your information, Clay wouldn't kill anyone, let alone April. Clay and I are tight. He's not wired that way."

"No way he could hurt April," said Janie in agreement.

Heather thought she detected too much emotion in Janie's response. Was that a wink she gave LaShawn?

LaShawn's gaze shifted to the mirror on the wall and then back to Janie. "I heard April started dating an ex-con." He shifted his gaze to Janie. "Didn't she take up with that guy who always hits on high school girls at the Melody Barn?"

Janie added, "Clay being in jail proves my mom was right. I'm glad we broke up a long time ago."

Instead of letting the conversation play out, Briann asked, "Why did your mom make you break up with him?"

All three of the older students seemed to wake up at the same time. Janie tilted her head. "You sure are inquisitive."

"Yeah," said LaShawn. "Too nosy. Do you think you're some sort of Nancy Drew or something?"

Steve spoke for the first time. "Get her out of there, Heather."

She was already on her feet, heading to the door. Within seconds, she was looking at Jack's daughter. "Briann, they're ready for you to try on your blouses. Come with me, please."

Heather brought Briann back into the observation room. Jack gave her a weak smile. "You did great."

"No, I didn't," said Briann. "I pushed too hard. They were talking, and I blew it."

Steve took over. "I picked up on several outright lies or attempts at deception."

"Like what?" asked Briann.

Steve ran a hand across his chin. "Your father will get a copy of these tapes. I want you to study them. Begin with this question: Why didn't Luke want to divulge who he dated in high school?"

Briann's eyes opened wide and groaned. "I shoulda' caught that. What else did I miss?"

Steve then added, "Watch the tape as many times as it takes until you can answer that question."

"I noticed something," said Detective Blake. "Rusty Brigs is moving up in my book of suspects."

Heather realized what Steve had done. By including the detective, she'd heard something that would prompt her to keep the case file open. Luke's reaction to the personal questions caused Heather to wonder if Luke had a relationship with April that he was hiding.

Jack put a hand on his daughter's shoulder. "You did very well today. I'm proud of you."

As expected, Briann let out a huff through her nose, showing she didn't agree with his assessment. He countered her reaction with a question. "Do you want to stick around and see if Bella can get any more out of these three?"

She shrugged half-heartedly. "You'll get a video, right?"

Heather answered for him. "I'll email the video to your dad, Steve, and Detective Blake."

Steve jumped into the conversation. "Why don't you and your dad go over the interviews tomorrow? I'll come by his office Monday after school and you can tell me what you found."

"I'd like that," said Briann.

Jack's bobbing head preceded his words. "I would, too." He smiled and said, "I believe this young lady has earned herself a nice lunch."

Steve grumbled. "You're going out for a meal and Heather's having sub sandwiches delivered."

"The lady thinks the man doth protest too much," said Heather.

"Nice play off Shakespeare," said Briann.

"Thanks."

Bella opened the door in time to hear the lunch conversation. She cast her gaze to Briann. "If you're not staying for lunch, I'll get your clothes. I hope you like them."

Briann smiled. "They're great, and so are you. Thanks for the modeling gig. It was a lot more fun than I thought it would be."

14

Heather escorted father and daughter to the elevator. As she bid them goodbye, she hoped by including Briann today a brick or two had loosened in the wall that divided them. It had been a good day of info-gathering and it wasn't over yet. Bella's interview Luke, LaShawn and Janie prior to and during the photo shoots might reveal another nugget or two.

Finally, Rusty was coming later in the afternoon. That could be fun.

Heather returned to Steve and Detective Blake. Bella had already found her way back to the interview room and stood facing Steve. He spoke in a calm, reassuring voice. "Remember, don't press too hard like Briann did. Silence can be your best friend when interviewing. Ask a leading question and wait for an answer. If you get something flippant, react with facial expressions and body language, but not words. It will make them uncomfortable, and people usually expound on their answers if you give them time."

Bella puffed out her cheeks and released a huff of air. "What else?"

"Spend more time with LaShawn Moody. We have a pretty good read on Luke and Janie, but LaShawn's deflecting. Keep showing that you know he's not forthcoming with his answers. Use gestures, silence, and if you must, come down on him hard with words."

"Like what?"

"Tell him part of his interview includes role play. The job requires him to communicate effectively with the public. Challenge him to tell a story. Make it relevant to the case."

Bella shot Heather a look that communicated she might be in over her head.

Heather threw her a lifeline. "Tell LaShawn that he's an ambassador for the sportswear company. He'll be required to brag about the company's products with all types of people everywhere he goes. Ask him to demonstrate how he would talk to Luke about the clothes he's wearing."

"I like that," said Steve.

Heather kept talking. "After he does that, tell him to pretend he's talking to Clay. We need to see how he reacts."

"You make it sound so easy."

Steve reached out his hand for Bella to take. She did, and he gave it a firm squeeze. "Pretend it's a game. Something like hide and seek, except you're searching for information."

"I can do that. Adam and I love to play board games with friends."

Steve released her hand. "Did someone mention sandwiches are coming?"

"Work comes first," said Heather. "Let's start with LaShawn."

The door clicked shut behind Bella, leaving Heather, Steve, and Detective Blake in the observation room. Loretta was the first to speak. "This is a wonderful refresher on interviewing techniques, but it hasn't changed my mind about Clay's guilt. I wish it wasn't him, but all the evidence points toward him."

"True," said Steve. "But we're still gathering evidence. In the meantime, I'm looking for a motive."

Bella led the way as she and LaShawn entered the room for the photo shoot. He was a handsome young man who looked like a model with close-cropped, curly black hair and chiseled facial features. Stunning green eyes competed with a dazzling, somewhat crooked smile.

Heather noted his lean build and erect posture. It was easy to imagine him as a professional model.

Bella pointed to a chair in front of the cameras and asked him to take a seat. She pulled up a chair and sat at a slight angle in front of him. The placement of her chair allowed the cameras to capture him and gave the occupants of the viewing room an unobstructed view.

Bella leaned back in her chair and lolled her left leg over the right. She began the interview by saying: "I understand you've never done modeling before."

"That's right."

"I love to work with new models. The first thing I need you to do is relax. The camera will capture any hint of nervousness." She uncrossed her legs. "Sit like I'm sitting and place your hands on your thighs."

He did as she instructed.

"Now close your eyes, take in a full breath, and hold it."

He followed her lead as she said, "Now release it slowly."

After four more cleansing breaths, she said, "Start with the top of your head and release any tension in your scalp. We're going to work our way all the down to the soles of your feet."

Bella named body parts from forehead to feet. Shoulders showed the most significant difference as LaShawn allowed them to drop.

"Keep your eyes closed and tell me about the most peaceful place you've ever been to."

It took LaShawn a few seconds to answer. "I'm alone by a mountain stream in Colorado. The only thing I can hear is water rippling over rocks."

"Very good," said Bella. "When you open your eyes, you'll continue to hear the water. You'll see the cameras, but they'll be like the trees by the stream, a part of the landscape."

"This is nice," said LaShawn.

Steve was the first in the viewing room to make a comment. "Now that he trusts her, she can begin her questions."

Loretta asked, "Did you teach her that trick?"

"I found a variation of that technique works well with teens, especially with those who are trying to hide something."

"She's off to a good start," said Heather as she and Detective Blake stood shoulder to shoulder, looking through the one-way mirror. "Let's see if Bella can get LaShawn to talk about himself."

Right on cue, Bella asked, "Do you really want to model sportswear?"

"I wouldn't be here if I didn't. The money seems good. The work may take up a lot of time, but I have plenty of that."

Bella consulted the questionnaire he'd completed. "One thing I insist on is absolute honesty from my models."

"What do you mean? I was honest."

Bella held up the three-page document. "You're a very handsome young man. Do you expect me to believe you've never dated?"

"We three decided that question wasn't relative to us being models."

Steve spoke up. "He's shifting the blame again. Let's see if Bella remembers how to respond."

Instead of speaking, Bella remained quiet but continued to hold up the questionnaire.

"Let's make a deal," said LaShawn as he held up his hands in a pretend surrender. "Tell me why it's important and I'll tell you about my love life."

Bella didn't drop the stapled pages or say a word.

LaShawn issued a smile that was more crooked than his normal one. "I have nothing to be ashamed of. I've dated plenty of girls. Now it's your turn to tell me why it's important."

"I'll need names if you want to work for me, but I'm willing to compromise. First names only. Make a complete list and when you dated them. I'll tell you why it's important at the end of our interview."

Heather whispered, "I hope she didn't paint herself into a corner."

Steve's chin lifted. "She didn't. We did a lot of role play."

Heather kept her gaze on Bella and LaShawn as he asked, "How far back do you want me to go?"

"High school only."

It didn't take as long as Heather thought it would for LaShawn to complete the list and hand the clipboard back to her. She ran a finger down the list, lifted her gaze to him, and kept it there.

"That's all. I swear." LaShawn crossed his arms. "I go for quality."

Bella dragged her finger down the page until it rested on a name. "Is that why you dated this girl named April when you were a sophomore? That's pretty young to date. I'm not sure I would describe girls that age as 'quality'."

Steve's whisper wasn't as soft this time. "Good job, Bella."

Heather shifted her gaze back to the interview room and LaShawn as he uncrossed his arms. "April was a great girl, lots of fun to be around. You know how sophomore romances go. Here today, gone tomorrow."

"If she was so great, why did you break up? Was there someone else for one of you?"

"We moved on by mutual agreement. My friend Luke was her next stop, but that was a one-sided relationship that didn't last long. I don't know what happened. Clay, another friend of ours, came next, but that ended, too."

Heather turned to Detective Blake. "Do you think he's lying?"

"No doubt about it, but which part?"

"Most all of it," said Steve.

Bella moved on. "I understand you and Janie Polk are friends.

If you like quality so much, why isn't she on the list of girls you've dated?"

"Her mom's her gatekeeper. I didn't qualify."

"Because you're black?"

He laughed. "Because her mother watches her like a prison guard. I never stood a chance for the same reason no one else does." LaShawn tapped his head. "Janie's mom is not right in the attic, if you know what I mean."

It came as a surprise to Heather when Steve said, "That's enough from LaShawn. Tell Bella to get on with the shoot. Then let's see what she can get out of Luke."

Heather sent Bella a text. Steve remained silent during the shoot, leaving Heather to carry on a conversation with Loretta. The session ended and the young men traded places.

Luke had changed his mind about withholding personal information and filled out his questionnaire. Heather snuck frequent glances at Steve during the second interview. He never moved, but sat with hands folded into something that looked like a church with its steeple resting on his lips.

Someone who didn't know Steve the way Heather did would think he'd lost interest. She'd bet a good sum that he heard something important and was putting it through a test of sorts. Perhaps Luke said something earlier that he was processing. It might be a stray word that LaShawn had uttered. Whatever it was, he went to a deep place to consider it.

Heather was so lost in her own thoughts that she didn't notice when Bella finished asking Luke questions and came through the door of the viewing room. "I've run out of things to ask him."

Steve came to life. "Do the shoot and move on to Janie."

Heather followed Bella into the hallway as the newlywed asked, "Is Steve all right?"

The flick of Heather's hand preceded her words. "He must have heard something important and needs time to put it in the right cubbyhole."

"How does he do that? I didn't hear a thing."

Heather shook her head. "Beats me, but there are people in prison who wish he wasn't so good at what he does."

"It's such a rush to think someone we're talking to could be the killer."

Heather ignored the comment, bringing Bella back to the task at hand. "We're running a little behind. Steve will growl if he doesn't get a sandwich soon."

Bella released one of her trademark giggles. "I'll fetch Janie. She's so beautiful, her shoot won't take long."

It came as a surprise when Steve joined them in the hallway. "Bella, we're running late. Cut out the questions for Janie and go straight to the photo shoot. I don't want any of the high schoolers or their parents here when Rusty arrives."

15

Submarine sandwiches weren't Heather's favorite meal, so she took off the top half of the bun and ate half a sandwich open-faced. Steve ate all of his plus her other half, along with potato chips and a cookie. After he finished the meal, he was in a more talkative mood.

With Bella sitting next to him at the conference table in their office, Steve leaned her way. "How have the photo shoots turned out so far?"

"LaShawn and Janie are the standouts. Both could make a career out of modeling if they wanted."

"Too bad Clay's in jail. I understand he's a handsome young man."

Bella shook her head even though Steve couldn't see her. "Heather showed me photos of him in the school yearbook. He's one of those guys who looks better in person. His eyelids droop too much."

"One more potential model and we're through for the day," said Steve. "Based on what we've told you, what's your opinion of Rusty?"

Heather broke in, "Don't answer. He's setting you up."

Bella spoke with confidence. "Steve's not the only person setting someone up."

Heather raised her eyebrows and grinned. "What are you up to?"

"Be careful," said Steve solemnly. "Rusty didn't spend time in prison for singing too loud in a church choir."

"I know. Would it be all right if I did most of the shoot and waited until the last change to ask questions?"

"That's a good idea. If there's a problem and you need to get out of there, Heather will come in."

"I'll be right there with her," said Detective Blake. "Rusty's been a boil on the backside of this county for a long time."

Bella burst out in a laugh. "That's quite a visual. I hope I don't think about it while I'm talking to him."

Lunch came to an abrupt end when Heather's PA came in and announced Rusty was waiting to change into his first outfit.

Bella faced the photographers, two wardrobe workers, and the hair and makeup artist. "Let's make the last shoot of the day the best so you can get back to Houston."

The workers didn't need to be told twice. Heather, Steve, and Loretta were soon in the observation room as Bella instructed Rusty on how to pose.

"He's stiff as a flagpole," said Heather. "What a dirtbag. He keeps coming on to her, but Bella's ignoring everything he's saying."

"I can hear," said Steve. "She's doing what I told her."

Bella and the photographer finished the first shoot, and the male wardrobe worker led Rusty to change into his second outfit. It didn't take long for the ex-con-turned-model to ditch a manly outfit of cargo pants, work boots, and a hooded sweatshirt. He returned wearing straight-leg trousers, deck shoes, and a collared shirt with the tail worn out.

Rusty reminded Heather of a snake slithering as he walked across the room and stopped beside Bella. If he got any closer, she was going in. "That's a nice ring on your finger, but I don't think it means I can't take you for a spin around a dance floor. There's no harm in that. I know a nice place not far from here."

Bella's response was quick. "Focus on what you're being paid for."

Rusty gave her a lecherous smile. "If you'd rather take a ride in the country, we don't have to go dancing. I'm open to just about anything. What about you?"

"Look to your right and don't smile."

Loretta stood by Heather and said, "I'd like to take him for a ride... straight to county jail."

The camera clicked and Rusty continued his suggestive banter until the photographer said, "That's plenty. Let's get him into his last outfit."

When Rusty returned, he wasn't smiling.

Heather covered her mouth to stifle a laugh. Loretta said, "He looks like an Easter egg."

Bella had chosen a special outfit for him—an Easter-bunny pink jogging suit with white high-top tennis shoes. He carried a pink baseball cap in his right hand with the company logo embroidered across the front.

"I ain't wearing this stupid hat."

Bella said, "The contract you signed calls for you to wear whatever we tell you to."

"I don't care. You're nothing but a tease. I should have known better when you called me and said you were looking for a real man to model." His eyes narrowed into thin slits. "I'm not having my picture taken wearing pink."

Bella tented her hands on her hips. "For your information, that outfit represents breast cancer awareness. There's an entire advertising campaign designed around it. If you don't pose in it, you'll not only forfeit your salary, but you'll go to court for the cost of the outfits and our time."

"I make plenty of money. I don't need this. If you think the threat of a petty civil case means anything to me, you're wrong.

The only reason I agreed to come today was because I could tell you were looking for a good time."

"Would you like to talk to one of our attorneys?"

"You're bluffin'."

Bella responded with silence.

Steve spoke, but only Heather and Loretta could hear him. "Say nothing, Bella. Let silence work for you."

The seconds ticked by as the impasse stretched on and on. Rusty was the first to bend. His crooked smile returned. "Perhaps we could compromise."

Bella tilted her head. "What do you have in mind?"

"You can take my picture in this if you agree to go dancing with me."

Bella hesitated. "You didn't fully fill out the questionnaire. You'll also agree to answer questions we ask. The answers must be true and there's nothing off limits. Do that, and I'll dance with you."

"Where's that form?"

Heather said, "No, Bella."

"Tell him he has a deal," said Steve.

"What?" demanded Heather.

"Trust me."

Heather's gaze shifted back into the room as Bella extended her hand. "It's a deal. You agree to answer questions and complete the photo shoot, and I'll dance with you."

The two shook hands. Bella jerked hers away.

Bella stood behind the camera and directed the shoot. "I'm going for something whimsical. Stand in front of the green screen like you did before, and we'll be able to put various backgrounds in the pictures. Put the baseball cap on sideways and mount the tricycle we brought."

"No way."

Bella pouted. "I thought you wanted to dance with me. I was looking forward to seeing your moves."

The shoot progressed when Rusty mounted the undersized

prop. Heather asked Steve, "What kind of backgrounds will she put in the photos?"

Steve's smile threatened to stretch his face. "Prison cells and scenes of Texas prison farms. She has no intention of using him as a model. This is her insurance policy against him coming after her."

"Sweet!" said Loretta. "He'd be the darling of the cell block if other inmates got hold of them."

Further discussion ceased as Bella announced, "That's a wrap. Now it's time for you to answer some questions."

"Not until I put on real clothes."

"Go ahead. I'll be right here."

It didn't take long for Rusty to get back into jeans, a black T-shirt with a country-western singer's face on the front, and boots. He covered the shirt with an unbuttoned denim shirt.

Bella looked up from the chair she'd set a safe distance away from its mate. Rusty flopped down in the identical chair and extended his legs in front of him. "Let's make this quick. I want to give you plenty of time to get ready for our date. It's going to be a night you'll never forget."

Bella took out the contract. "I see you've signed this. Did you read and understand it?"

"Yeah. I read it."

"Good. Let's go over a couple of items. You admit to only one arrest, but you didn't say what it was for."

"Put down whatever you want. It was a long time ago."

"I can't do that."

Rusty took his time answering. Steve said, "Here comes a lie."

"Hot checks. Put that down, even though it was the bank's fault. They lost a deposit I made."

Bella then asked, "You work as a heavy equipment operator?"

"Yeah. You saw me. I can operate anything you can name."

The interview progressed, with Bella verifying that Rusty was working in the general area where they found April's body. She then shifted to ask questions related to the victim.

"Ms. McBlythe told me they found a girl's body at the construction site. That must have been awful. Was it you that found her?"

"Nah. I wasn't operating the digger that day."

"Did you know the girl? Was she someone local?"

"Yeah, she was local. Her name was April Brewer, but I didn't know her. Not really."

Heather, Steve, and Loretta all came to attention like well-trained bird dogs. Steve said, "Bingo."

From the other side of the glass, Bella asked, "What do you mean *not really?*"

Rusty shrugged. "She liked to dance. There's a dance hall I go to. Quite a few high school kids go there. The place has good burgers and the bands are decent."

Loretta shook her head. "It looks like I'll be going home very late tonight. I have all I need to detain him for further questioning."

Steve held up a hand. "Let's see if Bella can get anything else out of him."

Heather's gaze shifted back to Bella as she asked, "So you whirled April Brewer around the floor from time to time. Did you also leave the club with her and show her a good time like you want to show me?"

"Are you kidding? I'm not into girls." His gaze swept over her like he was picking out produce. "You're more my type."

"I heard she was eighteen."

Rusty rubbed his chin. "What are you up to? This has nothing to do with modeling clothes. I think it's time for you and me to take a ride."

"Wait. We have a deal and I want to fulfill my part." Bella pulled her phone from a back pocket and soon had an up-tempo song playing. She stood a suitable distance away from him and gave a halfhearted attempt to sway from side to side. She looked at him. "Aren't you going to dance? It was your idea."

"Hilarious. That's not the dancing we're gonna' do." He

reached into the waistband of his jeans and pulled out a black semi-automatic pistol. "You and me are leaving right now."

Detective Blake burst out of the observation room with pistol in hand. Heather followed with her pink-handled .9 mm pointed toward the floor. Come what may, Rusty wasn't leaving the building with Bella.

Heather and Loretta stopped outside the door. Heather asked, "How do you want to handle this?"

To her surprise, Steve stood behind her. "Don't shoot him. I had Bella go into the room where he changed clothes and unload his pistol."

Heather wanted to slap him, then hug him. He'd thought ahead but once again hadn't included her in his plan. Both she and Loretta let out a huff of relief. Not only had Steve taken precautions to protect Bella from a dangerous man, but he gave the police a viable suspect other than Clay. Jack would be thrilled.

A crash from inside the room brought Heather back from her musings. The two women entered and found Rusty doubled over in pain. Bella looked satisfied with herself. "All it takes is one good kick where it hurts and guys fold like a cheap lawn chair." She pointed to Rusty's empty pistol on the floor.

Detective Blake pocketed the empty weapon, then flipped the writhing man onto his stomach. After snapping handcuffs on him, she escorted him out the door.

After Heather's pulse slowed, her anger came alive. Steve had planned and executed the most dangerous part of the plan without telling her how it would play out. By the time they were back in their office, she had her speech all ready to deliver.

Before she could open her mouth, Steve's phone came to life. The mechanical voice said the call was from the fire department.

"I'd better get this."

"Mr. Steve Smiley?"

"Yes."

"This is Lieutenant Roberts with the fire department. We're at your condo. There's been a fire. The damage is significant."

"Max!" shouted Heather.

"Bucky Franklin," said Steve.

16

Heather burst out the front door of her office building, barely aware that Steve and Bella were in her shadow. They piled into her Mercedes SUV with Steve in the back seat. Tires squealed as Heather took the turn out of the parking lot and headed for I-45.

Traffic kept her from achieving more than fifty miles an hour, regardless of how much she weaved in and out of honking cars. They were halfway to their condos in Spring, a city located a mere ten minutes south of The Woodlands, when the revelation hit her. She raised her voice so it would reach the back seat. "Why did you say Bucky Franklin's name?"

Steve cleared his throat. "I think he torched my condo."

Heather gripped the steering wheel tighter. "Surely he wouldn't go to such lengths because of some digital books? Are you positive he did it?"

"Not yet."

Heather drove another mile before speaking again. "You're too quiet. There's more to this story. What did you do to him?"

He cleared his throat again. "I was going to ask you the same thing."

Heather had a bad feeling about what was going on. Steve

was being deceptive, and her beloved cat might be dead or seriously injured. This was no time for verbal jousting.

"Mr. Smiley," said Heather in her best lawyer voice. "You're not being forthcoming, and I don't appreciate it."

He heaved a sigh. "Answer two questions, and I'll tell you the whole truth and nothing but the truth. When was the last time you spoke with Constance Banks, and what did you discuss?"

Heather glanced in her rearview mirror, then brought her attention back to the road. "She called me last week and asked if I wanted to delay proceedings against Bucky Franklin. I told her to proceed."

"That explains it."

"Explains what?"

"Why we're rushing to a fire at my condo."

She wasn't going to let him get by with such an incomplete answer. "Keep talking."

"While he was assaulting me, I led him to believe I'd drop the civil action against him."

This wasn't what Heather expected. She tried to keep panic and anger out of her voice. Anger won out as she spoke through gritted teeth. "When, where, and how did he assault you?"

Steve sounded calm. "The day after he was served with papers for copyright infringement. Bucky pretended to be a delivery driver. I made the mistake of opening the door for him. Once inside, he showed me how vulnerable I am and gave me a taste of what he's capable of. After a brief conversation, he dumped semi-hot coffee on my head. After that, he grabbed my right wrist and shoved it up my back farther than it's meant to go at my age. I haven't touched that spot between my shoulder blades since I was in the tenth grade."

Bella turned in her seat to look at him, her blue eyes filled with alarm. "Why isn't he in jail?"

"He will be, in due time. Leo's working on it."

Heather was ready to explode, but first she needed the full story. Once again, she pretended this was a courtroom and not a luxury car. "To follow up on Bella's question, why the delay? You could, and should, have filed charges against him that day."

"He said he had two cops ready to give him an alibi. I was in no position to argue. Besides, I needed to get more on him than a simple assault and a civil case."

Another revelation hit Heather. "That's why your face looked like you'd stayed in the sun and wind too long."

"Yeah. I'm glad he didn't come earlier when the coffee was scalding hot."

Heather thought he'd finished his confession, but she was wrong. "I had him bluffed. It would have worked if you hadn't talked with Constance and told her to proceed."

His last statement popped the cork on her emotions. "No, you don't, Mr. Smiley. You're not putting the blame for this on me. Part of being a business partner is not keeping secrets from each other. This assault happened while we've been working a case. It's not like you haven't seen me lately. You should have kept me informed."

Steve shifted in his seat. "You're right, but we both keep secrets from each other. It's the way we're hard-wired, or haven't you noticed?"

Deep down, Heather knew he spoke the truth, but she wouldn't give up without a fight. "What secret am I keeping from you?"

"How about the duplexes you're planning to build on Lake Conroe? One of which concerns me. If you hadn't let it slip, I still wouldn't know about that."

"That's different. I was planning to surprise you with it."

Steve spoke in what she took to be a condescending tone. "You have more to say. Go ahead and get it all out."

"You didn't tell me you snuck into Rusty's dressing room and unloaded his pistol."

Bella spoke up. "Uh... that was me who took out the bullets. Steve just told me to check to see if he had a weapon."

The steam in Heather's emotional teapot had reached full

boil and was screaming to be released. Her words came out clipped when she said, "You involved Bella, but didn't bother telling me?"

Instead of coming back at her with another argument, Steve chuckled. "It looks like everyone kept something to themselves. Unloading the pistol was a nice touch, Bella. Everyone's safe, Rusty's in jail for attempted kidnapping, and Clay may not have a bond hearing on Monday morning."

With some of the tension between the two detectives ebbing away, Bella asked, "Why not?"

Steve explained, "Rusty is on tape admitting to working in the same area as Clay. He had just as much opportunity to kill April and bury her body under the drainage pipe. We got lucky when he admitted to knowing April and dancing with her at a club. Until we see the forensic results, I'd say he and Clay are equal on evidence, with the exception of Clay's letter jacket. It wouldn't surprise me if Clay was back at work by Monday or Tuesday."

Heather's thoughts were fixed on the murder suspects when Steve said, "You're coming up on our exit. If you miss it, you'll be madder at yourself than you are with me."

Her anger and frustration slowly subsided, like a boiling kettle with the heat turned off. "We'll delay this conversation but it's not over."

Two fire trucks with lights ablaze stood in front of their condos with hoses snaked across the parking lot. Ladders reached to the roof where firefighters stood. She pulled into an empty parking space when an officer stopped her forward progress. Steve leaned forward. "Check on Max. I'd only be in the way."

Bella stayed with Steve as Heather quick-walked to the condos they'd called home for several years. Steve's condo had a hole cut in the roof. Her side did not. This told her that his side of the duplex received the bulk of the damage.

Heather had attended enough fires when she was a cop in

Boston to understand the hole was there to vent smoke. Fans sat in the doorways of both dwellings.

She approached a man wearing a white fireman's hat. "The condo on the left is mine," she said, trying to keep the panic out of her voice. "My cat was inside. Is he all right?"

The man replied to something on his radio and turned his attention to her. "Was that a cat? The first crew to arrive didn't know what it was because of its size. He's probably all right, but when they kicked in your front door, he shot out so fast nobody could get a hand on him."

"Where did he go?"

The man pointed to a wooded area a hundred yards away. "That direction."

Heather almost ran into Bella, who said, "I put Steve on a bench near the trees." They turned at the same time. Bella took loping strides with her long legs. Heather was glad she'd worn sensible shoes with her slacks and blazer but wished she'd worn running shoes instead. Both hollered for Max when they got to within fifty yards of the trees.

"Let's split up," said Heather. "Go left, and I'll look to our right. He should answer us if he's not hurt or too afraid."

Heather slowed her pace to a fast walk when she came under a canopy of pines and oaks. She called out to Max repeatedly, hoping he'd make his presence known. A glance over her shoulder revealed Steve approaching with his white cane leading the way. He, too, was calling out for Max, but he tried a different tactic. He moved to a spot barely within the tree canopy and sat down. Now and then, he'd holler Max's name, then wait and listen.

It only took a few minutes before she heard Steve shout, "Over here!"

Heather was out of breath after sprinting to where Steve sat. "Where is he?"

Steve pointed skyward. "Up high. It's a good thing the fire department is already here with ladders. You may have to climb up to get him. I don't think he's happy about being in a house fire."

Bella arrived and Steve had an assignment for her. "Go tell the firefighters we found Max and we're going to need a very long ladder."

Bella jogged back to the firetrucks, leaving Steve with Heather. He spoke while resting his hands on his cane. "If he ran all that distance and climbed as high as he sounds, old Max may have lost one or two of his nine lives due to fright. Otherwise, I'm sure he's unharmed."

"I'll feel better when he's on the ground."

She glanced back toward their condos. "We need to find somewhere to stay for quite a while. Our places aren't habitable."

Steve spoke in a tone that sounded like the loss of their homes didn't faze him in the least. "I called your PA when you were talking to the firefighters. She's looking for a furnished rental we can get into tonight. I told her to make it big enough for us three and Adam. He'll be here tomorrow."

"You called him, too?"

"Of course not. Didn't you see Bella text him on the ride from your office? She told me when you rushed to talk to the firefighters about Max."

Heather stared at her partner. Steve was always one step ahead of her. His composure in tense situations was both impressive and infuriating. Her anger had blocked out Bella's presence in the car with them. She longed to be more like him in stressful situations, but with her hot-headed Scot personality, she wasn't sure if it was attainable.

Her kettle was starting to boil again. She wasted a perfectly good glare on her blind business partner and asked, "Who else have you talked to while I was chasing my cat?"

The answer came in the same matter-of-fact tone. "Only Leo." Steve issued a chuckle. "He's quite amusing when he goes into one of his screaming fits. You should hear him cuss in Spanish. It rolls off his tongue so fast I can't understand him. Bucky made a powerful enemy. There's no telling what will happen to him by the time Leo and Constance Banks are through."

"Did you call her, too?"

Steve switched to his questioning voice. "Why would I do that? It's Saturday, and most attorneys don't like phone calls on their days off. Besides, you're responsible for the litigation side of dealing with Bucky."

The revelations were coming so fast Heather wasn't sure she could keep up. Steve didn't help when he kept talking. "I told Leo he'd need to explain everything to the local police and the fire captain. We can come back tomorrow and give formal statements. No use in us hanging around here since this is now a crime scene."

Heather wanted to gain a victory of some sort to counter his barrage of information. "I have a better idea. Why don't I depose you tonight and email the police your confession of keeping information from me?"

Steve shrugged. "That's a good idea. We won't have to come back."

Max let out a screeching howl from far above them. Heather kept her gaze on the black fur while she asked, "Anything else you did without consulting me?"

"Only one more. I had tiny video cameras installed inside and outside my condo after Bucky attacked me. Leo has access to the recordings. He'll give them to the police and arson investigators. Others will take care of Bucky. I should be able to devote myself full-time to solving the murder starting tomorrow morning." He pointed upward. "That's assuming you can get Max down from that tree."

Heather turned her gaze to him. "I'm surprised you haven't solved the murder by now." She paused. "Or have you?"

"Almost. We still need the forensic report from the secondary crime scene where Clay discovered April. Then we have to find the primary crime scene, find the vehicle the killer transferred the body in, discover motives, and fill in some gaps in background information on all the suspects."

He gave his head a nod. "That should keep us busy a while longer."

Heather gave a huff and walked away. "I'm leaving you here. I need to get my cat."

17

Heather pulled her car into a parking space at a store that carried everything she, Steve, and Bella would need to make it through a couple of nights. She announced, "This shouldn't take long. We'll all need sleepwear and two or three outfits. Bella and I need makeup. Steve, don't forget all your bathroom supplies. You're starting over from scratch."

"I'd rather shop at a second-hand store for clothes," said Steve. "They're more comfortable. Besides, I don't answer to the fashion police."

Heather shot back. "You're still on my Christmas naughty list. You'll wear what Bella and I pick out for you."

He responded with a tongue-in-cheek response. "Isn't there a perfectly good pink jogging suit in your office? I could wear it for a couple of days."

"The wardrobe people took it back to Houston," said Bella. "I can get one for you. It could be a conversation starter for supporting breast cancer awareness."

Heather grumbled instead of offering a response. She unfastened her seat belt.

Steve's door opened, but he didn't get out. "Your cat smells like a chimney."

"Be nice to Max. He's had a hard day."

"He's not the only one. You know I hate to shop, especially in a full-price store. Let's get this over with. I've overworked my brain, and I'd like an early bedtime." He took a quick breath. "After supper, of course."

Heather looked in the back seat. Max raised his head and hissed.

"I know, my sweet boy. You've had the worst day of all. Mommy will get you several cans of tuna, your favorite cat food, a new bed, the kitty treats you like so much, a scratch box, and a brand-new litter box. I'll order some toys from the online catalog tonight."

"You won't order anything unless we stop by your office," said Steve. "That's where we left our laptops."

Heather hated to admit he was right again. They'd fled the building in such a rush, she'd left everything behind but her pistol and car keys. She didn't even take her purse. She groaned. "Does anyone have a credit card or cash on them?"

"Not me," said Bella. "My purse is at your office."

"I don't leave home without it," said Steve with too much swagger in his voice for her taste.

He topped off his comment with, "I was wondering when you'd realize your purse is in the bottom right drawer of your desk."

She'd heard enough. "Congratulations, Mr. Smiley. You get the privilege of paying for this outing. Since you hate shopping so much, stay here with Max." She gave Bella a stare that didn't invite comments and took Steve's credit card as he handed it between the seats. "Let's go. We'll leave the men here to talk about manly things."

Heather was still mad enough to spit. She tried to take the first shopping cart out of a long line, but it was wedged tight. She jerked two more times. Three carts shot out, bonded together like someone had welded them.

Bella came to her rescue by taking hold of the handle of the next cart in line. It slid from the line with ease. They walked in silence to the area near the pharmacy. Heather tossed an assortment of personal items into the cart, barely taking time to look at what she was buying. Bella came along behind her, adding her own items to the growing pile.

Next, they went to the clothing section. It didn't take Bella long to pick out three complete sets of pants and shirts for Steve. Then came sleep shorts, socks, underwear, two pairs of shoes, a jacket, a belt, and a knit cap.

After putting her haul into the basket, she turned to look at Heather. "I know it's been a hard day for everyone, but why are you so mad at Steve?"

Heather closed her eyes for several seconds. It wasn't the first time she'd been angry with him and she couldn't promise it would be the last. She searched for an answer that didn't sound petty and couldn't come up with anything. A response occurred to her but she didn't like it.

"You asked an excellent question and I wish I had a better answer."

"Does it have to do with the fact that you like being in charge?"

"Yes."

"And is it because you're very competitive?"

Heather nodded. "Keep going. You're two for two."

"And it bothers you because he can think of a hundred things at once and keep them all straight in his head?"

"Not only that," said Heather. "Sometimes he doesn't need me at all."

"That's not true and you know it. He couldn't make it without you when you two work a case. You're just not used to someone who can see what needs to happen before you do in murder investigations. Your strengths lie with business."

Heather considered the young woman's words and found them to be true. Steve was a master at solving crimes, but he had his limitations. She could turn little stacks of money into large ones. Bella used her beauty and unshakable optimism to brighten people's lives. Everyone had their place.

Before she knew it, Heather wrapped her arms around Bella. "When did you become so wise?"

Bella flashed a wide smile and joked, "It came in a flash the moment I met Adam."

It was such a ridiculous answer that she couldn't help but laugh and say, "You've identified my problem. If I was married, all my frustrations would melt away."

Bella ignored Heather's joking statement and returned to their original subject. "Steve really is amazing. He knows so much about me, and about you, too, but I know hardly anything about him other than his late wife's name was Maggie. I don't even know if his parents are alive or dead."

"They're dead," said Heather. "I asked him the year we started working together. He changed the subject and never spoke of them again." She tilted her head. "I don't even know their names."

Bella asked, "Do you think Steve could be an angel?"

Heather shook her head. "He's more like a benevolent ghost. An angel wouldn't enjoy seeing me get so frustrated."

The basket was almost full, so Heather said, "This should get us by. Let's get back to our angel ghost."

The talk with Bella gave Heather something to think about other than making up a speech to say to Steve to put him in his place. Like it or not, Bella was right. Steve hadn't said or done anything worthy of her wrath except not including her in a plan to take care of Bucky Franklin. It occurred to her that Steve considered Bucky a nuisance and not a serious problem.

Once again, Steve was right. Leo was a competent senior homicide detective with contacts, friends, and even supervisors who wouldn't take kindly to a shady ex-cop. Bucky had stolen from Steve, assaulted him, and now, he'd probably set fire to his home. He'd gone too far and would pay a steep price. She'd done her part by hiring Constance Banks.

Heather issued a malevolent smile as she considered possibilities of Bucky's fate. One more phone call to Constance and Heather would wait for justice to pay a visit to Bucky.

Bella pushed a full cart across the parking lot. Max had moved to Steve's lap to receive strokes. The emotionally rattled cat didn't bother to open his eyes when Heather and Bella returned. Deep, sonorous purrs showed he was on the road to recovery.

Heather injected a touch of hope into the words she directed at Steve. "We won't have to sleep in the car tonight. I received a text from my PA. She found us a five-bedroom home in a gated community that's half the distance to work as our condos. The pictures she sent show a separate bedroom with an en suite bath, living area, and a kitchenette. It should be adequate for you."

Bella chimed in, "The backyard will make a great place for Max to play. There's even a pet door he can use."

Steve answered with a grunt of approval. Heather knew he didn't like change but would make a quick transition to his temporary home once he settled in.

It came as a bit of a surprise when he asked, "How long can we stay before we have to move?"

"Until we move into our duplexes on Lake Conroe. I'll either work out a long-term rental with the owners or purchase the house."

"Sight unseen? You might not like it."

"That's how you bought your condo."

Steve chuckled. "Good point."

18

Heather checked in with the guard at the gate and gained entrance to the neighborhood. The homes had the appearance of permanence. She'd describe most of them as colonial architecture, one notch below a mini-mansion. She imagined the residents to be successful business owners, middle-aged doctors still paying off student loans, or some other type of professional.

Her GPS told her to turn into a cul-de-sac. The curbs had the house numbers painted on them beside the driveways. Bella issued words of approval. "This is very nice. I love the triple garage. Plenty of room for storage."

Two vehicles stood in the driveway. The first was a Lexus coupe belonging to her personal assistant. The second was Jack's pickup.

Heather spoke as the garage door nearest the front door opened. Jack and Briann appeared from the cavern. Heather was out the door before he made it to her car. His face bore a wide grin. "Welcome to your new home."

She approached him and gave a quick hug. She then offered the same to Briann, not sure how she'd receive the gesture. Not only was the hug returned, but the girl said, "What a bummer to get your condos destroyed."

"It may be a blessing. You've been inside; what do you think of this home?"

Briann pushed out her lips. "I'm not a big fan of the wallpaper in the bathrooms. Otherwise, it's exactly what you need. The rooms are a nice size and there's a lot of them. It even has a separate apartment-type area with its own small kitchen. It's like a home inside a home."

Heather asked, "Wallpaper, huh? That sounds a little outdated." She decided to test the relationship between her and Briann. "If I purchase the house, maybe you can help me bring it up to date."

"Ooh. That would be fun."

Heather breathed an inward sigh of relief. Maybe that wall between them would eventually come down.

Jack gave a nod of approval but changed the subject. "What took you so long to get here?"

"We stopped at a big-box store and picked up clothes and essentials."

"Your PA took care of that. The three of you have a week's worth of new outfits to try on. If you bought shampoo and toothpaste, too, you'll have enough to last a year. Briann and I stocked your pantry and refrigerator. If you need a glass of wine to help you unwind, I have bottles chilling in the fridge."

Max brushed by Heather's leg as he made his way toward an open door. Apparently, his ordeal wasn't going to keep him from exploring his new home.

Briann spoke next. "I can show you the house. There's really not much left for you to do."

Bella approached with bags of clothes in one hand as Steve held on to her free arm. He spoke as they passed. "Has anyone ordered pizza? If not, you violate rule number one of the unofficial handbook on moving. 'Thou shalt not move into any home without pizza.'"

Jack turned to Briann. "You're the pizza expert. Get enough for everyone and salads." He pulled out a credit card and handed it to her.

As Briann took the card, she looked up at her father through long lashes. "You know, it would be easier if I had a credit card of my own."

"I think that may be a topic for another day." He turned her toward the house and said, "Lead the way. I'm sure Heather and Steve are ready to see their new home."

Briann sighed but turned to lead the way. "Let's not go in through the garage. Heather needs to use the front door to experience what guests will feel the first time they come here."

Heather stepped into the home's foyer and nodded her approval. No stairs in sight. She wasn't a fan of encountering a stairway as soon as you entered.

"Come look at the home office," said Briann.

The evening was going better than Heather thought possible. Max was scoping out his new abode without a meow of complaint. Briann pointed out details like a used car saleswoman. Steve wasn't grieving the loss of his condo, and food and shelter were no longer a concern.

After touring the home, lingering concerns about the property melted like a spring frost. The doorbell rang and Briann retrieved their supper. She spread the feast down the middle of the table and took her place beside Jack.

Steve lifted a glass of water to make a toast. "To new adventures."

"New adventures," came an echo of voices.

"And speaking of," said Steve. "I have some ideas on how we can proceed to solve the murder. But first, let's eat while it's hot."

The glass prisms of the chandelier over the dining room table caught the light and threw it in all directions. Pizza boxes dotted the center of the table while paper plates made a partial border. Heather drank wine from a long-stemmed glass while Jack's bottle of beer rested on a folded paper towel. Plastic glasses filled with water sat in front of most of the other place settings. The diversity of formality and blue-collar comfort couldn't have been more pronounced.

Steve sat at the head of the table, flanked by Bella on one side and Briann on the other. Heather took her seat by Bella with Jack across the table from her. The only one missing was her personal assistant, who'd left to salvage something of her weekend.

The day's activity left everyone ravenous, so talk was virtually non-existent until salads and pizza worked their magic.

Steve took a drink out of a plastic glass and resettled it at the two o'clock position above his plate. "Briann, you missed the excitement this afternoon."

She gave a nod that Steve couldn't see. "It's a shame about your condo."

"That's not what I'm talking about. I meant at the office, before we received the call from the fire department."

"Oh? What happened?"

"Your dad didn't tell you?"

"Briann and I went home," said Jack. "I parked myself in front of the television and watched a basketball game."

Briann spoke around a bite of pizza. "He was sleeping."

"Guilty. What happened?"

"I'll let Heather tell you."

"Thanks," said Heather with sarcasm seasoning the word. "You'll be pleased to know we gave Loretta Blake another suspect. It's a good thing Clay hasn't had his bond hearing."

Heather told her version of the story of Rusty Brigs knowing April Brewer and having access to heavy equipment to bury her. She conveniently left out the part of him bringing a pistol to the photo shoot. That detail could wait until later.

Her reticence to tell Jack she'd almost stared down the barrel of a pistol didn't stop Bella from filling in the most interesting part of the story.

Jack's expression clouded over as he lowered the half-eaten piece of pizza onto his plate as his gaze locked on Heather. "Let me get this straight. You arranged for Rusty Brigs to come to your office."

Heather let out a meek, "Uh-huh."

"And he brought a loaded pistol with him?"

"Correct. I didn't consider that possibility, but Steve did."

Jack ran a hand over his mouth. "What would have happened without Steve?"

Heather looked down at her plate. The tone of Jack's last question told her he thought she'd played too fast and loose with a dangerous man.

Bella took over. "Steve told me to look for a chance to check his clothes after he changed. He had to go to the bathroom before he went into the photo shoot. While he was in there, I found his pistol and unloaded it. No one was ever in danger. Detective Blake and Heather were both armed. He was already on the floor because I kicked him where it would really hurt. They had no trouble putting the handcuffs on him."

Jack shot Heather a withering stare. "He brought a loaded pistol to a photo shoot."

Steve eased a hand upward. "All the blame is on me. I didn't discuss the possibility of him being armed with Heather or anyone else. It didn't occur to me until he arrived, then I made a quick plan for Bella to check for a gun. It was her idea to take the shells from his pistol."

Heather jumped in, "That means Steve gets all the credit for you being able to get Clay released. As things stand now, Rusty replaced Clay as the primary suspect."

Jack's eyes seemed to dance as he fought conflicting emotions. They stopped shifting from right to left and settled on Steve. "I appreciate what you've done to help Clay, but I can't say the same for putting Bella, Heather, and everyone else in danger."

Bella shot him a questioning look. "I wasn't worried. I'm never worried with Steve and Heather around."

Jack countered with, "You don't know what kind of man we're talking about. He's a walking crime looking for a place and time to happen."

Steve nodded. "Jack's right. Rusty's a very dangerous man. I took a big chance today. Guys like him sometimes carry more than one weapon."

"Then why did you do it?" demanded Jack.

"It was the only way I could think of to get him out of circulation. After his encounter with Bella and Heather, I thought it would only be a matter of time before he attacked one or both of them. It was a calculated risk, and I took it. If given the same circumstances, I'd do it again."

Jack pushed away from the table and stood. "Briann, get your jacket. We're leaving."

"I don't want to go."

"You heard me, young lady. It's time to go. I'll wait for you in the truck."

It took coaxing, but Briann left after a few minutes of pouting. Steve and Bella did the convincing as Heather remained silent. She'd made headway with Briann and didn't want to sink their tenuous relationship. For once, she was glad Steve hadn't included her in his plan that day.

The mood had shifted from jovial excitement to something cloudy; like the smoke the fans pulled from the burned condos that afternoon. Steve lifted his chin and said, "I could use a cup of coffee and a recliner. Please tell me there's a nice recliner somewhere in this castle."

Bella perked up. "There's two in your living room sitting side by side."

"Perfect. One for me and one for Max. Is there a couch?"

"A couch and a love seat. It's a big room."

"Let's go there after we clear the table."

Heather looked at the remains of dinner. "You two go ahead

while I clean up. Show him where everything is in his apartment. You might as well let him make the coffee. He'll complain if it's not strong enough."

Heather thought long and hard about Jack's reaction. He and Steve held the same fears. They both recognized the danger posed by Rusty Brigs. Steve had played offense and eliminated the threat, at least for the time being.

After putting the kitchen to rights, Heather followed the smell of coffee brewing to Steve's apartment. The door stood open and revealed the living room with a bank of windows overlooking the backyard. In addition to the furniture Bella mentioned, a large television hung on the wall, taking the place of artwork or photos. It was a good use of the wall for Steve.

She strode into the bedroom and saw Bella arranging Steve's hanging clothes. "Pants on the left in order of light to dark colors. Shirts on the right. Short sleeves first, then long. Colors are the same as the pants—light to dark. Sweaters go in the bottom drawer of the built-in dresser. Questions?"

"Nope. The closet is bigger, but the arrangement is the same."

Heather backtracked and went into the kitchenette. She opened cabinets until she found the one holding coffee cups and mugs. It wouldn't take Steve long before he mastered the arrangement.

She heard the final gurgles of the coffeemaker and announced, "Hot coffee is being served in the living room."

Muted words about where to place shoes in the closet preceded Bella and Steve's return to the living room. His cane guided the way to the first of the two recliners. Unlike his charred leather one at home, the twin recliners had coverings of durable fabric. Steve settled into one and gave a nod of approval. "Nice. Max won't poke holes in this when he jumps up."

Heather said, "I'm putting a towel on his. Summer will be here before long and he sheds like crazy."

Steve said, "There's not a table between the chairs. Where

am I supposed to keep the television remote or put my coffee mug?"

Bella came to the rescue. "I saw one in the den that should work. I'll go get it. After that, I need to call Adam and verify when he'll arrive tomorrow."

She scurried out of the room while Heather poured three cups of coffee. Bella returned with the table and placed it between the two recliners. She left again after issuing a promise to return.

Heather's thoughts drifted to her former fiancé, who still kept the title of boyfriend. At least she believed the relationship was still on. A need to console Steve came over her. "Don't worry about Jack. He'll be all right after he processes everything."

Steve pulled off his sunglasses and rubbed his sightless eyes. "I took Jack into consideration when I laid a trap for Rusty. He reacted tonight the way I thought he would."

"With anger?"

"Anger sometimes comes from fear or frustration. He got used to the idea of being married to you. There's a caveman urge within most men to protect women and children. The role of protector grows stronger the deeper the relationship. You two were engaged. In some cultures, that means you were already married."

Heather shook her head. "That's not rational. We agreed to break off the engagement." She tried without success to look into the future. "I'm not sure we'll ever be married."

Steve put his sunglasses back on. "Love isn't rational, and once the kind of ties that lead to marriage are created, they're not easily broken. Besides, you're missing the point. Jack was upset tonight because he believes you and Bella were in danger. He won't say it, but deep down, he doesn't like us solving murders. We can't avoid dealing with dangerous and deceitful people, and I can't protect myself, let alone you. That leaves you to pull double duty and protect both of us."

Heather heard the words and recognized them as true but

didn't know what to do with them. "It's obvious you've given this a great deal of thought. What changes do you recommend I make?"

Steve held up open hands. "That's up to you. I'm giving you an explanation of why Jack became angry when no one else was. He sees himself as Briann's protector, and yours, marriage vows or not."

He lowered his hands. "Jack's a smart guy. I know he'll get over being angry soon enough."

Heather picked up her cup of coffee and took a tiny sip. "How do you think of me? Do you think I'm capable?"

His answer came without hesitation. "You're the most highly skilled and resourceful partner I've ever had or could hope to have. When we have a case to solve, I view you as an outstanding cop. When we aren't working on a case, I view you as a trusted friend."

"Thank you. I can live with that."

"Good. It's time for us to put the day's distractions aside and prove who murdered April Brewer."

Heather responded with the names of suspects. "I have Rusty Brigs, Clay Cockrell, Luke Paulson, LaShawn Moody, and Janie Polk as persons of interest."

Steve lifted an index finger. "I have those, plus I've added the parents of all the high school seniors."

Heather tilted her head. "Even Lee and LeAnn Cockrell?"

"For now. What we really need is to find the original crime scene and the vehicle the killer transported April in."

Heather put the pieces together. "I'll work on getting a list of the vehicles owned by all our persons of interest. After that, we can interview each of them and ask permission to search their vehicles."

Steve held up a hand. "Leo's already working on it. He's supposed to email me a list of all the vehicles and their owners tonight."

"When did you ask him to do that?"

"Early this morning, before we went to your office."

Heather shook her head. "That seems like it was a year ago."

"It's been an eventful day." He took another drink of coffee. "Once we get vehicles matched to names, I want you and Bella to call all the high school kids. Come up with a reason for them to come to the office. You and I will interview them individually."

"Their parents won't like it when they find out, especially Janie's mother."

Steve flipped away the comment with the back of his hand and moved on. He leaned back in his recliner. "You mentioned the parents. Let's give Bella something to do. We need background checks on all the parents we mentioned."

"I heard that," said Bella as she walked into the room. "I'll get on it tonight." She paused. "By the way, Adam says hello. His flight will land at twelve thirty tomorrow afternoon."

Heather stood. "Bella and I will get started. I bet you're worn out after the day you've had. Do you want to take something to help you sleep?"

"No, thanks. Other than coming close to committing entrapment, listening to a lot of high school kids try to hide the truth, my home burning, and making Jack mad at me, it was a pretty uneventful day. I should be able to sleep, eventually."

"What you did doesn't fit the legal definition of entrapment. Rusty threatened Bella. He did that on his own."

"I know that's true, but I still may lose a night or two's sleep over it." He grinned. "Only one night. I don't feel that bad for a guy like Rusty."

19

Heather cracked an eyelid open at 7:00 a.m. It was two hours past her normal time to get up, but she didn't panic as it was Sunday. She and Bella had worked into the early hours of the morning and completed a fair portion of the background checks on everyone under twenty years of age. She lamented that there were no great surprises. In fact, April Brewer, the victim, had been the only young adult who gave a hint of living on the wild side. Her social media posts showed she had a taste for beer, tight jeans, and older men.

She thought about calling Jack but remembered an old saying about the danger of rousing sleeping bears. Her thoughts shifted to Briann, and she hoped the girl and her father hadn't experienced a *battle royal* on the way home. Her mind drifted back to some arguments she'd had with her father when she returned from boarding school, especially the one in Germany. Talk about brutal teachers. Thankfully, Briann didn't have to endure that.

It was time to rise, shine, and stretch out the kinks. While still in her sleep shorts and tee, she reached toward the ceiling and inhaled a huge breath. After a slow exhale, she brought her palms almost flat on the floor. "Not good," she whispered before repeating the movements and deep breathing. This time her palms went flat on the carpet without a bend in her knees. "That's better. Time to spread my mat and do a complete yoga workout."

Forty minutes later, she rolled up the thin mat she'd purchased the night before, put on sweats, and went in search of coffee. She found Steve rummaging around the main kitchen. "What are you looking for?"

"You bought an apple strudel last night. I need something to soak up the pot of coffee I drank this morning."

"You've been up long enough to drink an entire pot of coffee?"

"Half a pot. You know me. I'm the very picture of moderation."

"Right. And I'm the Easter Bunny."

For once he didn't have a pithy comeback, so she said, "Sit at the bar. Would you like bacon and eggs with your strudel?"

"If it's not too much trouble."

"What would you say if I told you it was?"

Steve didn't have to think long. "I'd probably tell you I was calling Uber to take me to a restaurant. That should make you feel guilty enough to scramble two eggs, fry three slices of bacon, and heat a large slab of strudel in the microwave."

Bella came in and settled on a barstool next to Steve. She raised a hand. "Waitress, I'll have the same, please."

Heather raised her eyebrows. "You'll stand a much better chance of eating if you help."

The good-natured banter continued until Bella asked, "Have you heard from Jack this morning?"

"Not yet."

"I have," said Steve.

That took Heather by surprise until she reconsidered. Knowing Steve and Jack the way she did, they probably worked on the case. She lay a strip of thick-sliced bacon in a skillet and asked, "What's the latest?"

"Clay's being released this morning. He's not out of the woods, but focus has shifted to Rusty."

"What does that tell you?" asked Bella.

Steve slipped his finger through the handle of his coffee cup. "Forensics found little or nothing of value at the site where someone buried April. Clay gave a plausible answer for her wearing his letter jacket. Once he graduated, he knew he'd never wear it again. If she gave it back, he'd just throw it away."

Heather turned from the burners and spoke to Bella, "They can always go back and rearrest Clay if there's additional incriminating evidence."

"That's not double jeopardy?"

"That only comes into play after a criminal trial and they find the suspect not guilty. As a general rule, they can't try a person twice for the same offense. There are some exceptions, but that gets complicated."

Steve said, "Don't confuse her. She doesn't need to clutter her mind with federal civil rights violations, especially with Adam arriving today."

Bella asked, "Does anyone want to go with me to the airport?"

Steve raised his hand. "I'll ride along."

"Count me out," said Heather. "My list of things to do keeps growing. This home is too big for me to keep clean. I'll also need someone to cook and look after the yard. Believe it or not, I've never owned a house, so hiring for anything except a housekeeper is unfamiliar territory."

Steve took the slack out of his spine. "I never realized that. You own hotels and properties all over the world, but you've always rented until you bought the condo next to mine? This really is a new adventure for you."

Hot grease popped from the frying bacon. Heather jerked back her hand, but not in time. She let out a squeal and took quick steps to the sink to seek relief from the minor burn with cold water.

Steve moved on. "Heather, let's go to the Cockrell's later today. I'm not sure we have the full story of Clay's past relationship with April Brewer. Call Jack and let him know what we're up to. In fact, let's take him with us. You two could question the parents while I have a talk with Clay."

"I'm not sure Jack's ready to talk to me yet."

"He is. We had a good talk."

Heather shook her head in unbelief. "Have you added counseling to your resume?"

"It won't fit on my braille business card."

Sometimes there was nothing to do about Steve but accept him for who he is, and move on. "What about you going to the airport with Bella?"

"I'm still going. It won't take long to pick up Adam. We could let the newlyweds have some alone time this afternoon." He issued a sly smile. "There's that joint on the way to the Cockrell's. It's been too long since I've had a brisket sandwich."

"That place you're talking about is a combination beer joint and dance hall. They only sell food on the weekends."

"Right. And today's Sunday. Bring a photo of April. If memory serves me right, that's where she liked to go boot-scootin'."

Heather took the bacon out of the skillet and placed it on paper towels. She took two more towels off the roll and patted the grease from the bacon.

"You're ruining the flavor by taking off all the grease," said Steve.

They'd had this discussion a hundred times, and Heather remained constant with her reply. "Cook it yourself next time."

All the while, Bella was scrambling eggs in a second skillet seasoned with butter. Steve loved eggs scrambled in real butter. He could taste the difference and didn't hesitate to comment about the deficiencies of oil or margarine.

Breakfast ended in a tie. Steve raved about the eggs and

Heather enjoyed extra-crispy bacon, thoroughly drained of artery-clogging fat.

HEATHER HAD A FRUSTRATING MORNING, LEAVING VOICE messages with companies and individuals as she searched for a housekeeper/cook and lawn care workers. She also had to wait for Steve's return. Waiting wasn't one of her strengths.

The newlyweds and Steve hadn't been home long before Heather told Bella and Adam that she and Steve had an appointment with the Cockrells to keep. The couple traded looks that told Heather it didn't disappoint them to be left alone for several hours.

Heather led Steve to her car in the garage. He'd already mastered the floor plan and furniture placement of his apartment and much of the house. Another trip or two to the garage and she would no longer need to guide him.

After a brief trip up the interstate and into Conroe, they arrived at Jack's home. Instead of going in, Jack met them in the driveway. Steve exited and took up residence in the back seat, as was his norm when someone else joined them.

"How's Briann today?" asked Heather after Jack shut his door.

"Sequestered in her room, experiencing a crisis of historic proportions. She has her first pimple. I told her I could barely see it. That slip of the tongue put her into a complete meltdown."

"Has your mother talked to her yet?"

"She's on her way." He turned to look at her full-on. "I don't get it with you girls. Puberty for me included its share of facial eruptions and I didn't melt into puddles."

"I hope you didn't tell her that."

"No way. Mom said to walk a wide path around her and keep my mouth shut."

Steve spoke for the first time. "Wise woman."

Jack cleared his throat after they'd traveled in silence for a couple of blocks. "I apologize for the way I acted last night."

Steve and Heather spoke over each other. "Apology accepted."

Jack continued, "On the way home, Briann lit into me like a wildcat. She had her points all lined out and delivered them without ambiguity. She'll make a tenacious attorney."

Heather spoke in a soft voice. "Thank you for being concerned about our safety."

Steve's thoughts had moved on. "Jack, I'd like for you and Heather to keep Lee and LeAnn busy while Clay and I talk. From what I know of him, he's not the type of young man who will open up in a group setting."

"You're not kidding. He didn't say a word when they cut him loose from jail this morning. The only thing he told his parents was that he wanted to return to work as soon as possible."

"That'll be good for him," said Heather.

Steve settled back and seemed to go to his special place where he did some of his deepest thinking. Meanwhile, she and Jack planned ways to keep Clay's parents occupied.

20

When they arrived at the Cockrell's home, both Lee and LeAnn met them on the front porch. Heather remembered the earthy smell of the grounds. The builder set the home in lowlands chosen for an abundance of waterfowl. Lee was an avid hunter and outdoorsman. The hundred acres allowed him some of the best duck hunting in the nation.

Jack acted as point man for the trio as he was Clay's defense attorney. Once inside, Heather and Jack both accepted LeAnn's offer of coffee. Steve, however, had other ideas. He asked, "Is Clay here?"

"On the back porch," said LeAnn. "He hasn't said two words since we picked him up."

"That's expected," said Steve. "He's dealing with shame and humiliation. Jail is a very dehumanizing place, especially for people who have no experience with the criminal justice system. Do you mind if I go talk to him?"

Lee was the first to answer. "You can try, but don't expect much. He said he wants to be alone."

Steve rose from his chair. "LeAnn, would you mind leading me to the back porch?"

"Of course. I'll get Heather and Jack's coffee on my way back through the kitchen."

It was cooler outside than in the house. Another odor, that of a petroleum product, caught Steve's attention as LeAnn deposited him into a chair.

"Honey," said LeAnn. "Mr. Smiley wants to talk to you. He's here to help. In fact, he and Ms. McBlythe are the reason you're home instead of in..." Her words trailed off as if she couldn't bring herself to say the word *jail*.

The sound of the back door shutting came to Steve's ears and told him he was alone with Clay. Steve waited a full minute before he asked. "What kind of gun are you cleaning?"

"A shotgun. Remington, model eleven-hundred."

"Doesn't it shoot both two-and-three-quarters and three-inch shells?"

"Yeah."

"Vent rib?"

"Uh-huh. It helps me sight better. How could you tell I was cleaning it?"

Steve tapped his nose. "Nothing smells like gun solvent and spent powder on wads of cotton. Do you buy the cleaning patches or make your own from old T-shirts?"

"T-shirts."

"That's all I ever used back in my hunting days. One of the best chewing-outs I ever received was from my late wife when I butchered a new T-shirt instead of an old one with sweaty armpit stains."

"I go through T-shirts like crazy in the summer. Grease, diesel, dirt, and sweat seem to find me. I quit buying new. Garage sales are the way to go."

"You're a man after my heart, except I prefer second-hand stores."

Steve allowed silence to ebb back into the conversation. Experience told him he'd broken down the first barrier, but he couldn't press a deep-thinking young man like Clay.

When enough ticks of the clocks had passed, Steve broke the silence. "You realize you're not out of the woods yet with jail. Right?"

"Yeah."

"Do you know when and how that will change?"

The volume of Clay's voice decreased by a few decibels. "All I know is, I didn't kill April."

Steve answered his own question that Clay had sidestepped. "Things will change back to the way they were when Heather and I discover who killed her."

"What about the police? Isn't that their job?"

"They do their best, and it's possible they might catch this killer, but I don't think they will."

Clay didn't wait to respond. "You don't seem to have a high opinion of the police."

"They do an outstanding job at gathering and collecting evidence, but that's only half the job." Steve tapped his temple with his forefinger. "To be an outstanding detective, it's necessary to listen to what the evidence says to you."

"I think I know what you mean. What's the evidence said so far?"

Steve placed the palms of both hands flat on the table. "Great question. So far, there's not a lot of evidence, so it's mostly quiet. There is one thing that I'm hearing, but before I tell you what it is, I want you to describe what you saw when you took the drainage pipe out of the ground."

Clay took his time before answering. "Taking out concrete drainage lines is a pain in the neck. First, you have to uncover it without damage. That's not as easy as it sounds. There were eight sections of pipe to remove, then reset two feet deeper. The excavator dug down until the bucket scraped the top. Then, I took out the dirt on each side. I worked my way up the line, making the walls of the trench wider."

Steve gave occasional nods to encourage Clay to keep talking. The pace of his words picked up as he talked.

"I worked my way down the line and took out all the pipes that weren't buried deep enough. That required chains and a lot of patience. Then, I started back down the line, digging deeper."

"How much deeper?"

"The specs called for two more feet minimum, so I added another six inches for good measure."

"And then?"

"I started moving dirt. The bucket on the excavator is wide, and the teeth have no trouble sinking into the soil. I sank the bucket into the ground and curled it up toward me. All was going to plan until..." His voice cracked and he stopped.

"Take your time."

"Instead of lifting dirt, I lifted dirt and something blue. I stopped digging and cut it off."

"Then what did you do?"

"I climbed down to see what it was."

"You went into the trench?"

"Yeah. The smell was awful."

"Did you touch the body?"

"I pulled back the tarp enough to see hair. That's when I scrambled out and called 9-1-1. I was shaking so bad I'm surprised I could punch in the numbers."

The sound of Clay's chair moving away from the table reached Steve's ears. He wasn't finished with his questions, but he believed Clay was finished answering.

Clay confirmed his suspicions. "I'm sorry, Mr. Smiley, but I'm still feeling closed-in. I need to get into the woods."

"Only one more question," said Steve. "Do you think Rusty Brigs killed April?"

Seconds passed without a response. Clay finally said, "That question has kept me awake for days." He took a step. "I need to get in the woods where things make sense."

"Go ahead. We can talk again some other day."

21

Heather broke the silence as her SUV turned out of the Cockrell's driveway. "I hope you got something useful out of Clay. Jack and I were running out of things to talk about with Lee and LeAnn."

"I made progress," said Steve.

Jack didn't sound impressed. "Unless you got something concrete out of Clay, we still have three needles to find in haystacks: an original crime scene, the vehicle used to transport her body, and the murder weapon."

Steve sounded more optimistic. "Any one of the three things you mentioned may be enough. In my experience, all it takes is one breakthrough to get the ball rolling."

"Has the forensic report come back to the police yet?" asked Heather.

Jack gave his head a slight turn and cut his eyes toward her. "You and Steve did too good of a job in getting a replacement for Clay in jail. If we'd waited to implicate Rusty after a formal arraignment, I could have demanded forensic reports." He shrugged off the complaint. "Oh, well. It was best for my client to get him out of jail, but it might slow down your investigation.

I heard from a friend at the sheriff's office that they tested Clay's truck with luminol and came up blank."

"That's also progress," said Steve. "It all but eliminates Clay's truck as a transport vehicle. Do you know if they tested his parents' vehicles?"

"Neither Lee nor LeAnn mentioned it, and that would require a search warrant."

"What about Rusty's pickup?"

"I assume they did but don't know for sure. My source was off this weekend."

Steve's voice drifted to the front seat. "Heather, you and Loretta Blake seem to be on good terms. She might not have the full forensic report yet, but get what you can."

"That should be no problem, especially if they find traces of April's blood in the bed of Rusty's truck."

Jack broke in. "If they do, I'm glad I won't be trying to defend Rusty. The press would have a field day with that story."

Steve spoke in a low, deliberate voice. "For now, we need to keep going as if the police won't find anything to show April was ever in Rusty's truck—alive or dead."

As was his habit in an investigation, Steve changed the subject for no apparent reason. "Did Lee or LeAnn tell you anything today you didn't know?"

Heather made sure she spoke loud enough for him to hear. "I tried to focus on Clay's relationships with April and Janie. It wasn't what they said, but more what they didn't say. As you know, Clay is not the most communicative young man. Lee is like many successful business owners. As long as his kid isn't getting into trouble, he doesn't press for information. He knows next to nothing about Clay's relationship with either girl, other than Clay dated them for a while and the relationships ended."

"Lee sounds like my dad," said Jack. "Our common ground was hunting, fishing, and sports. We had an unspoken agreement of don't-ask, don't-tell with my social life. Mom was the family detective. She'd press me for information until I buckled and told her who I was dating. She'd relay what she thought was important to Dad. Otherwise, she wouldn't bother him with details."

The sound of a muted chuckle found its way to Heather's ears. "What's so funny?"

"Jack's dad reminds me of mine."

It was the first time she'd heard anything about Steve's father, and this could be the opportunity to find out more. No such luck. Steve moved on with another question.

"If we assume LeAnn pressed Clay for more information than his father did, what did you two learn from her this afternoon?"

Heather fielded the question. "It seems Clay ended both relationships. LeAnn hinted that April liked to make people believe she wanted to experience the wild side of life. Or, at least, she came across that way. In reality, she was a lonely girl trying to grow up as fast as she could. LeAnn heard through the mothers' grapevine that April's home life wasn't good."

Jack added, "Kids that age have a hard enough time finding their way. Add a crummy home life to the mix and they look for ways to escape."

Heather cut her eyes toward Jack. "When did you become such an expert on teenage girls?"

"I've defended my share of teens in court." His voice changed to one of sarcasm. "It's been over six months since I was told I'm a father. That means I'm a certified expert in family matters."

More chuckles from the back seat. Heather rolled her eyes.

Steve moved on. "What did LeAnn say about Clay's relationship with Janie?"

Heather knew she needed to choose her words carefully, as LeAnn's response to their questions left much unanswered. "It seems Clay fell hard for her. He came out of his shell and things seemed to go great. Then, one day, it ended. Clay stopped talking about anything but work and mundane subjects. He announced his decision to put off college for at least a year and presented it as non-negotiable. Anything personal was off limits."

A low "Ah," came from the back seat. Steve followed this with, "I'd like for you to get your three high school models back in Heather's office as soon as you can."

"Individually or together?"

"Both. Let's put them together and see how they act toward each other. Bella and I will interview them and you can watch."

"What am I looking for?"

"The things that make them who they really are. How they walk and talk, the way they carry themselves. Do the clothes they wear tell you anything about them? Are they fastidious about their appearance? Are they trying to be themselves or someone else? How do they act around each other when they think no one is watching?"

Steve shifted in his seat. "That's why I want to keep them waiting by themselves for at least thirty minutes. So much of communication is non-verbal. You and Bella need to be my eyes. Sometimes it's the little nuances that give hints to what's going on inside them." He paused. "The young also know how to push each other's buttons."

Heather allowed a half-mile to pass before she responded. "Do you think one of those three might have killed April?"

Instead of answering, Steve sniffed the air like a dog catching a scent. "The wind must be out of the south. I smell smoke, and you know what they say... where there's smoke, there's brisket."

Jack shot her a quick glance. "He has a nose like a bluetick hound."

Steve's phone came to life as the SUV pulled into the parking lot of the combination dance hall, beer joint, and weekend barbecue haven. The artificial intelligence voice announced the caller to be Leo Vega.

"Leo," said Steve. "I was wondering when you were going to get around to calling me."

"For your information, I've been burning the midnight oil, putting things in order to make Bucky Franklin's life miserable."

Heather shifted her car's transmission into park and cut off the engine. She twisted in her seat and spoke louder than usual. "Hi, Leo. Jack and I are listening in."

"Good. I needed to talk to you. What are you and Constance Banks doing to hit Bucky hard with the civil lawsuit?"

"I spoke with her and Kate Bridges yesterday on a conference call."

"You did?" asked Steve. "Why Kate?"

"Don't pay attention to him," said Heather. "Steve put me in charge of taking care of copyright infringement. It's driving him crazy, not knowing what I'm doing."

"It is not," protested Steve.

"I'll give you a teaser of what I've done," said Leo. "It didn't take me long to discover the two officers willing to give Bucky an alibi. When I informed my captain, he hit the ceiling and marched me to the assistant chief's office. She ordered a full investigation by internal affairs."

"Did you show them the video of Bucky breaking in and setting the fire?"

"I haven't seen that yet," said Heather.

Leo didn't respond to her. "It was a good thing you installed the new cameras inside your condo."

Steve spoke in a matter-of-fact tone. "I called a friend who could install two motion-activated cameras the same day."

"What friend?" asked Heather.

"You don't know him. He's a reformed burglar." Steve paused. "Well, he's mostly reformed. I proved he was at his home when a wife killed her husband. He'd burglarized the home earlier that day and left a cap behind. The man was a thief but not a killer. He told me to call him anytime I needed a great home security system. I finally cashed in the favor."

Heather huffed, "More secrets."

Leo broke in. "As much as I enjoy listening to you two argue,

I'd like to salvage something of my day off. Can you two meet me and the I.A. investigator tomorrow morning at your condos? The state fire marshal finished his investigation today and we can get in."

"How bad is the damage?" asked Heather.

"Mainly smoke to yours, except in the living room. The fire got in the attic there. They had to pull down the sheetrock, so there's significant water damage in that half of your condo. Steve's is a total loss. Fire, water, and smoke ruined everything."

Heather produced a mental picture of the scene. "It's a miracle Max survived."

"The fire marshal said he hid on the floor of your bedroom closet. The smoke never got that low."

"I need to find someone to salvage what we can from the condos," said Heather. One more thing to add to her list of people to call.

Jack spoke up. "I know someone I can call who does odd jobs. He hasn't paid me for getting him out of a DWI charge."

Heather tilted her head. "Is he trustworthy? I have several personal safes in my closet. I'd hate to lose my jewelry and emergency cash."

Jack held up three fingers in a pretend Boy Scout salute. "He's a paradigm of virtue until sundown. After that, he makes poor decisions."

"Tell him to meet us there tomorrow at first light."

Steve groaned. "Before breakfast?"

She believed his question didn't deserve a response.

Leo and Steve ended the call with Leo stating they shouldn't look for him and the internal affairs investigator before 9:00 a.m.

Three doors opened and dislodged the occupants. Heather noted the construction of the combination restaurant and dance hall on their way in. It appeared to be an old wooden barn as the main building, with multiple after-thought rooms added through the years. A tin roof, weathered by time to a rusty-gray patina covered the disjointed building.

Once inside, she took in the hodge-podge interior. A long bar ran along the near side of the wooden dance floor, with the kitchen jutting out the back. Opposite the bar, there was an oblong room dotted with picnic tables. Not the best design, as patrons had to cross the dance floor to get to a cold brew, place food orders, and pick them up.

Heather took three steps onto the dance floor and stopped. She leaned into Steve, who had his hand laced through her arm. "I didn't expect to see her here."

"Who?"

"Veronica Polk. She's working as a bartender."

"That's interesting," said Steve. "Bartenders see all kinds of things and can be an excellent source of information."

"Do you want to talk to her?"

"Sit where you can observe, but let's save our questions for now."

Heather took another look around the room. "There's another familiar face."

"Who?" asked Steve.

"LaShawn Moody."

"Even more interesting," said Steve. "I wonder what brings him to a dance hall on a Sunday evening."

"Let's ask him," said Heather.

Steve shook his head. "I have a better idea. We'll wait until you and Bella can set up interviews for all three in your office. This may be his home turf. I'd rather we have him in a place where he doesn't feel comfortable."

Steve's lip twitched ever so slightly. "Besides, I'm here to eat moist brisket, beans, and potato salad. Everyone knows that's brain food. We're going to need it to solve this case."

On the way out after dinner, Heather stopped by LaShawn's table. He stood and said, "I saw you come in. How did you like the barbecue?"

"I'm so stuffed I may not eat for two days. What does your schedule looks like the next few days?"

His head tilted. "I'm free after school."

"Bella needs you, Janie, and Luke to come back in to discuss something to do with the advertising campaign. Do you know if the other two will be busy?"

"Luke should be free. Janie has track practice, but she's finished by four thirty in the afternoon."

"So you think Tuesday about five thirty would work?"

He lifted his shoulder and let them fall. "It works for me."

"Bella will call you after she speaks with the other two."

"What about the little kids? Are they included in the meeting?"

Heather shook her head. "It's different with the children. She has to work around their parents' schedules."

LaShawn turned his head and released an inappropriate laugh.

"What's funny?" asked Heather in a normal tone.

"Don't be surprised if you have a helicopter parent at our meeting."

"Oh? Who's that?"

"If Janie's mom finds out, she'll show up, for sure."

"Is she that bad?"

LaShawn's eyebrows raised as he leaned over and spoke as if what he had to say was a secret. "She can either be sweet as pecan pie or a living nightmare." He paused and leaned back with a smug expression curling up one side of his mouth.

Heather said, "I'm assuming Janie keeps a lot of things from her mom. If I'm right, a phone call from either me or Bella wouldn't be welcome. Can you ask her to call Bella?"

"You're a smart lady." It was a declaration of fact. "You did the right thing by trusting me and avoiding psycho-lady."

"I'm also a determined businesswoman who believes adults should make their own decisions. For me, adulthood begins at eighteen. Can you assure me you'll tell Janie?"

He gave his head a nod. "She's very creative when she wants to sidestep her mom. If there's any problem, I'll call you."

Heather relayed the conversation to Steve and Jack on the way home.

"Uh-huh," said Steve. Sounds of slumber came from the back seat shortly after his short response.

22

The neon sign of DENNY'S restaurant shone brightly as Heather turned off the interstate's feeder road. She wheeled into the parking lot and turned her gaze to Steve. "Don't look so smug."

He held up hands to signify his innocence. "I had nothing to do with the salvage crew not being able to come until eight thirty. You should have known from Jack's description that the guy would be hungover after a weekend off."

She huffed, "And you get your wish for a carb-laden breakfast."

"I'll order whole wheat toast if it makes you feel better." He exited the vehicle and met her at the front of the car. "What's got you in such a foul mood this morning?"

She hesitated to organize her thoughts. "I may have to take Max to a pet therapist. He thrashed half the night before insisting on sleeping on my stomach. Do you have any idea how heavy he is?"

"No wonder you're in such a bad mood. He weighs as much as a blacksmith's anvil."

She smiled despite a desire not to. "Not that much, but it felt like it when I woke up. All the loud noises and smoke from the fire messed with his little mind. I don't know if he'll ever be the same."

"It's only been a few days, and he's adjusting to a new home. Give him time and he'll be back to normal."

"I'm not so sure."

"Then take him to the vet and get some kitty Valium."

"I wonder if I could give him a small amount of mine? It's about eight years old, so I don't know if it's lost potency."

Steve tapped his cane in front of him as they entered the restaurant. "He might like it too much, but I'd try it. You won't be at the top of your game without sleep."

They settled into a booth and ordered coffee. Heather took up the conversation where they left off. "I'm ready to get through this ordeal and put the condos behind us. It seems like Bucky tainted everything I owned."

Steve nodded his initial response but added, "I didn't realize I was in such a rut. The new place is a welcome change, and I'm really looking forward to living at the lake."

Her mind shifted. "What do you make of what LaShawn said about Janie and her overbearing mother?"

"Not much until I get a better read on both of them. LaShawn has another motive for saying what he did."

"Do you mean about Veronica?"

Steve's head went from side to side. "I mean about him giving us the impression he's not interested in Janie. It seemed like he didn't want to talk about himself and Janie but was very willing to talk about her mother. I get the idea he might have shaded the story to suit his own purposes."

"And what would those be?"

His shoulders shrugged. "Anger, jealousy, petty rivalry, guilt for killing April, you name it."

Heather believed he threw in the last reason to give her one more out-of-the-box thing to mess with her mind. It was his way of keeping her on her toes, and it worked. She tucked that item away for later.

Steve kept talking. "From what you've told me, April was an attractive young woman. Perhaps she turned LaShawn down for a date. Who knows?"

"I'm back to a question that's nagging me. Do you think any of the four teens are capable of murder?"

"It seems unlikely but I'm not ruling any of them out. The only thing I know for sure is, they're not forthcoming with information."

The server, a young woman with a baby bump, returned to their table to take breakfast orders. She covered a yawn as she wrote on an order pad and made a fast retreat.

As she watched the young woman walk away, it occurred to Heather that everyone had a story to tell, some happy and others not so much. More often than not, she and Steve were in the business of unhappy stories. How would the tragedy involving April Brewer turn out? Finding the killer would change lives and send ripples through families.

Steve interrupted her musings. "I'm not looking forward to what we have to do today. I always hated to go to a crime scene where someone covered their tracks with a fire. Not only did it make it difficult to find evidence, the smell of soggy ashes stays with me for days."

"Hopefully it won't take long."

Breakfast was a leisurely event, with Steve unobtrusively quizzing the server about her life. It turned out she was happily married. This was her first child, and the yawns were well earned. After the night shift in the restaurant, she attended college. Only two more months and she'd receive the pin of a registered nurse.

It boosted Heather's spirits to hear a cheerful story.

With breakfast finished, Heather left the server a generous tip and led Steve to the car. They traveled to their former homes in silence.

As they approached their condo complex, Steve said,

"There's a bench beside the walking path. I'll be there if you need me."

Heather parked a suitable distance from the place they called home and set him on a bench with a green iron frame and wooden slats. He assured her he preferred to wait outside as opposed to in her SUV. She left when a man arrived, driving a car bearing the logo of an insurance company. He introduced himself and confirmed he was an adjuster.

The scene put an end to her happy thoughts. The front windows on her side of the duplex were intact, but not on Steve's. Both front doors gaped open. Firefighters had kicked them in and they stood askew, covered in soot. Splintered wood around the locks meant the doors couldn't be properly shut. Only police tape kept people from walking in.

It might have been one of the quickest inspections of all time. After a quick trip through the charred remains of Steve's condo, the adjuster clicked off the video feature on his phone. "That's a total loss for dwelling and contents. Let's see about the one next door."

His trip through the front portion of the condo went without a comment. Only when he arrived at her bedroom did he say anything. "Since you're making no claim on the contents of the safes and the jewelry, you'll receive a check for replacement value on the structure and furnishings."

Heather asked, "Did the fact that my father is a major stockholder in your company influence your adjustment?"

He kept a straight face. "Not much. I was told to make sure you received prompt service and adjusted up for inflation." He slipped the phone in his pocket. "Do you want the checks now, or should I mail them to you?"

"Mail them to my office in The Woodlands." She tilted her head. "Do you need to film the men taking things from the condo?"

"I'll stick around and film them removing the safes and jewelry cases. That's for your protection."

They exited her condo as two vehicles backed up as close as they could to her front door. The driver of the van wore a dirty baseball cap over longish hair the color of a field mouse. The only difference was, a mouse's hair wouldn't look slick from poor hygiene. After stomping on a stub of a cigarette, the man noticed her and asked, "Heather McBlythe?"

She nodded.

"Tell me what to do so I can get that sorry lawyer off my back."

Heather wanted to jump down his throat with both cheap tennis shoes she'd purchased at the discount store. She decided he wasn't worth it. Instead, she pointed to the door. "Most everything salvageable will be in the condo on the left. Start with the safes and jewelry boxes in the master bedroom. Put them in my car. Also, there are some personal photos and paintings. Everything else goes, and I don't care where."

She led the way. Steve was right. The smell of wet ashes would cling to her through two or three hair shampoos.

Leo arrived a few minutes after the workers loaded the last of Heather's personal items into the back of her SUV. She knew her car would bear the smell of smoke on the ride home, but she couldn't help it.

Heather received an unenthusiastic introduction to a rat-faced man named Palmer. His receding hairline almost met a bald crown, but not quite. The wisps of blondish-brown hair reminded her of a land bridge between two lakes. The wrinkles in his pants and shirt indicated he hadn't been in a hurry to take them out of the dryer. With his second chin in the way, the knot in the necktie was closer to the second button than the first.

"Where's Smiley?" he asked, without acknowledging the introduction.

Heather pointed to the bench some distance away.

"Tell him to come here."

Heather shifted her gaze to the man's legs and shoes. If he'd been more slue-footed, his shoes would point in opposite directions. "You're ambulatory. I'll walk over there with you."

He gave her what she thought was a well-practiced glare. It might work with a cop who was in peril of losing his job to Internal Affairs, but she was having none of it. She changed the tone of her words. "I know how long trips through Houston traffic can leave your legs stiff. It will be good to walk out the kinks."

"Look, lady..."

She shot back. "McBlythe, Heather McBlythe."

Leo added, "That's attorney Heather McBlythe, former Boston P.D. Detective, Heather McBlythe. She's Steve's partner in their private investigation firm."

Heather issued a plastic smile and said, "Shall we go talk to Steve?"

"Not we. I'll go. You stay here."

"You're mistaken, Mr. Palmer. You'll not speak to him without his attorney present."

"Why? What's he got to hide?"

"I don't know. Let's go ask him. I'm sure he wants to cooperate with you. I'm also sure you understand he's under no obligation to do so."

"He filed a complaint charging two cops with crimes."

Leo joined the conversation. "No, he didn't. He called me, and I took it to my captain, and he brought it to the Assistant Chief's attention. She's the one who called Internal Affairs. Call her if you need verification. I'd love to see that."

Heather said, "Now that I see you haven't done your homework on this case, I insist on being present during your questioning. I'll make an audio and video recording of the interview to make sure there's an accurate account of what transpires." She paused and took her phone out of her jacket pocket. "I already have an audio recording of our conversation thus far."

They'd set the stage. Palmer could refuse, but if he did, he'd have to explain why he didn't get a statement from Steve and why he was too lazy to walk to where a victimized, blind former detective sat.

Palmer took off at a quick waddle. By the time he reached Steve, he needed to catch his breath.

Heather's phone captured the conversation.

"Mr. Smiley, I'm Detective Palmer with Houston P.D.'s Internal Affairs. Tell me about the suspected arson of your condo."

"Have you seen the video of it?"

"Not yet."

"It's my understanding local detectives have identified the person who poured gasoline in my living room, dining room, and kitchen. He started the fire with a match."

"I didn't know that."

"Why not?"

"I was off this weekend."

Steve tilted his head. "Are you interviewing before reviewing readily available video evidence of the crime?"

"Uh..." A pretty hue of pink rose into his wobbly chin and cheeks. "Never mind about that. What does Bucky have on you?"

Steve leaned forward. "How long have you known Bucky Franklin?"

Heather kept her phone trained on Palmer. It was cool enough to wear a light jacket, but beads of perspiration formed on his upper lip.

Steve waited for an answer that didn't come. Heather took over. "It appears you're either grossly incompetent or you have a conflict of interest, Mr. Palmer. I call you mister instead detective, because of what's going to happen to you. I'm willing to bet you spoke with Bucky Franklin prior to today. Were you aware of his plans to commit arson?"

"What?" His jowls shook as his head jerked from side to side. "Of course I didn't know."

"That's not true," said Steve. "You didn't look at the video because you already knew what was on it. Bucky told you what he was going to do. Were you so stupid as to think you could somehow cover for him with a sham investigation?"

Leo stepped into the conversation. "Palmer, you're an idiot. Phone records show you spoke to Bucky at least twice before today. Once around the time he assaulted Steve and again close to the time of the fire. I've already verified everything we said, so you might as well come clean."

"I've got nothing to say to you, Vega."

"It's Detective Vega, and I have something to say to you. Put your hands behind your back. You're under arrest for conspiracy to commit arson."

"No way. You're not puttin' cuffs on me."

"It may take two sets to get those fat hands behind your back, but we'll make it happen."

Palmer pulled back his coat to reveal a pistol in a holster on his side. When his hand wrapped around the grip, Heather didn't hesitate. She closed the distance, lifted her left knee to her chest, and buried her foot into his squishy midsection. Air shot from his lungs like a blown tire. He fell face down to the damp ground. Putting cuffs on him was no problem.

Leo marched Palmer to his unmarked car and put him in the back seat. With threats of reprisal rising from the soon-to-be former internal affairs investigator, Leo met Steve and Heather at the front bumper. He put a hand on Steve's shoulder. "Like old times. Thanks for telling me to see who IA would send so I could check phone records."

"I never cared for internal affairs investigators."

Steve smelled the air. "Is it all right if we email statements to you? The odor of wet ashes is drifting this way."

"Go ahead and leave. The captain's waiting on me to call. I'm not sure if he wants me to transport Palmer back to Houston or let the locals handle him."

Steve rubbed his chin. "Keep as low of a profile as you can. Palmer's arrest is going to put egg on the face of internal affairs.

You don't want those sharks circling you. If it were me, I'd call the locals then tell the captain I suggested you look at more of Bucky's phone calls. I'm sure I'm not the only active or former cop he's tried to intimidate."

Leo nodded. "The arson took place here. It makes sense the locals should get the credit. I haven't read Palmer his rights yet, so he's only detained."

Heather spoke up. "I didn't hear you arrest him."

"All I heard was he's being detained," said Steve.

Heather added, "Tell the arresting officers to call me for witness statements. We're headed back to our office."

After parting words, Heather and Steve were soon headed north on I-45. Steve broke the silence. "Have you noticed how many distractions we've had?"

"I haven't thought about it, but you're right. One thing after the next has kept us from bearing down on this case."

"Let's refocus and get serious."

"I've scheduled interviews with the three high school seniors this evening. Luke, LaShawn, and Janie said they couldn't come to our office until six thirty."

Steve responded with a grunt and remained silent.

Miles clicked by and they made it to the parking lot of the McBlythe building without speaking. Heather's phone rang as she pulled into her reserved parking space.

"Hello, handsome," said Heather after seeing Jack's name on the caller ID.

"Big news. The cops found traces of blood in the bed of Rusty Brigs's truck. I'm glad he's not my client."

Heather said, "No blood in Clay's truck, but blood in Rusty's. I'm also glad Rusty isn't your client. He's toast."

She heard Steve whisper, "It's not that simple."

23

Heather spoke to Steve as the elevator whisked them to the fourth floor of her office building. "Why doesn't the discovery of blood in the bed of Rusty's truck mean the case is over? He had motive, means, opportunity, and a long history of convictions."

Metal doors slid open, and Steve stepped into the hallway. "I can't explain it other than to say, my gut is telling me this case doesn't want us to solve it."

The statement stopped Heather in her tracks. "You lost me. How can a case not want to be solved?"

Steve countered with, "Tell me you haven't noticed the conspiracy of circumstances that keeps us from focusing on the case." One at a time, he held up a finger. "First, Bucky publishes my stories, which causes you to get involved and hire Constance Banks to file lawsuits." He held up another finger. "Bella makes a surprise visit long before she planned to."

Heather shook her head. "Bella doesn't count as a distraction. She's helping us with the case."

"I'll grant you that much, but my point is, her coming was unexpected and led to a complication."

"What complication?"

"Not only what, but who... Rusty. I had to devise a plan that put Bella, you, and others in danger."

"But that plan may have solved the case."

Steve shook his head. "It's not that simple. There's too much deception from others."

"Who?"

"Let me finish answering the question of circumstances that have kept us from devoting ourselves to the murder case."

Heather realized he had a point to make and wanted her to hear him out. With jaw set and feet spread shoulder-length apart, he said, "Next. Bucky comes to my condo and assaults me."

A fresh surge of anger shot through Heather. "And you didn't tell me about it."

Steve ignored her and carried on. "You and I get our wires crossed and Constance doesn't temporarily drop the civil action against Bucky. He retaliates by setting fire to my condo, which affects both of us."

"That problem was quickly solved."

"Distractions," said Steve in a firm voice. "We're talking about a conspiracy of distractions. I recruited Leo to find out about Bucky after he assaulted me. He did that on the down-low until Bucky mixed gasoline with fire and had two Houston cops lined up to lie for him. The captain took the information to an assistant chief who brought in internal affairs." He shifted his weight to his other foot. "What are the chances of Palmer, a crooked internal affairs detective, coming to investigate a case involving Bucky?"

Heather shrugged. "I'll admit it seems unlikely."

Steve pursed his lips into a straight line. "I'm normally a guy who deals in facts and evidence, but I'm telling you, this case is unique. We have to push all these distractions aside and drill down until we find our killer."

Heather thought for a few seconds before responding. "We also need to find out why."

"We won't solve it standing here in the hall. Let's see what this evening brings when we interview Luke, LaShawn, and Janie."

Steve had memorized the steps to their office a long time ago. He waited until the door closed behind them before speaking. "Just because there was blood found in Rusty's truck doesn't mean it's April's. The DNA tests will take time. Meanwhile, I think Detective Blake will believe she has the killer and won't pursue other possibilities."

"Why don't you think Rusty killed her?"

"He received a different kind of education during his two trips to prison. Rusty knows what it takes to remove all traces of blood from the bed of his truck. If nothing else, he'd have set fire to it. From the way Bella described the old beater, the loss would have been minimal, and he makes good money for a replacement. He's too clever to hang on to something that would put him back in prison for the next thirty-plus years."

"Are you saying you believe someone set him up to take the fall for April's death?"

Steve settled into his chair. "Let's proceed as if that's the case. If additional evidence surfaces, we can always change our minds."

As expected, a stack of notes related to business ventures waited for her. She'd need to do some serious delegating if she expected to give much thought to the evening's interviews.

Her personal assistant came through the door and took long strides to cover the distance to where Heather was separating the notes into piles. The PA's first words were, "You smell like smoke. Do you want to shower and change before I give my report?"

"No time. Let's get to work."

One by one, Heather read the notes, delegated what she could to her staff, and made six phone calls for issues she needed to deal with personally. She skipped lunch while Steve had a deli sandwich delivered. He left half of it uneaten—a sure sign he was struggling to make sense of the case.

The hours slipped by as she solved problems and took action to prevent others. Steve sat in silence at his desk. She occasionally wondered if he had nodded off to sleep. It wasn't unusual for him to confirm her suspicion with light, sonorous expulsions of breath, but they didn't last long. He called them his brain breaks.

The vibe of the office changed at five o'clock when her clerical staff left for the day. To her, five in the afternoon was just another number on the clock. She and Steve would leave after they interviewed the three teenagers. The reluctant teens might divulge information that confirms Rusty's guilt. Then again, they might know very little about him.

Bella arrived a short time after the secretaries and receptionist departed. As usual, she walked with a spring in her step and a bright smile parting her lips. "Adam said he's cooking something special but wouldn't tell me what it is."

Heather stretched. "Does he know we may not be home until late?"

"I told him. He said it would be something he could keep warm."

Bella changed the subject. "How are we going to handle the interviews?"

Steve took over. "I want you to put the three teens in the interview room by themselves. We're going to watch how they interact when they think no one is watching. After that, we'll interview them one at a time."

"Let's make sure we're all on the same page," said Heather as she looked at Bella. "What reason did you give the teens for coming here tonight?"

"I laid it on thick," said Bella with a trickle of conspiracy in her words. "They'll arrive with the expectation of doing pretend interviews with the press and public. I told them they needed to act like the celebrities they might become and have opinions on current events."

"That's brilliant," said Heather. "That way we can weave in questions about April's murder."

"It was Steve's idea."

An incoming text concerning the lake project put an end to Heather's conversation. As usual, phone calls continued to pester her like mosquitoes at a nudist colony. At six fifteen she sent all messages to voicemail and focused on the questions she'd ask the teens. Ten minutes later, Luke Paulson and LaShawn Moody arrived at the same time.

Heather and Bella met them in the receptionist's outer office. "Did you two ride together?" asked Bella.

LaShawn swaggered toward her. "Nah, we met in the parking lot. We both have our own cars."

"They're sort of like real cars," said Luke. "More like wind-up toys from a garage sale. I have what used to be a Corolla until the first two letters broke off. Now I drive a 'rolla.' It fits 'cause she once rolled over on her side. She still drives, so I guess I shouldn't complain."

LaShawn was quick to respond. "At least you have a cool story to go along with the new name. The badge on my relic of a Mustang lost a letter in a car wash. The *s* went down the drain. Now I drive a Mutang."

Luke shot back, "You're lucky you have anything to drive after totaling two nice cars."

"That's what my dad says," he scoffed.

Bella put an end to the banter. "Ms. McBlythe will show you to the same room where we did the photo shoot. We're still waiting for Janie to arrive."

The two young men looked at each other with raised eyebrows. "Are you sure she's coming?" asked LaShawn.

"She said she'd be here," said Bella.

Heather wondered why the two young men looked on with skepticism.

LaShawn shook his head. "I hope she can get away from her prison guard."

Bella asked a question using only her raised eyebrows.

"Her mother," said Luke. "We call her that for a reason."

Before he could explain, the door jerked open. In walked a scowling woman with a mane of jet-black hair. "Where's Janie?"

24

Heather and Bella were at a loss for words, but not Steve. "You must be Janie's mother. My name is Steve Smiley."

Bella took over. "Your daughter has an incredible presence in photos. She's a natural model for sportswear. Did she show you the proofs?"

Veronica shot back. "It must have slipped her mind." Her eyes narrowed. "I gave my permission for her to take part, but only to take pictures. What's this meeting about and why wasn't I notified?"

Heather nodded to Bella, who took the hint. "LaShawn, why don't you and Luke go down to the room where we did the photo shoot? I'll be down in a few minutes."

"Stop!" said Veronica. "Why are they here?"

Bella issued a wide smile. "They're here to discuss future photo shoots, how to respond to the press, and what to expect from their future fans. Would you like to see Janie's photos now?"

"No."

Heather took over. "They're fabulous. Janie has such a presence in front of a camera. Believe me, she has that something special that catches people's attention. It's a quality that can't be described, but for those who have it, it's pure gold."

"What do you mean?"

While Heather sprayed compliments, she opened her tablet and pulled up photos from the shoot. Meanwhile, Steve went into a coughing spasm and dropped his cane. Bella herded the two young men out the door while Veronica was distracted.

Heather never skipped a beat. "Look at Janie's eyes. They have so much mystery in them. From a sales point of view, that translates into marketing gold. There are so many pretty girls her age, but there's something unique in Janie's eyes. It makes potential buyers want to go on a hike with her and wonder where she'll take them." She flipped to the next shot. "And look at her wearing this fall jacket, and her expression. She has a secret that she wants to share with whoever is looking at her."

"My daughter doesn't keep secrets from me. I don't permit it."

"Of course not," said Heather. "What I'm saying is, she communicates without words. That's what I meant by advertising gold. That ability can mean real money to Janie."

Veronica lifted her chin and tilted her head. "How much, and what are we talking about in terms of time commitment? She's going to get a full-time job after she graduates, then go on to college in the fall. I'll not tolerate any distractions."

Heather asked, "What if I said she could earn thousands of dollars and only do photo shoots on school breaks and in the summers?"

Veronica raised dark eyebrows in question. "Is that possible?"

"Of course it is. Look at her." Heather kept scrolling through the photos. "I heard Bella say something about a two-year contract."

Steve broke into the conversation. "Why don't you and Veronica stay in here and discuss details? I'll step out and leave you two alone."

"Hold on," said Veronica. "How do I know this isn't a scam?"

Heather went to her desk and pulled out a checkbook. She returned to the table and spoke as she wrote. "I know you have to be careful these days. To prove we're not trying to scam you, I'm willing to give you a good-faith payment of a thousand dollars. If you and Janie negotiate a contract with Bella, this is yours to keep."

Veronica thought for a minute. "Make it two thousand, and Janie has nothing to do with the negotiations."

"Fifteen-hundred," said Heather. She added, "As a reminder, Janie is an adult and can enter into a contract with or without your permission. Bella and her company don't want to cause friction between you and your daughter, but this is business we're talking about. As an attorney, I'm telling you, the contract won't be binding if Janie doesn't agree to it."

Veronica's eyes shifted from left to right. Her words remained harsh and demanding. "I do all the negotiating and Janie will sign it."

Steve broke in. "It seems we're on the right track. Bella and Veronica will hammer out the details. Heather will write the contract, give it to Veronica and Janie will sign it."

"I don't trust anyone. I want my attorney to review it, and I insist Janie gets enough money to pay for all the things she'll need in college."

Heather knew Steve was up to something. She could have put together a contract in no time and had it signed that night. He wanted to delay the signing. Why?

Heather turned to Veronica. "After you and Bella come to terms, I'll give you this check. It will take me a day or two to write the contract."

"I want it now."

"The contract or the check?" asked Heather.

"The check for fifteen-hundred dollars."

"All right," said Heather. "I'll give you the check, but I won't sign it until you agree on the details of the contract. You'll leave with it tonight."

Veronica huffed, "You're a tough negotiator."

She gave a half-smile. "You're not so bad, yourself."

Heather tore the unsigned check out of the bound book of checks and handed it to Veronica. "I'll send Bella in so you two can hammer out the details," said Heather. She took Steve by the hand and left her office.

She leaned into Steve and whispered, "How do you think Bella will do with her?"

"Better than you. If you'd stood your ground, she would have agreed to a thousand bucks. I did some checking on Veronica. She's in debt."

"How bad?"

"Not horrible, but without Janie getting a full ride to college and earning her own money, she won't make it without a huge pile of student loans. Mom doesn't have the wherewithal or the inclination to help her."

"Should we tell Bella?"

"Her company told her how much she could spend on models. She'll do fine."

The door opened to the hallway and Janie walked in. "Is this where I'm supposed to be?"

Heather took a step toward her. "Hello, Janie. LaShawn and Luke are already here. Let's go to where they're waiting. Bella's going to be tied up in a meeting with your mother."

Janie's face dropped as fear shone in her dark eyes.

Steve said, "Drop me off in the spare office."

The three exited the main office and walked down the hallway until they came to the door leading into the room with the one-way glass.

"Here you are, Steve," said Heather. He waited to open the door until she deposited Janie into the room where the photo shoots took place. In a matter of seconds, she was back with Steve, who'd found a chair and sat listening to the conversation of the three teens.

LaShawn was speaking as Heather looked through the glass. "Does your mom know you're here?"

"She caught me... again. I tried to tell her I was going to the library tonight, but she kept hammering away at me until I told her I wanted to go to the library but had to come here first. She made me ride my bicycle."

"In the dark?" asked Luke.

"Punishment for trying to deceive her."

"Bummer," said LaShawn. "What's she going to do when you go off to college?"

"She'll probably find another loser to hook up with."

"She can really pick 'em," said Luke.

"Tell me about it."

Steve spoke softly from where he sat. "This is some good stuff."

Heather gave a soft, "Uh-huh."

Heather took note of what Janie was wearing. Apparently LaShawn did, too. He asked, "Isn't that the outfit you wore during the photo shoot?"

"It's one of them. Do you like it?"

Luke responded before LaShawn had a chance to. "What does it matter? You're only interested in what one guy thinks."

"Do you think he'll like it?"

"Sure. He likes anything you wear."

LaShawn cupped his chin in his hand. "I don't know. I think he'd like to see you in a white wedding dress instead of a red yoga outfit."

Janie giggled. "I can't wait until he gets his wish."

"Before you go to college?"

"The week before it starts, if everything goes according to my plan." She took in a deep breath and let it out in a worried huff. "He thinks it's best if we wait until after summer. And I still have to make valedictorian to make college a reality."

"You're home free with that," said Luke. "April's murder

pretty well assured you of it. You two were running neck and neck, but I was rooting for you."

"I'm not taking any chances of blowing it. It's back to the books when I get home tonight." She looked around the room. "Bella told me why she wanted to see us tonight. Did she tell you?"

LaShawn straightened his shoulders and raised his chin. "She wants to offer me a six-figure contract as the next male super model."

"You wish," said Luke.

LaShawn shrugged. "A guy can dream."

The subject changed to gossip about friends and teachers. Heather turned to Steve. "Do you know who Janie's mystery man is?"

Instead of answering directly, he said, "Go check on Bella and Veronica. Let's get the prison guard and Janie home as quick as possible. Miss Polk needs to hit the books; we don't want to ruin her wedding plans."

Heather went to her office and quickly returned to the soundproof room. "Bella and Veronica have a deal. Do you want to come back to the office or stay here?"

"I'll stay. It's been a long time since I heard high schoolers talk. It's making me realize how out of touch I am with this generation."

"You don't want to hear the discussion between Janie and her mother?"

"Veronica will be in a good mood. She's probably counting the dollars and thinking about ways to spend them all."

"I hadn't thought of that. She'll have a rude awakening when Janie marries and her husband helps her stand on her own two feet."

"It may not take that long. Often all it takes is a little taste of freedom to help a person find their backbone," said Steve.

Heather let the comment pass and left the room. She looked over the agreement, making sure it didn't mention Janie's mother. When Veronica objected again, Heather told her if she wanted her fifteen-hundred dollar check signed, she'd abide by the terms of their verbal agreement.

Heather sent Steve a text, asking him to bring Janie.

The verbal jousting continued until Steve and Janie came into the office. Steve must have explained the situation to Janie before they came through the office door.

Janie sat beside Veronica and placed her hand on her mother's arm. "Mom, listen to me. I took business law last year so I know about how this works. I'm the employee, not you. And I'm considered an adult. Even without your name on the contract, you have full access to my bank account. That means whatever I make is yours to spend."

Veronica looked like she'd taken a large bite out of a lime. "What about future deposits?"

"Same thing," said Janie. "The checks have to be made out to me because I'm the employee." She waited until her mother turned her head, then gave Heather a wink. Both of them knew all Janie had to do was open a new account at whatever bank she chose. It apparently didn't occur to Veronica that her daughter was miles ahead of her, with her own plans for the money she'd earn.

Bella and Heather walked mother and daughter to the elevator and bid them a good night. Bella maintained a wide smile that remained until the sound of the elevator descending seemed to pull her lips together.

"What an awful mother. If she has her way, Janie will work for her benefit the rest of her life."

Heather hooked her arm in Bella's and gave her a gentle tug. "You don't need to worry about Janie. She's a bright young woman with a plan. Her mother will get fifteen-hundred dollars, but she'll lose her daughter if she tries to get more."

"Are you sure?"

"If I'm not mistaken, Janie already has another bank account her mother doesn't know about."

"Good," she said with a firm shake of her head. "That's one less thing for me to worry about."

When Bella said she wouldn't worry about Janie, Heather knew she meant it. She could put things out of her mind and move on to the next thing with amazing speed. She proved it by asking, "What's next?"

"We need to interview the two young men separately. Let's check with Steve and see how he wants to do it."

They arrived in the observation room in time to hear LaShawn say, "What's taking so long? I have an overdue paper to turn in tomorrow and Mr. Finkbinder is on to me about copying from Wikipedia."

"Just Google the topic, find three sources and mix up the sentences. Old Fink only checks Wikipedia."

Steve stood. "Let's take Luke first, before he corrupts LaShawn more than he already is." He unfolded his collapsible cane. "Bella, are you going to offer him a contract?"

"One year only."

"Good. Don't tell him until you get to the office. After you do that, Heather and I will take over."

"You sound serious."

"It's time to scare some truth out of the children."

25

Bella ushered Luke into Heather and Steve's office and seated him in a chair on the long side of the conference table. Heather, Steve, and Bella sat facing him with plenty of space between themselves—so much space that Luke had to turn his head whenever a question from a different person came at him. Steve sat directly in front of him, with Heather off to his left and Bella to the right.

"Luke," said Bella. His head turned to face her. "I'm pleased to tell you I'm ready to offer you a one-year contract as a model. There is, however, one caveat. My agency only hires models of high moral character and who can communicate effectively with the public. This interview, while usually only a formality, is the last step before we talk money."

Steve added, "You'll be representing a company known for honesty and integrity. Please don't waste our time by giving false or incomplete answers."

Heather knew this was stretching the truth, but Luke and LaShawn wouldn't know. It was Steve's idea that Bella begin both interviews with her memorized preamble.

Bella continued after taking a breath, "Because my company is so serious about our reputation, I've asked Mr. Smiley and Ms.

McBlythe to assist me in verifying you're a person of outstanding character. Do you understand?"

"Uh... I guess so."

Heather took over. "Relax. Steve and I may both be former police detectives, but we're not here to cost you a modeling job. All you have to do is tell the truth."

"From here on, treat Mr. Smiley and Ms. McBlythe like they're reporters. I'll be a fan of yours," said Bella.

Steve leaned forward and spoke with emphasis. "The press wants the truth."

Luke shrugged. "Sure. No problem."

Steve asked. "I guess a kid your age likes a beer every now and then."

"Huh?"

Heather spoke in a soft voice. "When was the last time you had a beer? Please answer the question."

"Oh. I don't drink."

Steve shook his head. "You're off to a terrible start. Want to try again?"

Heather spoke next, which caused Luke to turn his head toward her. "We won't count that one against you. It's normal for people to test us, especially young adults. They have the mistaken belief that we can't detect simple lies. You should know that we do extensive background checks before we interview and have loads of training under our belts."

It was a partial truth because the various distractions during this case had kept them from boring down on background checks as deeply as they usually did.

"If I were a reporter, I'd want to know a little about you in your own words. Tell us about yourself. Say anything you want for the next three to five minutes."

Luke rattled on for four minutes. He had a gift for gab and gave a fairly complete account of his childhood that included place of birth, one move from Houston to The Woodlands, parents' occupations, participation in organized sports including a broken arm in the seventh grade, and a bothersome little sister.

Steve waited until Luke seemed to run out of things to talk about before asking two current event questions. The first dealt with the decriminalization of shoplifting, and the second was about global warming. Luke answered both with a word-salad made up of several sentences that dodged the issues.

"Who are you dating?" asked Steve.

"No one."

"What about Janie Polk? You seem to know her pretty well, and you both want to model for the same company."

"We had a very brief high school thing. It was a four-week crush."

"Were you the one who got crushed?"

"You could say that, but I got over her."

"Are you sure? She's a beautiful young woman."

Luke rendered a muted laugh. "She's so far out of my league, I'd need a telescope to see her."

Steve didn't waste a second. "What about April Brewer? I heard through the news she was your age. In fact, she went to your school. Did you ever date her?"

Luke rocked back in his chair. "April? I couldn't believe it when they found her. We didn't see her for a while, then there was a big search. Everyone had a different idea of what happened to her."

"What did you think?"

Luke raked his hair with his fingertips. "Man, it blew my mind. She liked to have a good time, but she was way too focused to run away."

Steve said, "Sounds like you knew her pretty well."

"I guess," Luke shrugged. "She was beautiful, fun, and really knew how to dance."

Heather took her turn. "Why didn't you date her?"

"She always went for older guys."

Steve hit him with another question. "How much older?"

"It didn't matter as long as they could dance."

"Twenty-five? Thirty? Fifty?"

"I saw her dance once with a guy who could have been her father."

"Where?"

"The Melody Barn."

"Tell us about the men you referred to."

Luke took the slack out of his posture. "There's one guy she danced with more than the others. I've never spoken to him, but he's the guy the cops arrested. I hear he works for Clay's dad as some sort of heavy equipment operator."

"Is he a regular at the Melody Barn?"

"I only go there about once a month, but when I do, he's there. April said she liked to dance with him because no one our age was any good." Luke seemed to look into the past. "Those two could really scoot across the floor. It was like they'd choreographed their moves."

"Did he also dance with women his own age?"

"Yeah, but only if April wasn't there."

"What about other high school girls?"

"He'd dance with anyone, but only to see if they were any good."

Luke tilted his head. "I know you're pretending to interview me like reporters, but what does this have to do with modeling sportswear?"

Heather broke in. "There's a reason for every question. The last group of questions was to test you on current local events. Please answer his question."

Her justification seemed to satisfy Luke. He continued, "He'd scope out all the women and pick out those who looked like they could keep up with him. Otherwise, he sat at the bar."

Steve took his turn again. "Did you ever see him leave with anyone, or did he stay until the place closed?"

Luke's eyes shifted to look at a spot where the wall met the ceiling behind Steve. "Now that you mention it, I can't remember a time when I saw him leave before I did. Even when I stayed until closing, he was still there."

In a sudden shift, Steve asked, "When was the last time you smoked a joint?"

The hesitation was too long. Luke rolled his eyes and let out a breath of resignation. "This may cost me a sweet contract, but I smoked one on my way here. I was a bundle of nerves and needed to mellow out."

"What about other drugs?"

"No, sir."

"Never?"

"No way. My dad sat me down when I was in the seventh grade and told me he knew I'd experiment with alcohol and weed. He didn't exactly give me permission, but said there'd be a death in the family if I did anything else. It worked. He gave me enough rope to test out what he called the forbidden fruits of my youth."

Heather took over, which caused Luke to turn his head and shift his gaze to her. "We understand you and LaShawn were good friends with Clay Cockrell. What happened to that friendship?"

Luke stammered before his words solidified. "He graduated before us. We used to be the three amigos, but I guess things change after graduation. He's working long hours, and me and LaShawn are coasting out of high school and going to college in the fall."

Heather believed him when Luke said they were coasting, but said, "Going to college is a good plan. I think it will help the sportswear company see you as a young man wanting to make something of himself."

Steve turned to face Bella and gave his head a nod to show he had no further questions. Heather did the same.

Bella issued a wide smile. "You've passed the interview. Since you're eighteen, you can sign the contract. However, I recommend you take it home and have your parents read it. They may want to consult an attorney, which is fine. I'll give you a week to have it back to me. Call if you have questions."

Luke left the office smiling, carrying a file folder with his one-year contract to model. Steve mumbled a word of parting while Bella and Heather congratulated him.

Heather wondered what Steve heard that caused him to retreat deep within himself. Her thoughts shifted to April and Rusty's relationship. Did the ex-con want more from the high school senior than dancing? Things weren't looking good for Rusty.

Bella retrieved LaShawn, who sauntered in with his curly black hair puffing out from the sides and back of a flat-billed baseball cap. His baggy jeans sagged over designer high-topped athletic shoes. A slouchy sweatshirt emblazoned with the logo of Bella's company completed the expensive outfit.

Heather offered her comment on his attire. "You wore that outfit in the photo shoot. It looks good on you. How do you think it will sell?"

"There's definitely a demand for the look. The logo on the sweatshirt isn't edgy enough for those wanting the full gangster look, but the cap, pants, and shoes are spot on."

Bella gave a nod of agreement. "The big money is in the shoes and pants. We're trying to appeal to the somewhat conservative parents who want to compromise with their teens on what, or who, appears on the shirts and hats."

As with Luke, Bella explained the purpose of the interview and how it would be role playing between two reporters, a fan and LaShawn. She also told LaShawn this would be the last step to get a one-year modeling contract. Steve opened up with a few softball questions, which LaShawn fielded with no problem. The young man showed himself to be articulate and self-assured without sounding arrogant.

The tone of the questions changed when Steve leaned forward. "Bella's company places high value on moral character. I understand you're good friends with Clay Cockrell, who is currently a suspect in a murder case. Is that right?"

LaShawn stammered out, "We're not... we used to be... we were closer before he graduated."

"I understand he put off going to college. Bella's company also values people who know what they want and stick to a plan. With friends like Clay, there may be some concern you could make bad choices too."

"But I... I wouldn't."

"Why do you think he changed his mind about college? From what we know of his parents, they have enough money to pay his way to any school he wants to attend."

LaShawn looked down at his hands and shrugged. "Clay's a real tight-lipped guy."

Heather said, "This isn't the time or place to follow his example. What are your plans for college?"

The young man looked up and said, "That all depends. I'll go, but my mom forgot to plant money trees."

"What if you get a nice contract to model sportswear?"

LaShawn flashed a wide smile of perfect teeth. "That would go a long way to me going somewhere besides a junior college."

"What do you want to study?" asked Bella.

The reply came back without hesitation. "Accounting. I'm good with numbers and I like business. You can keep the humanities."

It was Steve's turn to pepper him with another question. "Where are you working now?"

"I keep the books for a guy who owns a couple of local car washes."

"What's his name?"

"Uh... Mr. Clayton."

Heather said nothing but remembered an old social media post Briann had uncovered. Clay owned two car washes. Perhaps LaShawn was managing them for him.

Steve moved on before she could ask. "Are you involved in a serious romantic relationship?"

The smile came back full-force. "I have big plans for my life. I'll start looking for the right woman in my third year of college. Until then, I'm content hanging with a group."

Heather took her turn. "I did the same thing, except I waited until I was over thirty. I made it a practice not to date anyone over three times."

"That's so cool. I thought I was the only one who didn't think they had to be married by the time they were twenty-one."

Steve changed the subject. "Up to now, there've been two men taken into custody for the murder of April Brewer. One is a man named Rusty Brigs, and the other is your friend Clay Cockrell."

The smile disappeared and LaShawn shot back, "It wasn't Clay."

"We know he dated April."

"That's ancient history."

"He discovered the body."

"So? He didn't put her there."

"How can you be so sure? You say you're not in close touch with him anymore. He might have changed since you stopped hanging with him."

Fists clenched. "I know Clay better than anyone. He had nothing to do with April's death. The police have the right guy locked up. Everyone at school knows Rusty and April met up at the Melody Barn on the weekends. He's also an ex-con. Two trips to the pen, both for violent crimes."

"How do you know that?" asked Heather.

"Luke found out and is taking action to make sure the guy goes back to prison."

"Taking action? What action? Be specific."

The bill on LaShawn's cap dipped and returned three quick times. "Luke's good at stirring up people when he puts his mind to it. He started by organizing a bunch of us at school to write emails to the sheriff. They complained about the violent ex-con who could come to the Melody Barn and hit on high school girls. A YouTuber who hates cops heard about it and made a video that's gone viral. The sheriff told the guy to go back to Houston and mind his own business. That played right into Luke's plan. It made the cops look like they didn't care about April being killed."

Steve broke in. "I thought Luke's interest in April ended a long time ago?"

LaShawn snorted out his nose. "Don't let nobody fool ya'. Luke burned like a blowtorch for April. He couldn't stand to see her dance with that Rusty dude."

"What about Clay? Was his candle still burning for April?"

Before the bemused young man could answer, Heather quickly asked, "We're hearing talk you and Janie Polk had something going on."

LaShawn snapped back, "You heard wrong."

Steve added, "I think you'd like to go off to college with her."

The laugh shot out of LaShawn. He didn't elaborate on what made him explode in laughter.

Steve asked, "Were Clay and Janie Polk a better match?"

"Yeah, but it didn't matter. No one in their right mind would try to get past her mother."

"She can't be that bad," said Steve.

"Wanna bet?" said LaShawn with a challenge in his tone. "She has an app on Janie's phone and sometimes checks it several times an hour. She also has another tracking device in Janie's car that pinpoints her location. Janie has to ask permission to use her own car except to go to school. When she goes anywhere, her mom knows where she is, how many miles it should take to get there and back, and how long it should take. Any deviation and Janie loses the car for two weeks. Her mom didn't even buy it for her; Janie bought it with her own money."

Steve shook his head. "That's tough. How did Janie earn the money to buy a car?"

"Her mom got her on as a bar backer at the Melody Barn."

"Speaking of Janie's mom. Does she ever break away from the bar and dance with customers?"

Another laugh came from LaShawn. "Prison guards don't dance."

"Are you sure?"

"She's too busy watching Janie."

"Does Clay ever come to the Melody Barn?"

"Never. He's too busy earning money."

Steve laced his fingers together. "The cops first thought Clay killed April and he's still a suspect. Why don't you believe he did?"

The question took the smile off LaShawn's face. "Anyone with half a brain knows Clay couldn't harm anyone."

"Couldn't or wouldn't?"

"Both," snapped LaShawn.

"You sound angry," said Steve. "Explain why."

LaShawn's smile returned, but it lacked sincerity. "Clay and I might not be as tight as we once were, but I'd bet anything he had nothing to do with killing April." He paused. "The question I have is, who tried to set him up?"

Steve's face was an unreadable mask. "I've been asking myself that same question." He made a steeple out of his index fingers while resting his chin on his thumbs.

Heather knew he'd finished his questions and gave a nod to Bella that the interview was over.

"Congratulations, LaShawn," said Bella. "You passed the interview. You did very well under pressure, which is what we were really testing you on. I look forward to working with you this year."

Heather remained seated while Bella and LaShawn completed their business and he left.

Once the door clicked shut, Heather said, "That was interesting. What did you learn?"

Steve shifted in his chair. "Clay's lucky to have a friend like LaShawn."

Heather's phone rang. The screen showed the name and she announced, "It's Loretta Blake."

Steve said, "She's going to tell you that the blood in Rusty's truck belongs to April Brewer."

26

"Hi, Loretta," said Heather. "Steve believes there's a blood match."

"There is, and that isn't all. Not only was it April's blood on Rusty's truck, but we searched his mobile home and found a shovel under his porch. Forensics has it, and there's blood on it, too. They're also matching the dirt from the grave he dug."

"Do you have a confession?"

"Not yet, and he's not talking."

"Can you let us know if he tries to make a deal with the DA?"

"There won't be any deals on this one. Rusty's been stalking April for months at the Melody Barn. We're lining up a full dance hall of witnesses."

Heather offered her congratulations to Loretta and ended the call. Her phone buzzed again before she could ask Steve if he wanted to continue the investigation or not.

The call needed to be taken in private. Heather stood and walked toward the door to her tiny apartment. "Excuse me, while I handle this call." With long strides, she made for the bedroom, threw open the door, and shut it behind her. "Hold on a minute."

Heather went into the bathroom, closed the door, and ran

water in the sink. "Sorry, Kate. I didn't know if you wanted to keep this call from Steve or not."

Heather checked her makeup in the bathroom mirror as she pressed the phone hard against her ear. The call from Kate had taken her by surprise and she didn't want Steve distracted. Like two horseshoe-shaped magnets, sometimes the attraction between Kate and Steve was strong, but when circumstances changed the polarity, they pushed each other away. And she never knew which way their relationship was going.

Kate asked, "Is this a bad time to call?"

"Not anymore. We just learned the police seem satisfied they have the killer in the murder case we've been working on. The evidence is overwhelming."

"What does Steve think?"

"He's shifted into his silent, contemplative mode. I'm getting the impression he believes there's another layer I'm not seeing."

"That tells me what I need to know. I'm coming to Houston next week to give a formal statement to Constance Banks. Steve isn't returning her phone calls, so I'll steer clear of him."

"Oh, snap! I'd love to see you, and I know Bella would, too."

"Hold that thought. Let me tell you what progress I've made with Constance. I sent her my copies of the manuscripts Steve wrote that I critiqued and edited. Those and my testimony will prove the works are originals from Steve. I've also put the word out in the writer community that Bucky Franklin stole Steve's works and published them. His reputation is mud."

"Good. Did Constance tell you about the fire?"

"What fire?"

"It started in Steve's condo, but it got mine, too."

"No! Are you two all right?"

"We weren't home and we're collecting on the insurance. I've leased a large home much closer to work. It was a short-term rental and came fully furnished. Steve has his own private living area."

"What about Max? Was he injured?"

"He hid in my closet until the fire department broke down my door. It took a while to find him and get him out of a very tall tree. He hisses every time he passes the fireplace in the den."

"How did the fire start?"

"We have our friend Bucky Franklin to thank for that."

An audible gasp came through the phone followed by, "Is he in jail?"

"Out on bond."

Heather considered telling her about Bucky assaulting Steve with hot coffee but decided against it. Instead, she gave a piece of good news. "Did you know Bella and Adam are staying with us?"

"That's wonderful. I feel horrible about missing their wedding, but when I heard you and Steve were also working on a murder case, I knew I'd made the right decision."

"Plan on spending at least one night with us when you come."

Several seconds of silence followed. "I'd so love to see you and Bella, but I don't know if staying with you is such a good idea. You know how Steve is when he's working a case."

"The case is all but over. If you're not coming until next week, the coast will be clear."

Kate hesitated again. "Are you sure you have enough room?"

"More than enough, with extra rooms to spare."

"I'll come for one night, but only if the case is done and dusted."

"Perfect. We'll take you to where I'm building our future lakeside homes."

"Stop," said Kate. "Too much sensory overload. Don't tell me about your new homes until I'm there."

Heather watched herself in the mirror as a smile parted her lips. "I can't wait to see you again, Kate. I jumped for joy when I heard you were going to be Steve's editor and coach again."

"This time it will be a formal business arrangement. I don't want there to be any misunderstanding."

"Agreed," said Heather. They traded salutations and Heather left the room with a smile on her face.

Steve stood. "I'm starving."

"Nothing new about that," said Heather and Bella at the same time. Bella then asked, "Where do you want to eat?"

"What day is it?"

"Does it matter?" asked Bella.

"Not really. Let's get a burger and head home."

The week passed with Heather spending little time on the case while Steve didn't call or text her. She arrived home early Friday with the satisfaction of a wonderful week's work under her belt. The project was on schedule and budget. She knew that could change at any moment, and likely would, but for now, all was good.

Steve met her in the kitchen with an impish smile pulling up one corner of his top lip. "My taste buds have a hankering for a chopped brisket sandwich, and I wouldn't say no to a two-step around a dance floor. Why don't you call your dance partner and tell him to meet us at the Melody Barn? Make sure he brings Briann. I need someone to dance with."

Heather's jaw dropped as she traded glances with Bella, who squealed with delight. "What a great idea. Believe it or not, Adam is a wonderful dancer. I didn't expect that from a confirmed introvert."

Steve walked toward his apartment. "Don't underestimate us strong, silent types. You can make your phone call from the car."

Bella said, "Adam has another hour's worth of work. We'll meet you there."

It wasn't long before Heather had changed and was cranking the engine of her SUV. With Steve beside her, she called Jack. "Hey, handsome. Have you and Briann eaten yet?"

"She wants pizza again, and I told her no. I'm only good for three times a week and there's still the college and pro basketball games to watch tonight."

"Good. Put on your boots and meet us at the Melody Barn."

"Is this a celebration because the cops nailed a murder charge to Rusty?"

Heather searched for an answer and came up with something to goad Steve. "You-know-who is acting weird. He wants a brisket sandwich and to dust the cobwebs off his dancing boots."

"Hmmm. I'm intrigued. The only time I ever saw him dance was at Bella and Adam's wedding. One dance with Bella was all he had in him."

Steve cut into the conversation. "I don't want to show up you amateurs. Your egos are far too fragile."

Jack shot back, "That's big talk. I think Heather and I can give you a run for your money."

Steve rose to the challenge. "Briann and I will put you two to shame, and I'll do it with my eyes closed."

Jack shouted, "Briann, change into jeans and boots! We're going for barbecue and a dance contest. Me and Heather against you and Steve."

Briann must have been nearby. She responded with, "You and Heather are going down. Steve's an outstanding dancer."

"He is?" said Heather and Jack at the same time.

Jack followed up with, "How do you know?"

"He's been teaching me when you two go on your dates and he comes over here. At first it made me mad you didn't trust me, but he said dancing builds self-confidence, plus I won't embarrass myself when I date."

Jack cleared his throat. "You'll have many years to practice with Steve before you're ready to date."

Briann countered with, "Middle school dances start next year."

Jack and Heather groaned at the same time. The call ended. At times like this, Heather wondered if she had it in her to deal with a teenager. At least she wasn't living with Briann full-time like Jack was. Sometimes, the postponed engagement looked like a blessing.

Steve's chuckle brought her to the realization that she'd been mumbling to herself. She refocused on the road. "If you and Briann are better dancers than Jack and I, something's seriously wrong."

"I'm not going for a dance contest," said Steve in a flat voice.

"I didn't think so. Want to share with me the real reason?"

"Not yet, but keep your eyes open. I'll need you to tell me when you recognize people of interest and how they react when they see us."

"Anyone in particular?"

"Any of Bella's models, their parents, or anyone else we've talked to since Clay found April's body."

Heather puffed out her cheeks and let out a breath. "I thought this was going to be a pleasant night of dinner and dancing. I'll need to tell Jack I'm still working."

"You can tell him he's on the clock, too. I need both of you to tell me what you're seeing."

"You don't think Rusty killed April, do you?"

"All the evidence points to him, and that's the problem... *all* the evidence."

"I understand what you're saying, but without something to contradict what the police have, the district attorney has a slam-dunk case."

"That's why we're going dancing." He paused and smiled. "I also wanted a real good barbecue sandwich and fries."

27

U p-tempo country western music spilled into the Melody Barn's parking lot when Heather and Steve opened their car doors. It was relatively early, the time when patrons emphasized food over adult beverages and dancing. As the night progressed, the mood, volume, and vibe would change. Boot scooters and those looking to unwind from the week's work would take over.

As was their custom, Steve met Heather at the front of her car with hand outstretched. She bent her right arm at the elbow, took his hand, and placed it on her forearm. Steve was the first to speak. "There's nothing like the smell of hot grease and smoke from slow-burning pits."

"The wind is blowing away from us. How can you smell that?"

He breathed deeply. "It's swirling in the trees. I can smell beans, too."

Heather wove their way through three rows of parked cars. "Four steps up," she said as they made their way to wide double doors. Once inside the cavernous building, Heather led Steve to the side of the entry area, allowing others behind them to enter. She looked down at a darker path worn into the wooden floor before taking stock of the room. "The dance floor is empty. There's a good crowd at the picnic tables having dinner. A few people are at the bar."

"What about Veronica and Janie Polk? Are they behind the bar?"

"Veronica's pouring a draft beer. I don't see Janie." She paused. "Wait. Janie's coming from a back room carrying a bucket of ice."

Steve lightly pressed on her arm. "Let's go say hi to them. Slap on a smile and keep the conversation light. I'll come back later and spend some time with Veronica."

Heather whispered as she took a step. "You came with a plan. What is it?"

"Plans have a way of changing. Follow my lead."

"Who do you want to talk to first?"

"Only to Veronica. We won't be here long."

Heather found a spot near the beer taps with plenty of space between them and the next customers.

Veronica made her way to them. Before she could speak, Steve said. "Veronica Polk. Is that you?"

Her eyes narrowed and suspicion filled her reply. "How'd you know?"

Steve tapped his nose. "It's a sense I developed after I lost my sight. You wear just a dab or two of perfume that suits you. Most people don't realize it, but their body chemistry affects the way colognes or perfumes smell. March ten women by me wearing the same scent you're wearing, and I'd pick you out."

The explanation earned the upward curl of the corners of her mouth. It seemed to last too long, or did Heather only imagine that?

Heather joined in, "He has the nose of a bloodhound."

"Not that good," said Steve.

"What will you two have?" asked Veronica in a sweet voice.

Steve pursed his lips. "I think I'd better hold off until I get something on my stomach. We're meeting some others for a celebration and I need to pace myself. I have a date to dance the night away with a beautiful young lady."

Heather let out a boisterous laugh. "His date is my boyfriend's daughter; she's twelve years old."

Veronica's smile widened. "What's the occasion?"

"There are several things. One involves you and Janie signing the contract with Bella."

"I'm so glad you two decided to go forward with the contract. It's a smart business move," said Heather.

Steve leaned forward. "Doesn't surprise me a bit from a cautious woman like Veronica. Most people second-guess good fortune that seems to fall out of the sky." He leaned back. "Isn't that right, Heather?"

"Absolutely. People are hard-wired to question decisions. It's like buying a new car. As soon as you get it home, you notice minor imperfections and wonder if you made the right choice. I always wonder if I could have talked the salesperson into a better deal, even if it's only a few dollars."

"Not me," said Veronica. "But I'm curious. Did Bella really give Janie top dollar?"

Steve waved off the question. "You made the right decision to take what she offered. I'll be glad to explain later. In the meantime, I need to get a sandwich in my empty belly."

"I'll be working all night," said Veronica. "Come back and we'll have a proper talk."

"You get a break, don't you?"

"I'm supposed to get fifteen minutes at eleven o'clock."

"Perfect. Come get me and we'll talk while we dance." He didn't give her a chance to say no. "You wouldn't deny an old blind guy a dance, would you?"

"I rarely dance with customers, but I think I could make an exception."

Heather wondered how Steve had talked her into it with such ease. He placed both hands on the bar, leaned forward, and lowered his voice. "I tell you what, Veronica. Keep an eye on the dance floor. If I'm not the best blind dancer here tonight, you don't have to dance with me."

This earned a full laugh, followed by, "Aren't you the smoothest talker ever to come in here? I still want to know if I made a mistake on Janie's contract."

"What if I ask Bella to add another year?"

"Can you guarantee she'll do it?"

Heather answered for Steve. "What do you have to lose if Bella says no?"

Steve held up his hand as a sign to stop. "About our dance, there's only one catch."

Suspicion came like a cloud over Veronica's face. "What's that?"

"I can't lead. It's not safe for anyone if I do."

"It's a deal. I'll come get you at eleven o'clock."

Heather led Steve away from the bar. She waited until she had him seated at a picnic table and she took a seat beside him. "What do you hope to learn from her?"

"I already confirmed a couple of things."

Jack and Briann's arrival prohibited Heather from finding out more. The precocious twelve-year-old plopped down beside Steve. "Are you ready to dance?"

"Not until after we eat."

"Ok. Let's order."

"We're waiting for Bella and Adam."

"How 'bout we share an order of fries as an appetizer?"

Steve withdrew a money clip, pulled off a bill, and handed it to Briann. "Good thinking. Make it two orders so Heather and your dad will have something to tide them over."

Jack pointed to a counter on the other side of the dance floor. "You order and pick up food over there. Get something to drink while you're at it."

Briann unfolded her legs from the table and made for the other side of the dance floor. Her ponytail swished back and forth against her shoulders as she walked. Her jeans were tight over thin legs, giving her the look of a gangly colt. She was in the first stages of developing the curves that would separate the child from a fast-growing teen.

Heather rested her hand on Jack's thigh, hidden by the table-top. "She's no longer a child."

"Tell me about it," said Jack with an appropriate amount of sarcasm. His voice took on a serious tone. "She's trying to grow up too fast."

Heather wanted to debate him on the subject but lost concentration as a group of older teens strode across the dance floor. Luke Paulson was one of them.

Leaning to her left, Heather purposefully bumped into Steve. "Luke's here with a group."

"What about LaShawn? Is he with them?"

"I don't see him." She cast her gaze around the building. "Wait. There he is. He's at the corner of the bar talking to Janie. They're standing where her mom can't see them."

"Interesting." Steve seemed to gather his thoughts. "While I'm dancing with Veronica tonight, I want you to get Janie alone. Tell her you know about her secret and see how she reacts."

"What secret?"

Steve raised his shoulders and let them drop. "I'm counting on her having several. If she presses you for details, tell her you suspect her of a relationship with LaShawn because you saw them talking. Then, pay particular attention to how she reacts to that."

"Anything else?"

"Try not to let Janie's mom see you." He rubbed his chin. "Forget what I just said. It might be more interesting if she sees you two talking. I think I know how she'll react, but she might surprise me."

Heather scanned the room that was quickly filling. "Is this evening going to end in a barroom brawl?"

"Not between anyone we're interested in. Our people all have secrets they're trying to hide."

"All of them?"

"Every one."

Heather's focus on Steve kept her from paying attention to Briann until she placed two baskets of French fries on the table. "Here you go."

Bella and Adam arrived and sat opposite the foursome with their backs to the dance floor. As always, Bella turned heads with the platinum-blond rope of braided hair that hung down to the belt of her jeans. She grabbed a fry from the top of the stack. "I hope these are community property. I'm starving." She looked at Briann. "Are you ready to dance tonight?"

Briann gave her head a firm nod.

"Feed me first," said Steve.

Bella stood. "Come on, Briann." She shifted her gaze to the others. "Speak up or you're getting a chopped beef sandwich." She turned to her husband. "You're responsible for drinks. I'll take a Diet Coke."

Heather ate only half her sandwich, but it had nothing to do with the quality. The half-pound of meat spilled over the bun on all sides. Jack polished off his entire meal. Steve surprised her by only eating half of his. She searched her mind for a reason.

"What's wrong with your appetite tonight?" she asked.

He leaned into her. "Too much beef makes me sleepy. Briann's a quick learner on the dance floor. I don't want to be so full I make a fool of myself with a twelve-year-old. I also need to be on my toes when I dance with Veronica."

Heather accepted the explanations at face value. His response made her think about how she'd approach Janie and what questions to ask. She nudged Jack and asked, "Are you too stuffed to dance?"

He let out a muffled groan. "I think my sandwich needs to settle first. I skipped lunch today to interview attorneys. I'm happy to say I narrowed the search to two candidates. Both would be good, but I want your advice."

"Tell me about them."

"Charles Reed is fifty-five with three years' experience in private practice. Prior to that, he worked as a prosecutor in the Attorney General's office. He took an early retirement to escape the traffic and politics of Austin."

"Can't say that I blame him," said Heather. She considered what he'd said but waited for more information.

None came, so she said, "On the positive side, he sounds capable and stable. If he's receiving a state retirement, that includes most of his insurance coverage. That could be a big money saver for you." She took a breath. "Tell me about the other candidate."

"Sam Delgado is bilingual and has seven years' experience as a defense attorney in Waco. No spouse, no kids."

Heather asked, "Which one is the most aggressive?"

Jack didn't hesitate. "Sam."

"Did you schedule a second interview with them?"

A nod answered her question. "Do you want me to sit in on the interviews?"

"I was hoping you'd offer."

Steve joined the conversation. "Have you scheduled them yet?"

"Not yet," said Jack. "I didn't want to bother Heather until you two finished your investigation."

Steve pushed the remains of his food away from him. "Ask me again after I dance with Veronica Polk and Heather speaks with her daughter. It's possible we'll have everything wrapped up on Monday."

Jack sighed and said, "I hope Clay Cockrell isn't involved."

Instead of giving an immediate response, Steve turned to face Briann. "Are you ready to show these amateurs what a couple of real dancers can do?"

"You're darn right, I am." She spun on her rump, swinging her boots over the long bench.

Steve followed Briann's example but spoke to Jack before he did so. "Clay is still one of the main characters in understanding

April Brewer's murder. I'll let you know when you need to have him in Heather's office."

Heather held up a hand, signaling Jack not to ask any more questions. Briann led Steve to the dance floor, and the two glided in unison.

Jack took her hand. "Did you know he was so close to solving the case?"

"This is the point where he plays mind games with me." She spoke with certainty. "He's figured it out but needs verification. That should come tonight or this weekend."

"He's a complicated man," said Jack.

Heather gave his hand a squeeze. "Don't I know it? In the meantime, I suggest we put the case out of our minds and enjoy a couple hours of dancing. Nothing's going to happen before eleven, when Steve dances with Veronica and Bella and I speak with Janie."

28

Heather let out a breath of exasperation. She made it loud enough for Jack to shift his attention to her. "What?" he asked.

"Stop staring at Briann and Steve dancing. Not only are you making her nervous, you're ignoring me."

"Sorry," said Jack, but his gaze remained on his daughter.

Heather stopped in mid-shuffle. "That's it. You're fired as my dance partner. We're going to the table and I'm making you sit with your back to the dance floor."

"Let's negotiate. How about I only go to time out for one dance?"

"Two dances, and you can't be looking over your shoulder. Give your poor daughter a break. It's Steve she's dancing with, not some biker with a skull tattooed on his forehead."

The song ended before they made it back to their table. On the way, Heather's gaze shifted to the front door. Into the dance hall walked two uniformed sheriff's deputies.

Heather's gaze moved to where Veronica stood behind the beer taps. A scowl came over her countenance. Her gaze shifted to Janie, but she made no move toward her daughter, nor did she say anything.

The band took a break, and the dance floor cleared. Patrons were soon four-deep at the bar, going for another round. It wasn't long before their table was back to full strength with the additions of Bella, Adam, Steve, and Briann.

Steve was the first to notice the change in the seating. "Jack, why aren't you sitting by Heather?"

"He's in time out. It seems my dance partner is more interested in snooping on his daughter than waltzing with me."

Briann gave a firm nod to her head. "He deserves to stay there all night."

Bella, the peacemaker, changed the subject. "Steve, where did you learn to dance so well?"

He flipped away the compliment wrapped in a question. "Maggie gets all the credit. I had two left feet when we went to college. By the time graduation came, she had me whipped into someone who could hold his own. She had to endure sore toes the first semester but never complained."

Jack added, "I can't believe how good you and Briann are. How can I keep my eyes off of her?"

"You'd better learn," said Briann. "I can feel you staring at me."

Steve lifted his chin. "How close are we to eleven o'clock?"

"Twenty minutes," said Heather.

Heather looked up to see Detective Blake approaching. "Loretta, I didn't see you come in."

"We've been here for over an hour. I wanted to tell this young lady dancing with Steve that she does a mean two-step. You're even practicing spins. I'm jealous. My two-step turns into a three-step, with the last one being a trip."

Briann dipped her head. "Thank you. Steve makes it seem easy."

Loretta raised her eyebrows. "I'll have to ask Steve to teach me."

Steve said, "This could be the start of a new career for me if this private investigator gig doesn't work out. Are you a regular here?"

"I come now and then, but I wouldn't say I'm a regular."

Heather looked toward the bar. "I noticed there's a couple of uniforms here tonight. Is that in response to the YouTube video?"

"Ah, you heard about that."

Steve took his turn. "A minute ago, you said *we've* been here for over an hour. Who's we?"

"Other detectives and officers. We're celebrating the upcoming trial and conviction of Rusty Brigs. It's putting away guys like him that makes my job worthwhile."

"Do you think it's possible he had help in killing April?" Steve asked.

Loretta's head tilted. "Do you know something I don't?"

"Not yet, but we're working on it."

Loretta didn't respond for several seconds. "It wouldn't fit Rusty's M.O." She narrowed her stare. "Are you trying to ruin my night by making me think he had an accomplice when there's no evidence to support it?"

Steve erupted in a boisterous laugh. "Why would I do something like that?"

Heather answered. "I can't tell you how many times Steve's done the same thing to me. It's a nasty habit of his to get me to second guess what I know."

"Guilty," said Steve. "Early in my career, I refused to consider a gang-banger would include an eleven-year-old cousin as an accomplice. The young kid shot two other people before we got him off the street. One died, and the other took a bullet in the spine. Never walked again. It taught me to keep asking questions."

Loretta stared at Steve. "Are you free to talk tomorrow?"

"Can we make it Monday morning?"

"Where?"

"Come to Heather's office."

"I can be there at seven," said Loretta.

"If you do, you'll be waiting for two hours."

Jack asked, "Do I need to be there?"

Steve placed his hands on the table. "I want you to bring Clay."

The band gave the opening riff to a fast, toe-tapping song that caused the crowd to let out a whoop. More time had passed than Heather realized. A glance at the empty bar told her the crowd had shifted back into dance mode. Veronica wiped a spill off the bar, placed the towel below the bar, and walked away.

It wasn't long before Veronica approached Steve. Her voice was at a near shout because the band had increased the volume to that of a private jet taking off.

"Well?" said Veronica. "What about that contract for a third year?"

Steve directed his voice across the table to where Bella sat. "Veronica wants to add another year to Janie's contract. Are you willing to consider it?"

Heather gave a sly nod to Bella.

Bella took the hint but voiced reservations. "I'm all for recommending it, but I'll need to get special permission from the director of marketing. I don't think it will be a problem because Janie's more impressive than any other models I've found."

"More than me?" asked Briann with what looked like a pretend pout.

"You were second, but only because girls your age change so much and many get braces."

Steve stood. "Instead of dancing, why don't you and I find a quiet place to talk?"

"That wasn't the deal."

"You're right, and I really feel bad that you won't experience the best dance of your life." He followed this with a wide, cheesy smile.

Steve's ability to disarm was on full display. Heather wondered how he did it so effortlessly.

Veronica, however, was a tough negotiator. "We can talk, but Bella has to give me something in return."

"As long as it's within reason," said Bella.

"I want the first year paid in advance."

Heather answered for her. "I'll guarantee the first year."

"What about the second?"

"One year at a time, or Bella tears up the contract and looks for another pretty girl."

"She can't do that."

Heather set her face like flint. "I drew up that contract. It has more ways for Bella's company to get out of it than you can imagine. She doesn't want to use them, but if you keep pushing, you'll end up with no money. That's not to mention attorney fees you can't afford if you sue. Believe me, there are plenty of escape clauses written into that contract."

Veronica's eyes narrowed to angry slits. "I don't like you."

"That won't cause me to lose any sleep."

Steve broke in, "I like both of you, and I think you both need to pull your claws in."

He took a step toward Veronica and spoke, "Veronica, Heather's worried about the contract falling through because Janie is showing poor judgment by having a close friendship with LaShawn Moody."

"Who?"

"LaShawn Moody. He was Clay Cockrell's best friend when Clay was in high school and interested in Janie. LaShawn's also under contract with Bella. From what we've learned, Janie and LaShawn are friends—close friends. In fact, we're hearing rumors of them being romantically involved."

"That's a lie. Where did you hear that?"

Heather jumped back in. "Steve and I are private investigators. We get paid for finding out things."

Veronica shifted her gaze from Steve to the bar. LaShawn

leaned against it as he spoke to Janie. The timing couldn't have been better.

"Don't go anywhere, Mr. Smiley. I have to take care of a pest."

Heather snapped her head to the side, a signal for Jack to follow her. The two lagged behind Veronica, trying hard for her not to see them. Heather said, "Block her view of me. I'll press against your back. Get close enough for us to hear."

"She's pushing people out of her way," said Jack.

"When we get close, keep your right arm away from your body so I can see what she does. I'll be looking through the gap under your arm."

"Get away from her!" shouted Veronica.

LaShawn spun on the soles of his tennis shoes. He raised his hands.

"Mother!" said Janie. "What's the matter?"

"It's him. He's the matter. This worthless creature is keeping us from making enough so I don't have to work in this stinking dance hall. I'll not have you spoiling everything by getting involved with trash like him."

LaShawn had his hands up, trying to blunt her words. He only managed to open his mouth before she grabbed him by the collar of his jacket. "I said get away from her." She pushed him toward the door. "Get out of here and don't come back."

A uniformed officer arrived. "What's the problem?"

"This creep is coming on to my daughter. I want him gone, and he's not to come back."

The officer took LaShawn by the arm. "Let's go outside and talk."

"That's fine with me. She's crazy."

Tears streamed down Janie's face. Her chin quivered, but she didn't speak. Veronica pointed an accusatory finger at her and said, "If you leave the spot you're standing on, say goodbye to your car. Don't talk to anyone."

Even though Veronica walked within inches of Jack, she

seemed to not see him. Heather had seen people in a blind rage before and recognized the look.

Jack turned to her. "Do you want to go back and make sure Steve's all right?"

Heather shook her head. "He orchestrated this and knew how everyone would react."

"Why would he want Veronica to go off like that?"

"To verify how she'd act."

"I don't get it."

Heather hooked her arm in his. "You will."

"When?"

"Monday morning at my office."

The conversation ended when Loretta Blake arrived. "What was that all about?"

"Steve's tying up loose ends," said Heather. "The young man the officer took outside is LaShawn Moody. He did nothing wrong tonight, but he's part of our investigation into April's death. Could you make sure he doesn't go to jail? Jack and I can give statements about what happened."

"Sure." Loretta placed her hands on her hips. "What about how it relates to April's murder? That's what interests me."

"I'd tell you if I knew. You can expect answers on Monday."

Heather shifted her gaze in time to see Veronica lead Steve toward the front door. What was he up to now?

Voices rose, followed by obscenities from the dance floor. It took mere seconds before a cacophony of high-pitched voices filled the air. The band played on while the crowd formed a circle around an unknown number of pugilists.

Loretta rolled her eyes. "Time for me to go to work."

"Need help?"

The detective shook her head. "Six of us are here in plain-clothes plus two deputies in uniform." She pointed. "My crew is already on their phones calling it in. Whoever picked a fight chose a lousy night."

Heather and Jack took a circuitous route back to their table.

They came to a quick agreement to gather everyone at their table and leave. They found Steve outside the front door, alone.

"How was the fight?" he asked.

Briann gave her opinion. "Kind of cool, but mostly stupid. It didn't last long and was nothing like fights in the movies."

Steve opined. "It doesn't take long to make big mistakes."

Once everyone said their goodbyes, Heather put the car in gear and pointed it in the general direction of home. She asked, "Did you find out all you wanted tonight?"

"I believe so. Now we have to put together a plan."

"We?"

"Yes, we." He shifted in his seat. "Do you want to represent someone accused of murder?"

"Not unless I have to."

Steve scratched his nose. "I didn't think you did. It would make more sense if Jack did it."

"He already represented Clay."

"That makes him well qualified."

"What if he doesn't want to?"

"Persuade him."

"Don't you think it's time you told me what you know?"

"I need to tell both you and Jack." He took a breath. "How does tomorrow sound?"

"You'll need to finish by noon, or you can forget about including Jack. His addiction to college basketball is almost as strong as his love of football."

"I'll adjust my schedule and get up early. There's a lot to do before Monday."

29

Heather hadn't been awake long when the ringing of her phone eliminated all chances of sleeping late on Saturday morning. She dragged it off the nightstand, or at least tried to. After retrieving it from the floor, she glanced at the caller ID and tried to clear her throat. Her voice still cracked as she said, "Ka... Kate. Good morning."

"I'm sorry if I woke you. I keep forgetting it's an hour earlier in Texas than in Miami. I'll call back."

"No." It came out sharper than Heather intended. "I mean, there's no need to call back. I'm awake and need to get up. You did me a favor by calling. Things are progressing well."

"That's why I called. Bella phoned me yesterday and said you were all going dancing last night. Steve wouldn't do that without a good reason. I could almost see the spider web he's weaving for someone to get stuck in."

Heather pulled another pillow against the headboard and sat up straighter. "He's still keeping his cards to himself, but Jack and I are to meet with him this morning to discuss a plan for Monday."

"Does it include Bucky Franklin?"

Heather's breath caught. Had she missed something? Her

heart seemed to stop mid-beat as she collected her thoughts. "Are you saying Bucky might have had something to do with April Brewer's murder?"

"Not that I know of." Kate took a breath and continued, "Don't pay any attention to me. I'm so used to critiquing book plots that I forget how lumpy life really is."

"What do you mean?" asked Heather.

"In fiction, everything and every character has a purpose. That's not the way of real life. Things such as luck, coincidences, and random events invade our lives. I've heard it said that things don't always have to make sense."

Heather still wondered if she had missed something about Bucky. She dismissed the idea as Kate talked on. "Bucky's attack on Steve wasn't random and had nothing to do with April's death, but what if it did?"

Heather hadn't had her first cup of coffee and wasn't keeping up with Kate's logic. Confusion reigned as her thoughts went in three directions at the same time. Kate must have sensed it from the silence.

"I'm sure you're right. The two aren't related. Forget I mentioned it."

Heather brought her knees up to her chest. "What made you connect Bucky with the murder?"

"It had to be my overactive imagination. I stayed awake most of the night thinking about the story Steve would write about this case. It occurred to me there's been something missing from his stories. Up to now, he's never faced a villain. Having an evil person or organization threaten to inflict physical harm on him brings a whole extra dimension to the story. It doesn't fit the plot of this one, but I'm wondering what Bucky will do after he gets out of prison."

The revelation that Bucky might seek to inflict harm on Steve in the future was like a kick to Heather's stomach. She blurted out, "Bucky didn't just threaten Steve with physical harm."

"What do you mean?"

"Bucky doused him with hot coffee and came close to dislocating his shoulder. It happened prior to him setting the fire."

The gasp from Kate preceded a long silence. She finally said, "I'm not a proponent of capital punishment, but right now, I'm having second thoughts."

Heather circled back to Kate's previous point about Steve's stories lacking a villain. It came to her that she'd not done a thorough background search on Bucky. Leo might have but she hadn't. Why did Bucky leave Houston PD? Why was he so intent on stealing from a blind former cop? What was his motivation? It was like he chose Steve specifically as his victim. Why? A phone call to Leo might satisfy her curiosity.

Another revelation came to Heather. She pressed the phone against her ear. "It occurs to me you're the perfect person to teach me about villains. Tell me the characteristics of one."

"There's a long list. I'll email it to you."

"Thanks. It will give me something to ponder. I need to make sure Steve's safe now that Bucky's out on bond."

Kate hesitated. "Now we're blending fiction with reality. A competent psychologist might tell you if Bucky's likely to seek revenge."

"It sounds possible to me that Steve could be in danger right now."

"That's out of my area of expertise. I write and edit stories with protagonists, antagonists, villains, sidekicks, and other supporting characters, but they're all products of people's imaginations."

"Life imitates art," whispered Heather.

Kate's voice rose to sound less glum. "The good thing about Steve is, he's probably already thought of this and has taken steps to protect himself."

"Now that you mention it, he insisted we put in an upgraded security system in the home I bought."

Heather glanced at the time on her phone. "I hate to cut this short, but Jack should be here soon, and I look like I spent the night in a roadhouse dancing."

"Did you?"

"Not *all* night, but long enough for Steve to stir the pot."

"Did the stirring result in a barroom brawl?" asked Kate.

"Only one, and Steve wasn't responsible. It was over almost before it started."

"That's perfect. None of Steve's stories have ever included a fight in a bar. When it's time to write this one, I'll need him to use a little poetic license to make it a real knock-down, drag-out." Kate chuckled, "He'll want to tell it like it really happened, but I know what sells."

Kate had one more question. "Do you know when you and Steve will wrap up the case?"

"It could be as soon as Monday, but that's an educated guess based on the way he's acting. I'll know more after today."

"Keep me posted."

The beep that signaled a text message interrupted the conversation. She pulled her phone away from her ear and read the message. "I just received a text from Steve. He asked if I was going to sleep all day or help him catch a killer. Listen to this: 'I'm leaving in twenty minutes, with or without you.'"

Excitement filled Kate's last words. "The hound is hot on a trail. You'd better saddle your steed and join the hunt."

Salutations flew back and forth. Heather threw back the covers and made for her bathroom to give her teeth and hair a quick brush. She sprinted into her closet and took out jeans, socks, hiking boots, a long-sleeved red and black-checked shirt, and a puffy vest. She might look like a lumberjack, but something told her it wasn't a day to worry about style. Her hair went into a ponytail as she walked into the kitchen. Steve was sitting at the bar, drinking coffee from a to-go cup. A paper cup with a lid on it waited for her.

"I'm ready," said Heather.

"What are you wearing?"

She told him and took the cup from the bar before asking, "What's our first stop?"

"Breakfast with Jack. After that, we're meeting Loretta Blake at the county detention center. Rusty Brigs has a new attorney and a private investigator on his team."

Heather groaned. "I was afraid you'd do this to me. I don't want to represent Rusty."

"You're not going to. Jack is, and I'll be his P.I. You're off the hook."

"Then why am I going to breakfast with you?"

"Jack enjoys your company, and I may need your help with something after Jack and I speak with Rusty."

30

Steve sat with hands clasped loosely together on a metal table. The smell of concrete, steel, and cheap industrial soap emanated from the jail's interview room. It was a room without audio or video surveillance, only a small window in a solid metal door. This ensured confidential conversations with attorneys stayed that way.

Jack leaned into him. "Heather's not happy you kept her in the dark about this interview with Rusty."

Steve waved away the statement. "She has too much to think about already."

The sound of Jack shifting in his chair reached Steve. "You know she thrives on staying busy."

"This case is different, with too many pieces for her to keep everything straight. There's the biggest project of her career, the murder case, and keeping me safe from Bucky Franklin. The least we can do is take a jail interview off her plate."

The metal chair squeaked as Jack shifted. "I forgot about Bucky. Do you think he'll come after you again?"

Steve shrugged. "The odds are that he won't, but I'll sleep better when he's delivered to Huntsville to start a long prison sentence."

Jack remained silent for a few seconds before he asked, "Why did you insist on Heather coming with us if you didn't want her involved in the interview with Rusty?"

"I have a hunch. If I'm right, Heather and Loretta will be busy today and perhaps tomorrow."

The door opened and in walked Rusty Brigs, followed by a uniformed deputy. Steve listened closely as the accused suspect sat on the opposite side of the table.

A deep voice said, "I'll be out in the hall. If he gives you any trouble, holler loud."

The door closed and the lock clicked shut. Jack was the first to speak. "I'm Jack Blackstock, a defense lawyer. Your attorney has asked me to help defend you. This is Mr. Smiley. He's a licensed private investigator and a former homicide detective."

"He's blind," said Rusty. "What good can he do, and why are you helping my attorney?"

Steve answered the first part of the question. "I'm a human lie detector. You'd be surprised how many attorneys pay for my services."

"I owe your attorney a favor," said Jack.

It wasn't a total fabrication, but Steve knew the favor was giving the attorney a ride from the courthouse back to his office on a cold morning.

Steve added, "You must be staying out of trouble. You're not handcuffed."

"How did you know?" demanded Rusty.

"If you were handcuffed, I'd have heard the metal clicking. It's not always standard procedure to handcuff prisoners once they're booked into jail. Only if they pose a risk to staff."

Jack broke in. "Don't underestimate Mr. Smiley. He enjoys putting people in prison who deserve it."

Steve followed up with, "Based on your record and the evidence, you'll take a one-way trip to the Diagnostic Unit in Huntsville and then on to one of the prison farms designed for lifers. You'll work the fields for a few months, provided you stay out of trouble. If you're lucky, you'll get a better job, but it won't be operating heavy equipment or anything with wheels or a motor. Of course, there's always the chance you'll rub someone the wrong way. There aren't that many homicides in Texas prisons, but there are a lot of assaults."

The sound of Rusty shifting in his chair reached Steve. Rusty asked, "Why are you trying to scare me? I know what prison's like and I know how to stay alive inside."

Steve leaned forward. "I wanted to make sure you've considered what a hopeless situation you're in. I happen to believe there's an outside chance you didn't kill April Brewer."

"I didn't," said Rusty with complete conviction in his voice. "Someone set me up."

"Who?"

Silence met his question.

Jack took over, breaking into the sound of a distant door slamming. "I'm a defense attorney. That means I'm to remind the cops and the jury that you're innocent until they prove you guilty beyond a reasonable doubt. Right now, I don't have anything to convince me that you didn't kill April. I'll be looking for things that will put doubts in the jurors' minds. Mr. Smiley will, too. It's critical that you answer all questions truthfully. I'm not exaggerating when I say your freedom depends on it."

Steve added, "I'm skilled in detecting deception. Don't think about bending the truth."

"You've made your point. Ask me anything."

"I'll write down your answers," said Jack. "Let's focus on the possibility of enemies wanting to pin a murder on you. You've been to prison twice before, in addition to several more arrests. Can you think of anyone who'd like to see you back in prison?"

"I've had my share of scrapes through the years, but who hasn't? I've been busting my brain trying to think of anyone who hated me so much they'd kill a girl like April in order to send me back to prison. I drew a blank."

Steve said, "You're not hearing what Mr. Blackstock is telling you. He wants names of people who don't like you. Give us names. We'll follow up with questions."

An hour and a half passed with Rusty giving names and reasons for people having a grudge against him. Steve listened carefully but didn't hear anything that brought the hair on the back of his neck to attention. He shifted his questions away from Rusty's juvenile, jail, and prison spats and scrapes.

"Let's talk about your affinity to be around younger women," said Steve. "It's widely known that you like to frequent dance halls."

"So?" asked Rusty. "I like to dance."

Steve moved on with the questioning, ignoring the last statement. "My research shows that you're fond of dancing with younger women, especially high school girls."

"I choose women who know how to dance. I don't care if they're young or older."

Steve tilted his head. "Doesn't that lead to after-dance activities?"

A hint of lechery salted Rusty's next words. "Of course, but not with girls. I learned a long time ago not to mess with any woman who wasn't old enough to buy her own beer." He paused. "It's even better when they buy one or two for me."

Jack took his turn. "What did you mean when you said you learned not to mess with young women?"

"I'll show you."

Jack narrated for Steve. "Rusty's unbuttoning his jumpsuit. There's a smattering of gray dots on the right side of his chest."

Steve asked, "Bird shot?"

"Yeah," said Rusty. "A rancher didn't like the idea of me becoming his daughter's baby-daddy. If I hadn't been wearing a winter coat and a puffy vest, that shotgun would've blown out my lung."

"What was your relationship with April like?"

"Only dancing." He took a breath. "The truth is, I'll dance

with the pretty young girls but I'll be looking for a woman with experience to go home with."

"Who are the best dancers among the local girls?"

"There's not that many. Janie Polk's a good dancer, but her mom limits us to one dance. As soon as the band starts, she's stuck behind the bar for her whole shift."

"Any others come to mind?"

"April was the best. That girl had moves and endurance."

Steve rubbed the stubble on his top lip. "I understand you have an old truck. Do you think it's possible that someone broke into it and hot-wired the ignition?"

Jack added, "And used it to take April's body to where she was buried?"

Several seconds of silence followed. "I like the way you think, Mr. Smiley. Could you get the cops to check on that?"

Jack responded, "I'm sure they know, but I don't have their full report yet."

"One final question," said Steve. "Did you have a spare key stashed somewhere on your truck?"

"You're sharper than I thought, Mr. Smiley. Tell the cops to look behind the front bumper. There's a key in a magnetic box."

31

Heather arrived at her office before anyone else on Monday morning. She went to her desk and slipped her purse into a drawer. She tried to focus on construction spreadsheets, but her mind kept slipping into the murder case.

When Steve arrived, the first thing she said to him was, "Let's hope Loretta finds the hidden key."

Steve took a sip of coffee from a travel cup. "I have a backup plan if she doesn't."

"It needs to be better than the wild-goose chase you sent me on yesterday. I didn't much like breaking into Veronica's garage and searching Janie's car."

"You worry too much. I told you the chances were slim you'd find the key to Rusty's truck, but I wanted to rule out Janie as a suspect. They left the garage unlocked and you weren't there but a few minutes. Besides, you had a legitimate reason for going there."

Heather snapped back at him. "Obtaining a copy of Janie's driver's license for Bella on a Sunday evening wasn't very creative."

"That's because I knew you wouldn't need something better." He eased back into his chair. "Everything worked out. Now we know one place not to look. I wanted to narrow down the search."

Heather remained skeptical. "Luke and LaShawn should be here soon. It's a school day for both of them, so let's try not to take long."

Steve waited as she stood. "You seem uptight this morning. Not enough sleep?"

"It's not that. Jack wanted me to meet the attorney he hired. They were watching basketball when I got there yesterday afternoon."

"Wasn't his name Sam Delgado?"

Heather huffed. "Sam is short for Samantha."

"Ah," said Steve. "I sense you're concerned about the ravishing Samantha."

"How did you know she was stunning?"

"Lucky guess. You wouldn't be upset if you'd been a part of the selection process like you planned."

"I couldn't. The architect needed my input on pickleball courts." A sigh of resignation escaped. "I'm considering getting Jack a blindfold so he can practice law alongside Lady Justice. Samantha is Latino eye candy."

Steve let out a raucous laugh. "There's nothing better to a guy who can't see than a clever way of describing a pretty woman. Well done." He continued to chuckle. "Tell me more about *Señorita* Delgado."

"I brought her file home. I hate to admit it, but she's more than qualified as a defense attorney. It certainly doesn't hurt that she's bilingual. What bothered me was how she matched Jack holler for holler during the game. She even knew the names and stats of all the players."

Steve contained his mirth. "How did she act toward Jack?"

"Like she was one of the boys. But believe me, she's all woman."

"You have nothing to worry about."

"How can you be so sure?"

"I checked her out. Jack's not her type."

Heather froze in place. "What do you mean, you checked her out?"

"I did a background check on her. Samantha hasn't dated a man under six-four since she was in the tenth grade. I hate to say it this way, but Jack doesn't measure up. He misses the minimum height qualification by at least two inches."

Heather didn't know what to say. All she could do was raise her bottom jaw to close her mouth.

Steve's head snapped up. "There's the elevator. It's time to get to work." He paused. "Let's squeeze Luke and LaShawn hard and see what squirts out of them."

Both Heather and Steve went into the hall. After a cordial greeting, they herded Luke and LaShawn into the interview room. Instead of allowing them to sit behind a desk, Heather instructed them to sit in chairs with plastic seats and metal legs. Steve sat in front of them in an executive chair.

Heather stood and stared until they squirmed. The plan was for her to make a slow circle around them to keep them off balance as she and Steve peppered them with questions.

Luke asked, "Are we waiting on Bella?"

"She's not here, and she's not coming today," said Heather. "We're not here to talk about modeling."

LaShawn tilted his head like a confused puppy. "Then why are we here?"

Steve responded as Heather took slow steps to work her way around them. "If you don't already know, Heather and I are private investigators. A prominent defense attorney has hired us to discover information related to the murder of April Brewer." He allowed the words to sink in.

After about fifteen seconds, LaShawn said, "What's that got to do with us? We don't know anything about her murder."

Heather was behind LaShawn when she bent over and issued a loud whisper. "That's not true."

Steve followed her comment with, "We need to reach an

understanding before we go on. Heather and I already know the answers to ninety-five percent of the questions we're going to ask you. If you think you're clever enough to hide the answers to the remaining five percent, go ahead."

Heather took a step to her right, leaned down, and spoke into Luke's ear. "We're also helping the police with their inquiry. You two know a lot more than you've told us, or them. They're ready to pull you in for formal questioning. Are you familiar with formal questioning?"

Luke shrugged. "They ask you questions, I guess."

Heather kept walking as the two locked their gaze on her. "In a formal police interview, if you lie, they can charge you with a criminal offense. We're giving you the opportunity to tell *all* you know and avoid an arrest for being stupid."

Steve immediately added to her words. "Lying to the police in a murder investigation is not a good idea. We're giving you an opportunity to avoid making mistakes that will land you in jail."

Heather watched as Luke's Adam's apple bobbed up and back down. LaShawn had too much swagger to show any sign of nervousness. "We don't know what you're talking about."

"Sit up straight when we're talking to you," shouted Steve.

The words seemed to bounce off LaShawn. Steve said, "That's just a sample of what a police interrogation is like." He turned to Heather. "Call Detective Blake and tell her Mr. Moody prefers a police interrogation to an informal interview."

Heather went to the door and opened it. "Get out, LaShawn. That smart mouth of yours just earned you a trip to the sheriff's office. Expect deputies to pick you up during school."

LaShawn didn't budge. "Wait. Let's talk."

Steve said, "Heather, make sure you call his parents and tell them what's going to happen."

LaShawn all but yelled, "No. My dad will kill me."

"He's not kidding," said Luke. "LaShawn got a speeding ticket Saturday night and his dad is ready to make him enlist in the army."

Heather's face was grim on the outside, but she was grinning on the inside. They had leverage over LaShawn. She closed the door and moved to resume her circular path around Steve and the two young men.

"Now that we understand each other, let's hear some truthful answers to our questions. LaShawn, does Luke know how much you liked April and wanted to date her?"

LaShawn looked at his feet. "Yeah. I told him after she died."

"Luke, how did that make you feel?"

"It didn't really surprise me. I can't say that I like it, but I understood why. She was everything a guy could want."

"I second that," said LaShawn.

Steve asked, "What did you two think about her dancing with Rusty Brigs?"

They looked at each other, but Luke answered, "We both told her he was trouble."

"Yeah," said LaShawn. "That guy wasn't one to mess with. An ex-con and a hot high school girl is a risky mix."

"How many times has Rusty been in prison?" asked Steve.

"Twice," said both of them at the same time.

"Who told you that?"

"Clay did," said LaShawn. "He worked with him and told us all kinds of things about him."

"Clay used to date April," said Heather. "Was he trying to protect her?"

"Probably," said Luke. "Clay's a great guy. It's like him to try to protect people."

"Why did he and April break up?"

Luke and LaShawn looked at each other, waiting for the other to answer. LaShawn finally mumbled, "It was a long time ago."

Heather had worked her way behind them. "Who did the breaking up?"

Luke gave a more complete answer than LaShawn. "It was mutual. April was a lot more social than Clay. He's a serious guy, and she was like a butterfly, always flitting around. I think they both realized they were too different."

Steve leaned back in his chair. "Are you saying they went their separate ways with no hard feelings?"

Both nodded, so Heather had to remind them to use words.

"That's right," said Luke. "No hard feelings."

Steve made a steeple out of his index fingers and tapped his chin. "That left April free for both of you to go after. I hear Luke took over where Clay left off."

Luke chuffed. "Not for long, and it wasn't for lack of trying."

LaShawn jumped in. "I'm the guy who goes places with a group and always leaves the same way. I've made it all the way through high school without getting serious about a girl. I wanted to date April, but I didn't have the guts."

This took Heather by surprise until she thought about it. LaShawn was lonely even when he was in a crowd showing off. She wondered what that level of loneliness would do to a young man.

She was considering this when Steve dropped his bombshell. "Luke, tell us about Clay and Janie. How long have you two been helping them keep their relationship a secret?"

An audible gasp came from LaShawn.

Heather added, "Where are they going to college in the fall?"

Luke quickly recovered. "You're wrong about them starting college in the fall. They're enrolled in the first summer session. How did you know they never broke up?"

"I wasn't sure until now," said Steve.

Both young men let out a groan. "Please don't tell." said LaShawn. "We swore we wouldn't tell anyone. If Janie's mom finds out, there's no telling what she'll do."

Luke added, "That woman's not right in the head. She'll do something that would keep Janie from being valedictorian."

Heather was now back in front of them. "You two need to get to school. Thanks for the talk."

32

The remainder of the morning passed with Heather and Steve going over details of the case. Piece by piece, interview by interview, they went through everything, making sure there would be no mistakes. Steve summed up the extended meeting. "I sometimes wish the truth wasn't such a bitter pill to swallow."

Heather rose from her chair and patted him on the shoulder on her way to the door of their office. "Jack should be here any minute with lunch. I need to check in with my PA."

Steve mumbled a response. Some cases took more of a toll on him than others. The murder of a teenage girl and having to deal with high school students and their parents stretched him to the limit. Combine that with the antics of Bucky Franklin, and his worry lines ran deep. She knew he'd recover his energy after a few days of rest, but what about the damage to his soul?

Jack's arrival brought a reset to her thinking. He barely slowed down long enough to greet the secretarial staff on his way through.

Steve addressed him with, "Glad you're here. Heather always waits too long before ordering lunch."

Jack placed sacks of food and drinks on the conference table.

"I wish I could take credit, but my new secretary took care of ordering this for me."

"Speaking of new staff," said Steve. "How's the latest addition to your legal team?"

"So far, so good. I tried to get her to talk about the latest college rankings this morning and she told me she wasn't there to waste time."

Heather gave an extended sigh. "A woman after my heart. I may have to hire her away from you."

"Don't you dare," said Jack. "I loaded her down with six clients this morning. She went into her office and I haven't seen her since."

"Speaking of clients," said Steve. "Is yours still scheduled to be here at twelve thirty?"

"Detective Blake is bringing two uniformed officers to make sure Rusty behaves himself."

"Did you have trouble talking the sheriff into it?" asked Heather.

"Not when I told him about the locked doors in the sound-proof interview and observation rooms. He agreed the security would be better here than before a judge. There'll be a minimum of three armed officers with him."

"Don't forget me," said Heather. "I'll be armed."

Steve added, "The orange jumpsuit will make him stand out like a Halloween Jack-O'-Lantern. With wrists and ankles shackled, I'd say he's not going anywhere."

"Time to eat," said Jack.

Steve remained quiet throughout the meal. So quiet that he was the first to finish. He lifted his chin. "There's the elevator. Let's get Loretta, Rusty, and the officers into the viewing room."

Jack swallowed his last bite of potato chips. "Are you afraid the others will come early?"

"It's unlikely, but let's not tempt fate."

It took mere seconds for Loretta and the two officers to whisk Rusty into the observation room. The murder suspect waited until the door closed behind him before he asked, "Is anyone going to tell me what this is about?"

Loretta did the honors. "This is about finding the person who killed April Brewer. I believe it's you, but others here aren't so sure. People you know will be on the other side of this glass, and all you have to do is sit quietly and enjoy the show."

Rusty thrust his feet out in front of him and leaned back. "This beats sitting in a cell. Could I get a cup of coffee?"

"No."

"Water?"

Heather pointed to a small refrigerator in the far corner of the room. "It's your call, Loretta."

The detective considered the request. "If I give you water, the next thing you'll ask is to use the restroom. You can wait for both."

Heather left the room without feeling sorry for Rusty. She went back into the hallway as Janie Polk and Clay Cockrell stepped off the elevator. She took them into the interview room and sat them on a love seat against the wall. Steve was already in the room, sitting in a comfortable chair.

"What's going on?" asked Clay. "Why did the cops take me from work?"

Steve said, "We have questions for you related to April's murder. Heather needs to run an errand. She'll be back in a few minutes and we'll get started."

Heather left the room and listened for the elevator. Long minutes passed until she heard the ding of a bell announcing the next participants in the drama they'd set up. Off the elevator stepped Lee and LeAnn Cockrell.

"Please follow me," said Heather. She took them to the door of the interview room but didn't open it. She looked into questioning eyes and said, "Clay and Janie Polk are in here. They're going to need your support today."

"I don't understand," said LeAnn.

"You will."

Heather opened the door and motioned them into the room. Clay dropped Janie's hand and sprang to his feet. "Mom... Dad. What are you doing here?"

"That's what we want to know," said Lee.

Heather motioned them to a second loveseat that sat at a right angle to the one Clay and Janie sat on.

"Please have a seat," said Heather. "We'll try to make this quick."

Heather took a seat beside Steve and spoke for his benefit. "There are four people looking at us with questioning expressions on their faces."

Steve nodded. "Heather and I spoke with two of Clay and Janie's friends this morning. Luke Paulson and LaShawn Moody confirmed what we suspected. They were hesitant to reveal Clay and Janie's clandestine relationship."

Heather interrupted. "It was obvious to Steve that they only pretended to break up. They did it to appease Janie's overbearing mother."

"We had to," said Clay. A plea for understanding was in his eyes, but he held back more words.

Janie wasn't so inclined. "Mom has serious mental issues. I've done a lot of research. She needs frequent counseling and to take her medication every day. When we run short of money, she cuts the pills in half or stops taking them altogether. I once worked up the courage to confront her about her mood swings."

Clay interrupted. "She sawed off the handle of a broom and beat Janie with it."

Janie nodded. "That's when she made me call Clay and break up with him."

Clay grasped Janie's hand. "We had to be extra careful." Clay looked at his parents. "So careful that we couldn't tell you."

Lee looked at his son. "But Luke and LaShawn knew."

Clay broke eye contact.

Janie's words spoke of her desire to protect Clay. "That's my fault. I needed help to forge college applications and do other things that would keep Mom from finding out about us."

Steve asked, "Whose home did the college acceptance letters come to?"

LeAnn gasped. "You're going to college?"

"Yeah, Mom. We start in June. That's why I've been working so hard. I had to earn enough so we could go together."

Clay turned his head to face Steve. "We used LaShawn's home address."

"Why?" asked LeAnn.

Steve answered for Clay. "To keep Janie's mother from finding out their plans. Clay knew if his acceptance letters were sent to your home, it would lead to a lot of questions that he wasn't prepared to answer."

Clay gave his head a firm nod. "No offense, Mom, but you'd be so excited you'd bombard me with questions. That would lead to lies about me and Janie."

Steve interrupted. "It's time you two told them the rest."

Clay and Janie clasped hands and looked at each other. Clay took in a full breath. "We're getting married after Janie graduates. Not right away. That's why I didn't go off to college last year."

Janie quickly added, "I'm doing my part by keeping my grades up. If I'm valedictorian, I'll get free tuition and other scholarships."

Lee leaned forward. "I still don't understand why you two didn't come to us instead of having Luke and LaShawn help you."

Clay straightened his shoulders. "Dad, we wanted to come to you and Mom but couldn't risk it. You're a problem solver. I knew you'd go to Janie's mom and try to convince her to let us keep seeing each other. You don't know how Janie's mom beat her and how serious her mental problems are. I had to protect my future wife."

Lee and LeAnn traded looks that caused each to break down. Lee was the first to speak through his tears. "I'm proud of you, son." He shifted his gaze to Heather and then back to Clay. "Heather told us we'd need to support you two, and that's what we intend to do."

"That's good to hear," said Steve. "You're about to be put to the test."

Heather stood. "I'm going to take the four of you to another room where you'll be alone. There are more interviews to conduct, and you'll be able to watch them on a monitor."

Steve added, "This won't be pleasant. Prepare yourselves."

33

Heather escorted the Cockrell family, which would soon add Janie to the fold, to a room with a wall-mounted monitor. LeAnn had her arm interlaced in Janie's before they left the room. How long would it take before LeAnn mentioned the word wedding?

The look and vibe of the interview room had changed by the time Heather returned. Jack sat next to Rusty on one of the short couches with a deputy standing behind them. Loretta Blake sat on the other with Steve facing them in the same chair he'd occupied during the previous interview. The second deputy stood by the door.

Heather took a seat next to Loretta as Steve asked, "Are you ready to start?"

"I'm ready."

Steve lifted his chin, making it appear he could see Rusty. "A few questions need answers. As the attorney by your side will tell you, you don't have to answer anything that's asked of you."

"Good," said Rusty. "It's doubtful I will."

Steve nodded. "I understand your hesitancy, but let me say, I don't believe you killed April Brewer and I intend to prove it today."

Loretta huffed a breath of unbelief at Steve's words.

Steve kept talking without responding to Loretta's doubts. "I'd advise you to follow the advice of your attorney. He's obligated to keep you from saying anything that will incriminate you."

Jack shifted his gaze and words to Rusty. "Give me time to respond before you say anything. The biggest mistake suspects make is thinking they can spar with trained interrogators. I'll tell you if it's all right to answer a question. Understand?"

"Sure. That's why lawyers are called mouthpieces. You'll do the talking for me."

"Not all," said Jack. "If I think it will help mitigate or absolve you of guilt, I'll give you a green light to answer in your own words."

Steve sat up straight. "Let's get started. Mr. Brigs, is it true that, until recently, you worked as a heavy equipment operator for a local construction company?"

Jack nodded for Rusty to answer. "That's right."

"And you had a satisfactory work history with that company?"

Jack nodded again.

"I operated anything and everything they told me to."

"Including an excavator?"

"I already answered that," said Rusty.

Jack interjected, "What my client means is that he, along with others, can operate an excavator."

Steve then asked, "Do you own a pickup truck?"

Jack whispered something to Rusty, who nodded. "There's one registered in my name."

"New or older?" asked Steve.

"I don't like new trucks."

"Do you keep it clean?"

Rusty laughed. "Only if it rains."

Steve took a deep breath. "How do you respond to the claim the police have made that they discovered traces of April Brewer's blood in the bed of your pickup truck?"

"My client has no comment," said Jack.

Steve quirked a smile. "He might the next time I ask him."

"I doubt it," said Jack.

Heather took her turn. "Mr. Brigs, how many sets of keys do you have for your truck?"

Jack signaled for Rusty to answer. "Two. One on my key chain and a second hidden in a magnetic holder under the front bumper."

"Do you ever loan your truck to anyone?"

"No."

"Have you ever told anyone about where you keep the spare key hidden?"

"No."

Steve followed close behind. "Can you tell us about your relationship with April Brewer?"

Jack wasted no time in saying, "I'm advising my client not to respond to open-ended questions."

Jack's hard response slid off Steve as he shrugged. "No problem. I thought it might save time. Let me be specific. There are multiple witnesses who say you danced with April Brewer at the Melody Barn. You also danced with other young women. None of these witnesses can testify that they ever saw you and April or any other young women outside the dance hall past closing time. There's no record of any phone communications between you and April."

Detective Blake gave Steve a hard stare.

Steve kept talking. "You told me in the presence of your attorney that you were only romantically interested in older women. Do you stand by that statement?"

"Don't answer that," said Jack.

Rusty ignored him. "Women under twenty-one are nothing but trouble. In fact, I'm partial to women between thirty-five and forty-five."

Heather asked, "Anyone in particular?"

Jack jumped into the conversation. "You're fishing for information. Please make your questions specific."

Steve's smile reminded Heather of a cat stalking a bird.

Heather took over. "Mr. Brigs, are you a regular patron of the Melody Barn?"

"Don't answer," said Jack again.

"Yeah, I go there."

"Do you know a young woman named Janie Polk?"

Jack held up his hand. "I'm calling an end to this. My client has nothing more to say."

"The heck I don't," said Rusty. "I know how the law works better than you. They're proving that I didn't kill April."

Jack shrugged. "If you know so much, represent yourself."

"That's the best thing to come out of your mouth today. You're fired."

Rusty's declaration earned a smile from Detective Blake.

Heather took over where she left off. "Again, Mr. Brigs, do you know a young woman named Janie Polk?"

"She's a high school girl who works as a bar-backer with her mother."

"Have you ever danced with her?"

"I used to. Not anymore."

Heather tilted her head. "Why not?"

"Her mom doesn't like Janie dancing with anyone. Veronica told me to never dance with or speak to Janie again."

Steve kept on the same trail. "Did you do something to offend Janie's mother?"

Rusty held up his hands with fingers spread wide. The chain that linked the handcuffs with the chain around his waist drew tight. "Veronica flipped out one evening when Janie and I danced."

Steve asked, "Do you know why she became so upset?"

"I asked Veronica about it after she'd calmed down. She said something about hearing that Janie was meeting Clay Cockrell on the sly. She's kept Janie under lock and key ever since."

"Would you say Veronica's concerned with protecting Janie?"

"It's worse than that."

"What would you call it?"

"Obsessed."

"Do you know why?" asked Heather.

Rusty looked to Jack for guidance, who said, "Don't look at me. I'm no longer your attorney."

Rusty turned to Heather and lifted his chin. "Veronica runs hot and cold. That's especially true when it comes to her daughter."

Steve followed up with, "Have you ever seen Veronica react with violence toward Janie?"

Rusty issued a rough laugh. "Yeah. She explodes like a barrel of gunpowder."

Jack's head snapped up, but he pressed his lips into a thin line and didn't say anything.

Heather asked, "Does Veronica take psychotropic medication?"

"Off and on."

Steve leaned back in his chair. "Perhaps we should wait for Veronica to arrive before we continue to talk about her."

Detective Blake pulled her phone from her purse and walked out of the room. She returned a short time later. "Deputies are following Veronica. She's pulling into the parking lot now."

Heather rose. "I'll bring her in."

34

I t wasn't a long wait. Veronica shot out of the elevator as soon as the door opened enough for her to pass. Heather blocked her path.

"Where's my daughter?"

"She's here, and she's safe."

Veronica's eyelids narrowed. "Why is she here?"

"Come with me and we'll explain everything."

Heather turned and walked toward the interview room. They passed the office where the Cockrells and Janie waited behind a locked door.

Heather moved on to another door and opened it. Veronica was in mid-rant when they stepped into the room. The sight of Rusty sitting on the loveseat with Jack brought her progress to an abrupt halt.

The deputy stationed at the door closed it and moved to form a human barrier with thick arms crossed.

Spittle came from Veronica's mouth as she pointed to Rusty and shouted, "What's that killer doing here? Where's Janie?"

Heather spoke in a soft tone. "Janie's in this building. She's been helping the police with their investigation."

"What investigation?"

Detective Blake responded, "April Brewer's murder."

Sparks seemed to fly from Veronica's eyes. "You already know who killed that tramp, and he's sitting right there." She pointed to Rusty.

Steve stayed seated. "Would you prefer we call you Veronica or Ms. Polk?"

Confusion filled her countenance, and she didn't answer. Heather took the time to inspect Veronica. She hadn't bothered with makeup or even to brush her long raven hair. She wore loose-fitting gray sweatpants and a man's flannel shirt.

Heather said, "I love the look. Is that one of Rusty's shirts?"

"Huh?"

Rusty answered for her with a quirk of a smile pulling up the corner of his top lip. "It's mine. A woman wearing a man's shirt always did something for me."

Veronica shook her head, seemingly to clear it. "I don't know what's going on, but I'm not having any part of it." She stomped her foot and said, "I demand you take me to Janie."

Detective Blake approached her. "Ms. Polk, you're being detained for questioning related to the murder of April Brewer. You'll sit on the loveseat." She pointed to the one vacated by her daughter and Clay. "Your only option is to sit with or without handcuffs. Which would you prefer?"

Steve spoke before the agitated woman could respond. "I'm going to call you Veronica. Ms. Polk sounds so formal." He smiled. "We've been talking with Rusty about you. I thought it wasn't right for us to do that without you being here. Do you want to know what Rusty's been telling us?"

"He's a liar and an ex-con. You can't believe anything he says."

"That's why we wanted you here. Have a seat and make yourself comfortable. After all, it's only fair that you should tell your side."

Heather reinforced Steve's words with an outstretched hand toward the loveseat.

Veronica kept a withering gaze on Rusty as she moved to the loveseat and lowered herself onto it.

Steve must have heard her settle. "Thank you for cooperating. What can you tell us about Rusty's relationship with April Brewer?"

"He tried to get her to go home with him."

"Did you hear him say that?" asked Heather.

"I didn't have to. I know his type and what they say to get young girls."

"Ah. That makes sense," said Steve. "What about Rusty and other girls of high school age? Did he come on to them, too?"

"Of course. He has the morals of an alley cat."

"That's rich coming from you," said Rusty. "You never complained when I went home with you."

"Shut up, jailbird."

Heather stood beside Steve. "It seems you two were in a relationship. It was close enough for you to end up with the shirt off Rusty's back."

Rusty responded with a lecherous grin. Veronica looked away but soon recovered. "We all make mistakes. I didn't know how dangerous he was."

Steve turned his face to Veronica. "The evidence against Rusty is substantial but not overwhelming. Did you ever ride in Rusty's truck?"

"I might have once or twice."

"Did you ever drive it?"

The answer came too fast and too firm. "Never."

"She's lying," said Rusty. "She used it once after I stayed the night with her."

"That's not what you said before," said Loretta.

"I forgot."

"Did you give her your keychain?"

"I keep a spare key under the front bumper in a magnetized metal box. She used the spare."

"He's lying again," said Veronica. "I took his keychain."

Steve scooted forward in his chair. "Let's go back to the scene of the murder. One or more persons placed April's body in the bed of Rusty's truck. Then that person, or persons, drove to the worksite and buried April in a trench that was scheduled to have a concrete drainage pipe installed the next working day."

Steve turned to Loretta. "Detective Blake, can you tell us what forensic investigators found in the bed of Rusty's truck?"

"Bleach was used to clean the truck's bed."

"Yet, there was still a trace of blood there?"

"That's right."

"And you found a bloody rag at Rusty's residence?"

"That's correct. And a shovel with April's blood on it. Forensics believe it to be the murder weapon."

"How do you explain the forensic report that shows April's blood was on top of the bleach used to clean the bed of Rusty's truck?"

"Well..."

Steve kept talking at a fast clip. "The only possible explanation is, after the cleaning, someone went back and smeared blood on the truck's bed. I believe that someone is trying to point the finger of guilt at Rusty. Tell us, Veronica, why would he clean his truck and then put blood on it?"

Stunned silence filled the room until Rusty stood and let out a holler. "I told you. I'm innocent. You just solved the murder."

Steve continued after the deputies settled Rusty back on the couch. He took in a full breath. "Like I said, the only way to explain April's blood in the truck's bed is that someone put it there after it was cleaned with bleach. The questions we must answer are who and why?"

Heather moved on before Steve could answer his own questions. "Veronica, what did you think about your daughter dating Clay Cockrell?"

Veronica's nostrils flared. "I put a stop to it. We have other plans for her life."

Steve took his turn. "We have testimony that you not only

forbid her from seeing him, but you beat Janie with a sawed-off broom handle."

"That's a lie. Who told you that?"

"You're the liar," said Rusty. "I had to pull you away, or you'd have killed her. All she did was talk to him on the phone. I know Clay and he's a good kid."

Heather directed her gaze to Rusty. "Was that one of the times she exploded?"

"Yeah. Like she's about to now."

The room went silent until Veronica launched herself onto Rusty, clawing his face with one hand and beating him with the other. Deputies moved quickly to remove her.

"Cuff her and get her to jail," said Detective Blake.

Heather put a hand on Loretta's arm. "She'll need to go for a psych evaluation."

Loretta nodded. "Call EMS."

It took three officers and two ambulance attendants to subdue Veronica and get her strapped onto the ambulance gurney.

Heather leaned into Steve. "One down. One more to go."

Rusty held out his hands toward Detective Blake and said, "It's obvious that Veronica killed April Brewer. I'd appreciate it if you'd take this hardware off me. I'll be expecting a full apology for false imprisonment." He turned to Jack. "Do you work on those types of cases? If you do, what percent of the settlement do you charge?"

Steve spoke up. "The only place you're going is back to jail."

Rusty spewed a laugh. "You know she set me up. Veronica wiped some blood on the rag and transferred it later to the bed of my truck. She killed April in the parking lot, wrapped her in a tarp, put her in the bed of my truck, took her, and buried her."

Heather looked at him and asked, "Do you expect us to believe that a woman Veronica's size loaded April into the back of your truck by herself?"

"She's stronger than she looks."

"I agree she likely killed April." Steve put a slight tilt to his head. "After that, things get murky. Let me give you a different version of what happened. You were going to follow Veronica home for your weekly rendezvous. When you reached your truck, she showed you what she'd done." He paused. "How am I doing so far?"

"Now you're trying to trick me."

Steve pressed on. "Then, all alone, Veronica covered April with a tarp and drove your truck to the job site and buried her. Is that right?"

"Yeah. I'll swear to it."

Steve continued at a quick pace. "I contend that it was you who drove your truck to the job site where drainage pipes were being buried. It was a place she wasn't familiar with. It had no street signs or lights and was closed to the public. You were the one who dug a grave in the bottom of the trench and buried April, knowing the next day a pipe would cover her."

Heather added details, "Months later, it was discovered that section of pipe had been set at the wrong depth. Clay was the one assigned the job of correcting the mistake. When he dug to the correct depth, he discovered April's body. If it wasn't for a simple construction mistake, you and Veronica would have committed the perfect crime."

Rusty leaned back and thrust his feet out as far as the chains allowed. "How are you going to prove any of this?"

Steve gave a sly grin. "You knew where to dig. You knew a pipe would cover the grave the next day. You cleaned the bed of your truck with bleach and left no trace of April's blood. What you didn't plan on was Veronica planting evidence at your residence and putting traces of April's blood on the bed of your truck after you cleaned it. I bet that took you by surprise."

Rusty's knuckles clinched in anger. "Yeah, I didn't think she'd set me up."

Steve grinned, "Thanks for the confession."

Rusty looked ashen but rebounded as best he could. "Veronica killed April."

Steve lowered his voice. "I believe that's true." He paused. "But you took over from there."

Loretta motioned to a deputy. "Take him back to jail. It's going to be a long time before he goes to another dance."

35

The evening sun made a kaleidoscope of the western sky as colors peeked through the trees of Heather and Steve's temporary home. They sat in lawn chairs that were more like recliners. The table between them held two glasses of iced tea, plain for her and sweetened with heaping teaspoons of sugar for Steve.

"It's too quiet," said Steve.

"It always is after Bella and Adam leave." Heather watched as condensation formed droplets and ran down her glass. "They'll be back next month. Did she tell you her parents are coming with them to help design their condos?"

Heather saw Steve nod out of the corner of her eye. She changed the subject. "I spoke with Jack today. He reminded me it's been a full month since he withdrew from defending Rusty."

Steve rubbed his hand on his pants. "What's the most recent news on the case?"

"The wheels of justice are turning. Veronica is back on her medication and behaving herself in jail. She can't afford the high bond so she'll stay in jail."

"What else?" asked Steve.

"Jack's new attorney must have connections in the D.A.'s office. Samantha told Jack the D.A. will start out by offering Veronica a thirty-year sentence for murder with a deadly weapon. However, it won't take much to get the sentence down to twenty years, non-aggravated because of her mental status and lack of criminal record."

Steve let out a sigh. "If she stays on her medication, she'll do less than ten in prison."

Heather moved on. "Rusty isn't so lucky. He's a habitual offender and is looking at a much longer stretch."

Steve shook his head and summarized the information. "The killer gets twenty years, and the accomplice will get double that. It's best that I not try to make sense of our justice system."

Heather replaced her glass on the table after taking a sip. "Jack said his office is humming right along. Between the new secretary, Briann, and the go-getter attorney, his profits are up despite the increased payroll." A breeze rustled spring leaves in the trees. "Unless there's an epidemic of morality, Jack will have more work than he can handle."

"Anything else?"

"That's about it. Samantha Delgado is bringing in so much business he may have to hire a third attorney."

Heather rested her head against the back of her chair. It was good to slow the pace of her life, if only for a day. She'd been working long hours on the project. This was her first day off since the arrests and arraignments of Veronica and Rusty.

"Have you heard from Leo?" she asked.

"I spoke with him a couple of days ago. Did I tell you Bucky skipped town a week after he posted bond?"

Heather jerked forward. "He's skipped town?"

"Leo said he closed all his bank accounts and cleaned out his apartment. He even sold his car. My guess is he paid cash for something and will sell it when he gets to where he's going. There's no telling where he is or who he's pretending to be."

Heather's gaze shot to her right. "There's something you're not telling me."

A frown pulled down at the corners of Steve's mouth. "Before he left HPD, Bucky investigated identity thefts. He knows all the tricks. If he lies low and plays his cards right, they'll never find him. My guess is, he's already moved to another state."

"That stinks. Does Kate know?"

"Yeah. By him skipping out, her trip was mostly a waste."

Heather slapped her forehead. "I'm such a dunce. She was supposed to stay with us. What did she do?"

"Don't be too hard on yourself. She stayed at one of the hotels by the airport. Constance drafted a contract and the three of us had dinner together. I guess her trip wasn't a total loss. Kate and I now know exactly what's expected between us and it's all business."

Heather slumped in her chair. It seemed as if all the air spewed out of her emotional balloon. "I'm not sure who I'm the most disappointed with, you, me, or Kate."

"Kate and I are fine. Good fences make for good neighbors, and good contracts make for good business relationships. If you want to wallow in self-pity for a day or two, go right ahead."

"It may take longer than two days. I can't believe I forgot she was coming."

"You were working twenty hours a day. Do you even remember you have a cat?"

"Barely. How is he?"

"I'm glad to report that Max is no longer hissing at the fireplace."

Steve may have delivered the last sentence in a carefree tone, but there was something in his words that caused goose bumps like clammy hands running down her spine. She rose from the chair and surveyed the backyard. Was it fatigue, paranoia, or simple caution that caused her to look for an intruder?

"Is Leo trying to find Bucky?"

"He's a homicide detective, not arson."

Heather wanted to stomp her foot but held back from launching into a rant. She tried using reverse psychology. "If you're not upset about him getting away with assault, stealing your work, or arson, I won't be."

Steve shrugged. "Being blind helps you become very patient. If he's as big a crook as I think he is, he'll eventually get caught." He took a sip of his iced tea. "I didn't tell you, but Bucky called me yesterday."

It took Heather several seconds to process and respond to what Steve said. She was on the verge of formulating a sentence when Steve added, "He told me to sleep with one eye open from now on. I thought it was a pretty good attempt at gallows humor."

Heather walked a circle around the yard before she came back and stood before him. "Who else knows about the phone call?"

"I called Leo and told him. Now, I'm telling you. I wanted to tell you first, but, like I said, you've been so busy with the housing development."

Heather huffed, "I wasn't that busy." Steel was in her voice. "What are we going to do about it if he shows up?"

Steve leaned his chair back. "I believe a guy who's capable of assault and arson is capable of much more. He counted on me being an easy mark and that I'd slink away like a scared puppy. So, I'm going to beef up security."

"How? I already have cameras and alarms all over this property."

"I'm looking to get a living, breathing bodyguard."

"You want to hire some muscled-up guy named Guido?"

"I was thinking more along the lines of the four-legged variety. Guido might be a good name for a guard dog. I'll think about it."

Of all the things Steve could come up with, she hadn't counted on him wanting a dog. "What kind of dog do you want?"

He stood and held his hand out at belt level. "One whose

back comes up to here. I'd like him trained to eat any intruder named Bucky in six bites."

Heather said, "I've done my part by securing the property electronically. You find the dog. Make sure he doesn't eat cats."

From The Author

Thank you for reading *Dig Deep For Murder*. I hope you enjoyed your mystery escape as you turned the pages to find out whodunit! If you loved it, please consider leaving a review at your favorite retailer, Bookbub or Goodreads. Your reviews help other readers discover their next great mystery!

To stay abreast of Smiley and McBlythe's latest adventure, and all my book news, join my Mystery Insiders community. As a thank you, I'll send you a *reader exclusive* Smiley and McBlythe mystery novella!

You can also follow me on Amazon, Bookbub and Goodreads to receive notification of my latest release.

Happy reading!
Bruce

Scan the image to sign up or go to brucehammack.com/the-smiley-and-mcblythe-mysteries-reader-gift/

A Killer On Christmas Cay

Palms swaying, tensions rising... and a killer's footprints in the sand.

Blind private investigator Steve Smiley is pulled into another case when his partner's father suspects corporate espionage. But after an employee is left battered and comatose, it's evident that more sinister forces are at play. To lure out the culprit, Smiley and his partner orchestrate an elaborate ruse—a high-stakes leadership retreat on a private Caribbean island.

The game takes a lethal turn when the assault victim succumbs to his injuries, confirming a cold-blooded killer lurks among the participants. As the weeklong gauntlet of grueling mental and physical challenges intensifies, suspicions escalate, and tempers flare.

The stakes skyrocket when two of the suspects fall prey to a mysterious assailant. Now, it's a perilous race against time for Smiley to unravel the twisted web of secrets and unmask the killer before more blood stains the pristine island sands.

Scan below to get your copy of *A Killer On Christmas Cay* today!

brucehammack.com/books/murder-on-the-brazos/

ABOUT THE AUTHOR

Drawing from his extensive background in criminal justice, Bruce Hammack writes contemporary, clean read detective and crime mysteries. He is the author of the Smiley and McBlythe Mysteries, the Fen Maguire Mysteries, the Star of Justice series and the Detective Steve Smiley Mysteries. Having lived in eighteen cities around the world, he now lives in the Texas hill country with his wife of thirty-plus years.

Follow Bruce on Bookbub and Goodreads for the latest new release info and recommendations. Learn more at brucehammack.com.